The Man in the Black Hat

By

R Kane

The Man in the Black Hat

By R Kane

Create Space Edition | Copyright 2015 R Kane

http://www.rkanepublications.com

This book is dedicated to all the crazy dreamers like me...never stop looking for the end of the rainbow, ever you guys.

The First Book

'I pressed my father's hand and told him I would protect his grave with my life. My father smiled and passed away to the spirit land'.

Chief Joseph

'Thought I walked a twisted trail
Till I saw where it led me too
Yeah, one foot in front of the other baby
And I came straight to you'

'Well it seemed like such a long shot
But somehow my aim was true
Like a moonbeam across the water baby
I came straight to you'
'I Came Straight To You ', Kevin Welch / Patty Loveless

And so it begins...

A gentle, low wind blew down the turn at 7th Street and Union Avenue, just a simple street in Brooklyn New York, nothing out of the ordinary. It was a beautiful spring afternoon, the clouds were few in the blue sky overhead which was nice because it gave one a chance to look up and see the mix of large and small air ships that passed just above the tops of the buildings. Some of the flying vessels were wood and some were metal, and a few were an amalgamation of both, but all looked just like ships that were moored at the docks by the river in the naval yards. Of course these whips could never be confused with the zeppelins, those large slow moving dirigibles with cylinder gondolas hanging beneath from ropes that still roamed the skies of the world in number due to a renewed popularity now among the rich. All of the air ships above were of varying design and each uniquely suited and built to a specific purpose from hauling goods and people to personal air travel for the wealthy to protecting and serving the great nation that is these United States. The steam driven turbines of the low flying air ships added to the breeze here and there kicking up small dust devils that tossed around debris as the children would stop and point at them, calling out the names of the types they knew. There were simple air haulers, long slow flying locomotives made up of box cars delivering pre-bought consumer goods around the city just a few feet above the roofs of the buildings. One of the kids looked up and screamed out gleefully at the smaller faster moving ones, was it a personal craft he asked. Yeah, his friend replied, just some rich fat cat heading up to the city to shop probably, look at the ship's sleek design and it's just made of wood. Then another friend pointed out one, an ominous steel ship with its shadow long and large, looming almost over the entire city it seemed as its wings were spread wide which meant it was patrolling and searching for something. All three boys gasped before the middle one whispered asking if this monster was one of the ships of the Protectorate, the Governments' military and national police force. The hull and large fan like rudder gleamed from being freshly washed as it floated by with the air wash from the seemingly endless number of the large steam driven turbine fans barely catching the attention of the people walking by the stunned children. If you had seen one flying metal war ship then you had seen them all the men and women thought while going about their daily business. One of the boys gasped again and pointed to the two turrets of three large barreled guns on its forward deck while another pointed at the tall tower of the structure as it rose from the main deck behind the guns. Is that a battleship the third asked in awe with a whisper as he saw the men on the decks look over the rails to the street below before going back to tending to daily chores? No, the other two whispered back in unison, the battleships are bigger...this one is smaller...might be a cruiser.

And with it being the almost perfect day the sidewalk was crowded. People were dressed in regular attire here though in this working neighborhood, nothing fancy like up town in Manhattan. The tail coats, top hats with gloves, and ascots were traded in for thick work shirts, wool vests and caps of men who worked hard with their hands for a living here in Brooklyn. The long billowy skirts and oiled leather corsets the ladies would wear in Manhattan were rarely seen among the modest and also hard working women here in the neighborhoods. A simple bodice and long chaste skirt was what these women who put in long days wore here. Young boys all wore pantaloons and shirts just like their father's before them with wool caps topping off the ensemble while young girls wore the handmade dresses and aprons of their mother's handiness. There was little money for expensive things here, even though if you looked around you would easily spot the new-fangled gas powered cars and bikes of visitors rolling by. Those were the folks who came down to 'visit' the regulars who lived here would say...and people not from the neighborhood were just that, visitors. There were the occasional high dressed individuals, 'seekers' they were called because they didn't live or work here in Brooklyn which meant you had to be down here looking for something, and if you were looking for something then the best thing for you to do was to find it and be on your way, 'understand' as the locals say?

So it was for the two men walking along the sidewalk this afternoon, their clothes drawing the usual curious gaze but not an overt look from the people who lived and worked here. The one in front was smaller than his companion who drew most of the eyes as the pair walked up to the turn and stopped. The smaller man was just over 6 foot tall and had the look of a well-built warrior who could throw down with the best of anyone if he had to. He wore a custom made leather single breasted waist coat over a white long sleeve shirt open at the neck showing off the chains and cords of several necklaces. The buttoned waistcoat he wore was tied down each side from arm pit to waist with similar cordage with ends which dangled a few inches down past the hem of the vest and bounced off the sides of his dark brown canvas pants, which were tucked into a pair of the strangest looking boots anyone in Brooklyn had ever seen. The moccasins were made of oiled leather but there wasn't one buckle or button anywhere on the shoes, no, the boots were laced right up the side and the soles looked thin and blank without grip or knobby wedges. How could a man walk around the deck of an air ship with those boots on, one might think? A pair of aviator goggles hanging around his neck from the leather strap jingled as he reached into the pocket of his waist coat and produced a large ornate pocket watch. A lady walking by took note of the smaller man and stared hard at his hat, a strange wide black brimmed felt job with a brightly beaded band around the base of the open crown and a single large Eagle father hanging from the back by yet another cord. It was yet something else you would never see here in Brooklyn. Or maybe it was the long white hair that streamed out from under that big black hat falling down his back to midway, a style you didn't see from many men these days and none here in Brooklyn.

One of the three boys turned from looking at the ship of the Protectorate and stared up at the new shadow with wide eyes, the larger man of the two. "Whoa mister, you're HUGE!"

"Yeah, will, keep drinking your milk and you will be too," the large man stated looking down at the boy. The remark might have been meant to be encouraging but it was delivered way too cold, too indifferent, and the boy sensed it immediately.

"My mother can't afford milk seeker and when she can she has to water it down so my brothers and sisters get some too." The boy shot back with a small sneer.

The large man squinted suddenly and eyed the boy, "what did you call me?"

"Yeah, you must be some kind of a rich seeker or something to buy all the milk you'd need to get that big." The second boy chimed in pointing to the large man before elbowing his friend. "Hey Charlie, look at this big gavoon!"

"He didn't get that big drinking milk. The putz probably paid some alchemist to hocus and pocus him to get that big!" The third boy said turning to look up at the large man.

The larger man had no idea what the boys just called him, either time, but he knew it sure meant nothing nice which is why he leaned in with a growl for all three. It was the first time the boys saw him full on, all six foot four two hundred and fifty pounds of him, and the two really large modified guns he wore low on his hips in holsters tied down to the tan trousers complete with canvas outer leggings he wore around his thick soled boots. They gasped again and looked up past the large single breasted tan waist coat made of expensive wool material, the buttons starting out in the bottom center of the vest then shifting slightly to the right before trailing up to the top of the left shoulder making a curved trail. The three continued on looking right up to the hard set features of the man's face as he glared, his tan skin made even darker by the long black hair surrounding his features and the pulled down brim of the large Stoker hat he wore with goggles sitting on top of the brim. The two adversaries faced off for another second staring at each other, the large man and the boys, till the man won by feinting with a snap of his hand toward the gun on his right hip.

"RUN FOR IT CHARLIE!" The second boy screamed as all three turned and ran out into the street dodging the gas piston powered bikes and cars. The large man chuckled deep and turned back to see his smaller companion looking at him with a raised eyebrow.

"What? Those kids called me...something that wasn't very nice!"

The smaller man chuckled then to himself checking the time on the pocket watch he carried while speaking, his words mixed with a slight southern drawl. "We better hurry to Carlo's."

"How much time do we have?" The larger man asked putting a hand to his gun again, and this time it wasn't because the kids were across the street screaming some of the neighborhood's more colorful and unique colloquialisms at him. No, it was because of something else entirely.

"Not much at all, by now the Umbra will be zeroing in on the crystal. Their Hounds have the scent of Joris energy and they'll be out scouring the neighborhoods searching for the source. When they detect the stone they'll have the Protectorate ready to drop on us in a minute."

"As long as the stone's in the pouch its hidden right, I mean we're safe." The large man asked quickly, apprehensively.

The man in the hat grinned, "Until we take it out, which we want. Remember, we need the Umbra to find us but not until the time is right."

"I got it...not till the time is right...yeah, I got that." The large man only nodded and followed the smaller one as the man in the black hat led the pair north from the turn back into town. Overhead the large Protectorate air ship glided along on powerful downdrafts from countless large turbine fans, slowly moving but not meandering in some random pattern. No, the large ship looked to be zeroing in on something...or someone.

John's hat, you know, I have never really been sure what drew more attention to him in a crowd, that damn big black hat or his pure white hair. I guess I should start this whole thing by telling you who's writing all this down or what might be better to say first is 'when exactly' I'm telling you all of this.

First things first though, I'm the larger fellow in the group and my name is Wahkan, its IP for 'Sacred'. I know, you're asking 'what does IP stand for?' Well, just keep reading and I'll get to that. My friend there in the hat, his name is John, John Greywolf, and he's a Shaman. Again, something I'll get to later if you keep reading.

The year is 1929 and at the present time every able country that could have has passed through the Steam Age has done so and thus built a society based around steam as well as amassed an Army and Navy that's foundation is based on some variant of Steam Technology. Every country that fought in the Great War also now follows either some form of Isolationism or outright

Authoritarianism, and by that I mean most adhere to the one new law of survival in this world which is one where you protect your own and your country by any means necessary. From tall concrete walls where sentries stand with weapons at the ready keeping anyone and everyone away from their borders to maintaining strict entry and exit lists for any and all foreign persons stepping on their soil, every nation maintains a curtain of intense security and internal order and they do it through force if necessary. The world was fractured before the war and afterwards those breaks only seemed to intensify and deepen, former alliances have grown cold with distrust and enemies seem to be everywhere you look. There are still relations between most countries, trading and travel and such, no nation would be able to survive if there wasn't, it's just now everyone has come to the realization after one long bloody war in which millions died that helping a friend isn't as easy as sending in one battalion after another of soldiers and hoping for a quick end. There's a harsher cost to war and it can't be measured until all the fighting is done and sometimes the butcher's bill comes out to be more than what you were willing to pay.

Our only true ally these days is Great Britain, face to face meetings by the respective leaders or visits by ambassadors from shiny gated embassies still happen, but the Brits are the only ones left we truly call 'friend' it seems. The President of the United States still talks with the Prime Minister of Great Britain and old King

George but anyone else, the French or the Italians or the Spanish,

well it's done through about a hundred different people and envoy's

in between whose only job it is to break down every syllable of the

messages being passed to see what each leader is saying, as if a

'the' in the wrong spot might mean something sinister. We officially

closed the southern border to Mexico in 1920. We built a wall and

shut it down with air ships, as simple as closing a gate, right after

the Brits told Wilson about the Zimmerman Telegram from the

Germans. I don't think a President has spoken a word to any official

from Mexico since. In 1922, in the middle of rebuilding after the

war, the French abruptly sent everyone, ally or not, home shutting

down embassies left and right and ending any visible diplomatic tie

with all due to discovering an espionage ring they found buried deep

in their own government, the spies may or may not have been ours.

No one will ever know because no can ask them now. The French

executed the four men and two women a week later quick and tidy.

The French people were trying to recover from almost being

decimated during the war when the spies were discovered so all

economic trade was kept in place afterwards of course, for the

purpose of reconstruction you see, only now with a ton of

restrictions and inspections in place. The Russians and the Chinese,

no one really knows what's going on behind their walls because

both make sure there are no leaks to give anyone an idea as to

what's happening. I've heard Stalin took over Russia after kicking some fellow named Trotsky and his boys the Bolsheviks out of the country and then closed the gates to everyone but the countries right next door like Lithuania. And China, what little I've heard is anything but good about the place. The only country we deal with in the Pacific is Japan and it's all on their terms. Who gets to come in and what comes in all determined after extensive negotiations. The Far East is a mystery and it's one we'll probably never figure out.

Yeah, it's a world where no one trusts anyone but after we almost destroyed this place we walk around on in the first Great War I'll live with a little distrust. Some people say with all of this Isolationism we'll all just end up right in the middle of another war, that it's inevitable with this new type of foreign and domestic affairs. Maybe we will and maybe we won't with this new attitude, this new national strategy where you only protect your own. All I know is now, because of the war, if your country gets into nasty spat with another no one's coming to your aid, at least not without a lot of begging. After spending my time in a trench in France with shells and bullets flying by I'll take some healthy second guessing before going back to war. Wait...guess I need to explain how we even got to this point in the world as well huh?

Like I said, after the Great War ended in 1918 every able country on this planet turned to some kind of Isolationism but even that policy didn't happen overnight. If you had to ask to me, and I guess you are if you're reading this, it all started long before that damn war. It all started on the night of April 14th 1865 when a man named John Wilkes Booth tried to kill the President of these United States at the time, one Abraham Lincoln, in retaliation for the South losing the Civil War. He came close did John, almost shot old Abe in the back of the head, only the pistol he had pointed at the President misfired. It was a Derringer and noted to be as reliable as the day is long and yet the damn thing still didn't fire and when it didn't that's when all this began if you ask me, that Derringer misfiring sent us all down this road of a single nationwide military police force and closed borders and the birth of the Steam Age. I will give John a nod for the effort. He sure died trying to kill Lincoln, after his gun misfired he tried to beat Abe to death with that useless Derringer but he was shot in the head by a soldier standing just in the shadows of the box the Presidential Party was seated in. Ironic some historian once said, to go shoot a man in the head only to be the one who gets shot, and the next day it began.

Old Abe changed the course of the country after that night and he did it with the Army and the Navy and Steam. Every coin and dollar he could get Lincoln spent on building the infrastructure of the country back up, to advancing the use of Steam and its technology among the populace and businesses and of course the Army and Navy. Lincoln moved quickly after the assassination attempt forming what he called 'The Protectorate', a single militarized force combining the Army, the Navy and Marines, and every law enforcement agency across the land. The only difference between a soldier and a beat cop these days is where you're stationed, a base or the jail of a local police station. I could spend a whole lot of time going over all the political and economic quandaries and ramifications of what Abe did with his Protectorate. All the here and there and all the good and bad of what he did would take me too long to put down in words, and in the end that's not why I'm writing this anyway. I could go into a deep thesis about the way he trounced Personal and States rights and gave Congress the thumb in the eye as he did it while getting every able bodied police man and soldier under one roof, how he forced young men into the Army or Navy through the draft to expand both and then used the combined might as a force to police the country but I don't really care to talk about it. It's all said and done now, no going back and getting a second chance so it's just best to move on as John likes to say. Was Abe keeping everyone in line, including anyone who opposed him with his new 'Protectorate', this national police force? I'm not really sure about that, I do know this new type of military started as an effort to keep the world out of our affairs while keeping everyone here on the inside of the US borders in line while we rebuilt. And with the progression of Steam Tech it all worked out just fine, the US came back stronger than ever. No one tried to topple the government and they probably could have *because after the Civil War the country was weak and trying like hell to just stand back up on her own two feet. After the country was strong again the Protectorate just kind of grew into the sometimes oppressive force we have today, forming new units and off-shoots under the same umbrella. There's the Protectorate Bureau of Investigation, an elite force of investigators in the Police division they say who are used to bring in the worst of the worst and I hear Congress is about to sanction an Air Force adding an aerial contingent to the Protectorate, which should fit right in perfectly. Think about it, police in planes, who wouldn't want that? What I'm sure of is today, in 1929, the Protectorate doesn't intrude on your life unless you give them a reason too and once the men and women in uniform are at your front door they don't leave unless the reason that brought them there goes away. Is the Protectorate heavy handed once they knock and come in? My honest opinion is hell yes, but then my history with them leaves me biased. Every police officer, cop, and constable is a member of the Protectorate from every community, city, and state. A single group covering the land and connected through wireless transmitters and receivers so running from say Chicago to escape capture doesn't really work anymore because the minute you do every justice bringer and soldier and marine in the country will be looking for you and what happens after they catch you probably won't be very nice.*

I'll say this about Abe too, forming the Protectorate to police the nation may have been over-reaching and wrong in some people's opinion but listening to the advisors who told him to focus on Steam Technology saved the United States. We grew this country and put her back on her feet after the Civil War almost damn near destroyed it and we did it in short time. Our factories in the North went into some kind of over drive due to steam driven machines that could make the goods we sold to the likes of the British and the French, and anyone else for that matter, faster and better thus putting much needed money in our hands. The coffers for the country filled up quick and just as fast we spent the profits rebuilding from the Civil War, the South rose again to match the North in manufacturing and all on the backs and brains of men and women who created bigger and more efficient steam machines to help do everything from lifting heavy loads to driving rivets into steel to shaping molten iron into parts to farming the vast Midwestern fields. Men like James Walsh and women like Ana Krieg whose minds seemed fixated to a single purpose, steam and the wonders it could do.

Transportation was changed by steam as well, or should I say the way people and goods get from point A to point B. The horse and buggy were cast aside in favor of the gas powered engine of the trike then the bike and then the car but the train, already propelled by steam tech, was truly changed increasing in power carrying longer lines of cars till the day came which transformed the Iron Horse forever, brought on by an ingenious mind. We had taken to the skies in zeppelins before 1900 and then in bi-planes but a woman altered the way we fly and with her vision great air ships took to the clouds and soon the steam locomotive joined right next to them using her designs. There was no longer a need for a metal track for the trains to ride on, no sir, all the newly flying Iron Horse needed was plenty of fire in her boiler and open sky to fly through.

Ana Krieg took her father's ship building business and with her knowledge of the new steam tech developed turbines with enough force to lift waterborne craft into the air. The Wright Brothers flew a twin winged plane made of Spruce 120 feet in 1903, Anna did them one better 6 years later. She flew the first air ship from her father's shipyards in Boston to New York non-stop on a nice sunny spring day in 1909, a small single mast sailboat stuffed to the brim with a boiler of her design and two large turbine fans on the bottom with a third in back by the rudder to propel the ship. With a single set of wings using rudimentary controls to go up and down she made the trip with spectacular ease. She even devised a way to take off from a floating stationary point and then to move forward by using the turbines independent of each other. Then Ana only improved the turbine and the way the steam powered the fans so her ships could gain in size and carry heavier loads. Soon, and to no one's surprise, the Queen of the Air Ships rolled out the first air borne warship for the flying Navy, the power of flight added to the might of an old wooden frigate which was capable of flying across the breadth of these United States. It's a sight to see now just twenty years after Anna started, the water patrolled by a heavy steel Cruiser and then overhead a giant Battleship keeping the air safe.

Gas lamps gave way to electricity and with steam there was no need for hydro-plants to be built by running rivers to house giant spinning turbines powered by Mother Nature. No, James Walsh revolutionized the steam tech needed to drive generators which created the electricity. He took the work of other steam pioneers like Parsons and De Laval and with his genius created a generator driven by steam which was so efficient and powerful a single set of his turbines could power an entire city with minimal effort. Now places like Chicago and Atlanta have so much energy they sell it when they find someone willing to buy.

Yes, as a nation the United States started to rise, and as we grew other nations saw us and those in power followed suit. The countries in Europe, Canada, and the Pacific Rim began their own ventures into the Steam Age. Each country developed and grew just as we did with steam technology, each arriving at the same point we were. And when you have so many nations with the power to create massive flying armadas of warships and rolling war machines *like tanks then all it takes is a single country and its ruler obsessed*

to bring the whole damn shooting match to the brink of disaster.

On June 28th, 1914 we all learned that the hard way...

"Are you sure this is the place?" Wahkan asked looking around noticing all the buildings looked like ordinary store fronts. He turned back to the large one they stood in front on Fulton Street, a building that looked more like an apartment dwelling than the grocery store which was just a few feet down the block or the restaurant the other way. There were no signs, no open windows or curtains to look through, and nothing but a brick front with a small set of steps leading up to a set of double doors.

John looked to his large friend and nodded, "it's Carlo's brothel, conveniently hidden in plain sight here in the neighborhood as a tenement."

"Yeah, but you'd think the neighbors might complain about it." Wahkan offered looking over his shoulder to a vacant lot that sat between two more ordinary buildings across the street. John did the same while answering his remark, both men nodding to the empty space as if there was someone there looking to them.

"Would you speak out about a business watched over by Charles Luciano or Don Masseria?"

"You got a point there. Still, you would think the boys from the Protectorate or the PBI might come down on this place like a steam driven hammer?" Wahkan commented looking back to the set of double doors that one took to gain entry into the brothel, or apartment building as everyone in the neighborhood chose to think of it. In truth they had to think of it that way because you didn't dare think of it any other way or a say a word against it.

"You would think so," John said reaching up and checking the other pocket on the left side of his vest with a pat of his hand feeling the bulge there and smiling, "but then the Protectorate is just an organization and all those like it have the same problem."

A shadow suddenly appeared in the draped windows of the double doors, stood there for a moment eyeing the pair of men standing out on the sidewalk obviously judging whether to give the strangers access to the realm on the inside. As the shade watched them closely from behind the drapes Wahkan just stared back with hard cold eyes as he whispered back. "Yeah, and what's that?"

The lock on the doors popped making an audible click as the metal latches were freed, seems we've been granted entry Wahkan assumed as John answered with a low voice. "Money is the great corrupter my friend and certain endeavors can be 'overlooked' for just the right amount."

"These Weavers, the special ones, both are in there?" Wahkan asked standing perfectly still on the sidewalk for a moment before looking left then right then back to the doors, scanning for someone following. "And Carlo Troisi is just going to trade them to us?"

"I'm sure Carlo will make a show of trading them to us, a very nice charade, but I'm also sure he has other ideas." John remarked turning to his friend and grinning while titling his head so the brim of his hat would block out the sun. "Are you having second thoughts about doing this?"

"Nope," Wahkan answered quickly with a snap of his head and with such assurance in his voice and eyes that there was little doubt as to where his loyalties lie. "I'd follow you through Hell soaked in gasoline carrying a handful of matches' brother. It's just, you know, we're about to take the food right out of the lion's mouth here."

"Oh both ladies are in there, nowhere else would they be," the shaman remarked after turning back and staring at the door waiting to be ushered into the king's presence, sort of speaking. "And the lion always get the best pieces of meat so who better to steal a meal from."

The wind blew across and down the street, a breath of fresh air everyone likes to say, and both John and Wahkan took a deep inhale of it as the door on the right opened. A man dressed much like they were appeared in the doorway, a wool waist coat and black trousers but with no hat, and gave a single nod to them. The man had a large gun under his right arm in a shoulder holster. John took one last look back at Wahkan still smiling his usual boyish grin before starting forward up the steps nodding to the gent at the door while Wahkan only exhaled with a deep rumble of his wide chest and whispered.

"I have all the faith of my ancestors in you my brother warrior, but this is pure crazy what we're about to do."

Overhead the shadow of the large Cruiser began to roll slowly over the buildings and street as the Warship passed by. The wind picked up as the downdraft from the turbines that kept the ship afloat grew and the shadow only expanded as the cruiser began to slow and then lower.

All it took to was one crazy man killing two people to start a war that damn near destroyed us all, one man shooting an Archduke and his wife. The assassin was man from a small country called Serbia and the man he shot was the heir to the Austrian throne. Yeah, when it happened you could see the writing on the wall, this wasn't going to be settled easily or amicably because no one wanted to do just that, settle it the easy way. The Austrians and Serbs tried to work it out but a month later they were at war and it wasn't just them. Everyone started to jump in, the Germans

and the Russians and the Brits and the French. It was as if all of Europe had been waiting for some excuse to get to fighting and when that Archduke died the excuse was right there for the taking. Everyone says the Germans pushed it but if you ask me everyone was just waiting for the fracas to start. In one month everyone had declared war on someone else, alliances were formed and brokered, sides chosen and players divided up like a bunch of kids playing stick ball. The only one staying out was us, the US, but we couldn't keep our noses out of it for long and old Woodrow the President at the time put all our chips in two years after it began.

I was 17 when it all began, just a big old boy on the Indigenous People's Home-Land in Kansas. I remember reading about it and wondering why I felt this need to go and fight. I didn't know anything about Europe or any of the places the news was talking about. I couldn't tell the difference between a French men and a Serb if you paid me. And it didn't matter at first cause Wilson kept us out of the war all together using Lincoln's already in place policy of Isolationism. It wasn't our fight he said, so we'll just keep trading with everyone involved as if this thing wasn't happening. That lasted two years and when we'd had seen enough of our sailing ships and airborne trains downed by German subs and planes Woodrow threw in with the Brits and the French. I was 19 by then and as an IP we were exempt from the draft into the Protectorate, still there were others on the Home-Land who felt the call to go and fight and I joined in with them signing my name to the ledger and becoming a soldier for the Protectorate.

Three months later I was stepping on French soil in an area the locals called with a pleasant smile the 'Western Front'. I can tell you now without blinking or hesitating that this was as close to the apocalypse as I ever want to be and live to tell about it. The ground was bare for miles and miles due to the ever present shelling destroying everything, not a tree or bush or rock broke the horizon for as far as the eye could see, and because of the constant bombardment the ground just shook and rumbled all day and night around our trenches. We were at a stalemate at the time with the German forces, the give and take of precious ground in skirmishes prior to these days ceasing and every soldier digging in, fortifying trenches and positions. The fighting never really stopped, just the movement of the Armies. We would attack in the mornings on foot in a great rush only to be driven back into our holes with machine gun fire before the Germans would counter with steam driven tanks at lunch launching shells into our fortifications that released deadly Mustard gas in yellow clouds. The trenches filled with the poisonous fumes and I watched as the men around me would scream in pain from having their skin blister and peel due to the gas because they were too slow to cover up bare arms and faces. And then late in the afternoon the flying Warships would appear, great floating behemoths firing shells into each other, fighting and circling overhead as fire from the air battle and the damaged ships would rain down on us in glowing showers of burning metal and embers. I once saw a German cruiser literally fall from the sky after a British frigate struck it just forward of the mid-ships with a full broadside of its 8 inch guns. The turbines holding the ship aloft failed and the metal air ship dropped right back to Mother Earth with its bow burning and men running around on the deck seeking safety. The ground shook at first as the ship hit then it began to shake and roll like an earthquake as the Cruiser drove father into the dirt of the bare battlefield. The metal hull crumpled and broke and bent inward from the weight of the aft following the bow down and then the boilers on board exploded which in turn ignited the powder magazine. The last I saw of the Cruiser before the whole landscape turned into a massive ball of fire were men jumping off the sides trying to flee from what they knew was coming...death.

Yeah, I'm pretty sure Hell would be a nice place to visit compared to the Western Front.

The destruction of the Cruiser was just about the worst thing I had ever seen and I swore I was never ever getting on one of those damn flying cans. Then one morning, six months before the Great War mercifully ended, the last and most secretive weapon that both sides had held back till that moment appeared. The Germans broke from the normal cadence of the war, instead of us attacking them they came at us with their tanks. It was an obvious push, a surprise *attack meant to gain as much ground as they could get as fast as they could, and it looked like it might work because while every able man took up spots along the trench walls in what we all knew would be a wasted last stand the commanders called HQ trying to get our tanks up and in place to counter the charge. It was obvious we were about to be overrun. A charge of troops into a wall of slow moving steel firing machine guns wasn't the way I had planned on dying but I wasn't about to meet the Great Spirit while knee deep in muck at the bottom of some trench crying for my life either. If I'm going to leave this world it's with both guns firing and taking no prisoners. The German armor moved right up on us, feet from the edges of the trenches, ignoring the fire from our rifles and with no armor of our own to push them back we were in a bad spot. Then the front of the tanks popped open and out of those metal maws lightning came right for us, arcs of long blue electricity that broke the morning haze with colorful flashes before cutting down swaths of men who thought they were safely hidden down in the trenches. Then men and women stepped out of the tanks with others following close behind step for step, coming right at us. I remember seeing the ones in front with their hands glowing throwing what I thought at the time was electricity while the ones just in back simply touched the ones they followed, hands glowing just as bright fueling the awful power of the ones in front.*

The Magi had come from the dark and they brought their Weavers with them strapped to their belts by long chains that were tied to the collars around the necks of the ladies and men who followed.

Everything changed after that morning...everything...

It took a moment for his eyes to adjust to the semi-dark, but when his sight returned Wahkan noticed he was standing in a very nice foyer, a word like 'opulent' would most certainly be used to describe it he thought. There were two lounges on either side of a small cramped hall and to the right was a window in the wall where another man stood dressed in a very nice jacket with tails and an ascot. And then there were the three men dressed in the same wool vest and black trousers and guns under their arms. All three had appeared suddenly from the end of the hall where a large red drape covered the entrance.

"You need to leave your guns with coat check, and that includes the knife on your back fella. No one gets in carrying anything bigger than a toothpick." The man who let John and Wahkan in ordered pointing a finger at the smaller man. He knows about John's knife Wahkan smiled inwardly, someone's been keeping up with the stories about The Man in the Black Hat. Yet the best part was if they really knew anything about John then they would know that knife is nothing compared to the damage his hands and feet can do.

"You don't have enough men in here to take my guns 'fella'," Wahkan growled low in response letting his hands slide down his body toward the guns on his hips.

If there was a man who could take Wahkan in a fight John hadn't met him yet, still there was no need for violence the shaman quickly considered. He began to hold up a hand to offer a compromise when a voice called out from the other side of that brightly colored drape. "The boss says to let em' in, no need to worry about their weapons."

"Are you sure about that?" The man yelled back while eyeing John and Wahkan both. It wasn't long before his answer was forthcoming being a little louder and more direct.

"The boss says if you make him wait another minute he's going to have you shot and buried out in Secaucus, capiche?" The voice demanded. John just smiled, not as cheeky as Wahkan, but just enough to make the man grumble and nod, once and only once, toward the curtain to follow.

The two men walked through following the man who let them in with the three new ones following and when Wahkan saw what was on the other side of the drape his jaw almost hit the floor. It was a Hotel's lobby he instantly recognized, it was done up like the foyer in deep rich red colors, only just so far over the top it made you rethink how you might live these days. The room they entered was large and wide open with no hint of a ceiling for the five floors the building was comprised of until one's eyes reached the roof, which was made of glass to allow in the natural light. The floor was marble John noticed, where it wasn't covered in some thick expensive rug and all about the center of the lobby were lounges like the pair out in the hall, only these long couches were the places where the 'workers' here at the brothel waited to be 'employed' you might say. And there on more than one of the lounges was a working girl dressed in only her underclothes and thigh high stockings, stark white girdles with tops and bloomers it seems was the best way to dress here in the brothel. It gave men a teasing view of what they were purchasing, a small taste with just the right amount of delicate pink circles displaying here and there under the tops. A large open staircase with steps made of the same marble led one up to the first floor and the beginning of the rooms where one could spend the night for the right amount of money. The railings for the staircase were solid Rosewood with Mahogany newels and volutes; it was extravagance times twenty John thought. Wahkan noticed along the walls to his right a raised floor had been put in and private booths had been erected with more of the thick drapes hanging down by the entrance to each one. Great ceramic pots which held tall Parlor Palm plants with large fronds were everywhere giving the former lobby a garden like feel, though which garden was up for debate.

"You think they're going for a Garden of Eden thing here?" Wahkan asked as he walked along.

"Probably, though if you stumble across a talking snake and it offers you an apple I would advise against taking a bite." John smiled as he pulled out his watch and noted the time again with a quick check.

"It's too late for that boss," Wahkan chuckled then turned to one of Carlo's men walking next to him and pointed a thumb to one of few empty couches and lounges. "Say, where are all the girls? You shut down during the day?"

The man didn't even look his way, just spoke in a tone that was detached and not remotely interested in conversing. "We give most of the girls the morning off and some of the afternoon to rest from the night before. We have a few available to entertain special clients who make special requests for day visits."

"Sounds like a better work schedule than mine." The large man pointed out, an obvious dig at the smaller one. John just chuckled taking one last look at his watch before putting the time piece back in his waistcoat pocket and looking up to see the group was about to enter the back rooms. A single door was the gateway to the suites and offices of the brothel and a man dressed in much the same garb as the coat check gent opened the door allowing the mass of men to walk through in single file. Wahkan made sure to stay right behind John as they walked into a hall decorated just like the foyer and lobby, over the top. It was all, the foyer and lobby and these offices, a display meant to show how much money the boss of the brothel made, meant to exhibit the fact Carlo was a success beyond anyone's dreams. At the end of the hall was one last door and as if on cue the portal opened just as the group reached it, passed through into the last room. It was the personal office of the boss and it was even more opulent than what Wahkan had seen out in the lobby.

Behind a large desk made of the same dark rosewood and mahogany wood sat a man of obvious Italian descent. His hair was held in place with pomade of some exotic sort and his dark blue expensive suit looked straight out of one those Victorian shops in Manhattan where every meticulous stitch and cut is done by hands trained to do only one thing, make a suit a man would kill for. Carlo Troisi sat in a chair that looked more like a throne behind that garish desk drumming the fingers, each digit adorned with a large gold ring, of his right hand on the top. He scowled as the group entered and stopped by the large circular table in the center of the office, looked to the couch where a girl sat dressed in nothing but her unmentionables and stockings like the ones out front, and nodded for her to take a powder in the next room. Her long curly brown hair draped over one shoulder she stood up and sauntered past the men of the room with her hips swaying just the right amount to make their hearts skip. Her high heeled white Victorian boots crossed each other with a quick sweep as she walked and it matched the smoldering smile she gave Wahkan then the man in the black hat.

"Ma'am," John politely offered with a tip of his black hat as she passed. The lady just looked him up and down while smiling seductively still before exiting the room leaving the men to talk.

The drumming of the mafia boss's fingers stopped as Wahkan took a look around focusing past Carlo and his office's decorations for the first time to take note of the surroundings. He saw two men on either side of Carlo, both dressed in the same black attire as the other guards and both carrying large revolvers under their arms in shoulder holsters. A third man, young and dressed in clothes like Carlo stood on the other side of the room by some potted flowers. He was leaning up against the wall while playing with a deck of cards in his hands. As the other men piled into the room filling it up halfway the young man called out Wahkan while aimlessly shuffling those cards still, "you a real IP, right off the range and everything?"

"What kind of question is that?" The guard who led them back into the office hissed walking past to stand by Carlo's desk.

"I've never seen a real Indian before Mikey. We don't get many IP's here in Brooklyn...just want to make sure he's the real deal is all."

Wahkan sighed letting the air rumble out of his wide chest again as he noticed of a second door on the other wall adjacent to the one they came in. "Yeah, I'm a real IP right off the Home-Land and all."

"Really...Hey I hea-" the young man started to say when an abrupt 'Boom' stopped him short.

Everyone turned back to the desk, back to the man in charge after he slammed his hand down on the desk, as Carlo eyed the room with a glare that told the people present he was done with the pleasant conversation. "Where's Bentley?"

Before anyone could answer the other door Wahkan had spotted opened and a thin man entered quickly, obviously flustered from being late, adjusting and straightening his long black jacket that covered his whole body down to his ankles with fidgets and jerks of his hands. "Sorry, I was preoccupied."

"Alice just wouldn't let you go upstairs, huh?" The young man laughed but then stopped just as fast when Carlo turned his glare on him.

The man, Bentley, adjusted his long coat one more time getting all the buttons and both cuffs just right, the gold embroidery that flowed along every hem perfectly straight. Everyone waited, impatiently, as he then moved to fixing his greased hair before nodding to the mafia boss to continue. Wahkan only smiled thinking the skinny man was kind of funny with his machinations before he asked a question. "I thought Mr. Masseria said you fellas weren't allowed to use a Magi, you know, being from the old country and all?"

Carlo looked from John to Wahkan, those hard eyes trying to beat into the large IP, but the daggers both orbs were throwing failed to touch the large man as the IP only stared back just as hard. The boss of the brothel sat quietly for a moment before answering, "I decide who works for me and who doesn't, but you know what I don't like? People who ask a lot of questions, I really don't like that."

"Sorry about the intrusion, guess I'm a little too curious. I mean I've never been in a 'Family' run brothel before, you know, being from the 'range' and all." Wahkan smiled and the dig was instantly picked up by the guard Mikey who had escorted them into the back office. The man just sighed and shook his head.

IP, or Indigenous People, is what we the first ones to this land named the United States now call ourselves these days. We don't go by Redman, Native, or any other such low term. We are one tribe, one people, and we are strong. In 1874 Lincoln's lengthy

Presidency came to an end, his heart finally giving out as he sat at

his desk one night by himself working. What Booth's Derringer

failed to do that evening in Ford's Theater nine years earlier was

finally completed by being the tireless leader of this country and it

was done with quiet peace in a single moment. And before Mr.

Lincoln was taken to the other world he did one last act for us, the

first ones to walk this land, its Native People. He met with a

Hunkpapa Lakota holy man by the name Sitting Bull one night in

secret in 1872 in a small town in South Dakota in a vacant hotel

room. What Abraham heard in that meeting changed the course of

where we the IP stood in this country and it changed our history in

this new land of the United States. For years and years we had been

forcibly removed from our lands, our homes, and dumped onto what

the white men called Reservations. The promises of letting us live

our lives by our ways were never kept, never honored, and as such

we were a people ready to go to war to save ourselves. In that

room, sitting and talking like men, Sitting Bull told the President of

the United States to let his people be free and to let them live their

lives as they saw fit by their laws and ways or pay a dire

consequence.

Sometimes at night I sit on the deck of the air ship we live on

and look up at the stars wondering what really happened in that

meeting, what old Sitting Bull really told Lincoln? I wasn't born when it happened and what I know of it only comes from tales my grandfather would tell me and what the history books describe. Both stories, with all due respect to my grandfather, probably had more than a few embellishments that favored either Sitting Bull or Lincoln. What I think happened was simple. Sitting Bull gave Abe a choice, gives us our land and let us be or face another Civil War, another uprising. To make his point, my grandfather told me with a gleam in his eyes, the holy man handed over a carefully wrapped bundle of buckskin. When Abe opened that bundle he saw the emblem from every tribe from all across the lands, from the Lakota to the Blackfoot to the Cherokee to the Ojibwe, and as he looked up the holy man whispered with all the truth in his voice he could bring, 'we are one tribe now Great Chief of the White Man, we are strong and we will fight you to our last breath to be free'.

Maybe it was the fact Lincoln was older, wiser now than he was before the war with the Southern states or maybe he was just too damn tired to want any more bloodshed? Maybe it was the look in the holy man's eyes, the intent and meaning there not easily confused or missed? Whatever it was the President of the United States gave in. He shook hands with Sitting Bull promising the man that if he kept his people calm he would give them their land. After Abe returned from the meeting he kept his promise, a first for us, and pushed through the Indigenous People's Land Grant legislation giving us our land. From the badlands in South Dakota and stretching down through all the states right down to the pan handle of Texas is ours, three hundred and fifty miles at its widest point to a mere hundred miles in a small spot in Colorado, Sitting Bull had won us our homes and we did not sit back celebrating this accomplishment. We couldn't celebrate or rest. My grandfather said there were those white men who did not honor Lincoln's decision and I'm sure a few in the Congress back in those days had an obvious resolution to take all the land back. We were low, less than the white man those in Congress thought, but what everyone seemed to discount was our own intention and resolve to keep what was ours.

We built our own walls and fences and then towns and then cities behind those walls. We made our own economy inside our now new nation, we traded and bartered with each other and just as Sitting Bull told Lincoln we were one tribe now living our lives by our ways. We practiced our own religions, we honored our own Gods and ways, and we kept it all away from the eyes of the white man for as long as we could. We policed ourselves refusing the aid of the newly formed Protectorate, who by the way made sure no one made trouble for us outside of our walls. After Lincoln's passing Johnson never tried to resend the bill or come to take our land back, probably knew better because by then we were hunkered in and leaving was not an option. We, the Indigenous People, live peacefully now behind our walls. We trade with those outside our boundaries and we travel so don't think we're locked away on our land, but never forget we would have and will die to keep our land.

There's probably only one other group besides us, the IP and the Magi Society, who are more reclusive and secretive and it's the very men we ended up meeting with that day. There's not much I know about them but I'll give you what I do. There are five 'Families', groups of men more like, who pretty much run all the crime in New York. Any kind of gambling or prostitution or extortion or the-what-like, it all happens at the behest of one of the five Families. There are similar 'Families' in Chicago who do pretty much the same kind of work, run the same kind of enterprises. No one knows much about the Families and that's because they don't let their secrets get out. This fella here, Carlo Troisi, is a member of one of those Families. The word is the man over him is one Charlie Luciano and rumor is over Charlie is his 'Boss' or Don Masseria who runs that Family. It's all speculation though, smoke and mirrors, no one knows who is with whom really or who runs what in which Family. John told me that Luciano wants to organize all the 'Families' into one giant nefarious group...a Mafia is what he said someone called it. If that's the case then it's a bit scary if you think about it, look at the IP and what happened when we became one tribe.

"Is he the real deal?" Carlo asked staring hard at John.

Poor Bentley was still tending to the adjustment of his coat on his skinny frame so it took a moment for him to look at John then answer. "Yes, it is the Shaman Greywolf in the flesh."

"Shaman Greywolf," Carlo asked back before looking to John with a small sneer taking an obvious exception to the title before the name, "is that what they call you, Shaman?"

"It's just John," the man in the black hat replied with a smile.

Carlo drummed his fingers one more time thinking and looking over the two men who just walked into his office. He finally spoke with a curt and quick question getting to the bones of it you might say. "You told my associate you had a trade in mind, something that would make me some nice coin?"

"Yes, that's what I told the man in the butcher shop just a few blocks from here. I have a proposition, a trade for the two Weavers you have for the Joris stones I have." John answered truthfully. It hadn't been a chance meeting between the two. It was a well-planned encounter the shaman used to bait and draw in Carlo here...or better yet the Magi Bentley who watched carefully.

"Yeah, about that, how do you know about my girls when no one else does?" Carlo asked locking eyes with John.

"I wasn't totally sure you had the ladies, but then you did agree to this meeting rather quickly and with you asking how I knew about them...well that makes me feel a little more confident that you have them." John responded. The lie was perfect, not enough to show his hand and yet just enough to keep everything moving forward.

"All right, you got me on that one, but you better not be wasting my time. My man Bentley says these Joris stones are rare and very valuable, but it's going to take a lot to get my girls away from, me, understand?" The boss of the brothel finished coldly, setting the tone once and for all. Carlo didn't like being misled but John just smiled on. He was already in the door and that was the really hard part of all this.

"You truly have a pair of crystals infused by Joris the Misguided himself? This is not some...flimflam? To have one Joris stone is remarkable but to possess a pair is very auspicious, almost to the point of being questionable." The Magi asked and Wahkan smiled just a little. The bait worked like a charm because who could resist two Joris stones the large man thought as John nodded to the young man.

"This is not a ruse, I have one of the crystals with me as proof, but I don't see the Weavers? You keep them nearby I assume?"

The drumming of the fingers stopped as Carlo squinted just a bit, "What, you don't trust me John?"

"This isn't about trust Mr. Troisi, it's about business." The shaman said shaking his head causing the large Eagle feather hanging from the back of his hat to twirl and the aviator goggles around his neck to jingle. "I just want to make sure the Weavers are the 'real deal' as you say. You know, like Bentley here when he told you I am the true Shaman Greywolf."

The office went quiet for a moment as Carlo's face, which had been in a permanent snarl since before the meeting for some reason, changed to a somewhat happier one. A small smile, the kind where respect is given begrudgingly, crossed the man's face and he spoke without such a hard tone. "I have to respect a man who knows when it's time to shut up and deal. Michael, have Vincent and Joe bring our girls in."

The guard who led them into the office nodded and went back out the door to the small offices but he was only gone maybe a half-a-minute. Carlo's office went quiet again as everyone waited for the other party to this meeting to arrive, and the men didn't wait long. The door Michael, or Mikey depending on how old and thus how respectful you were, went through suddenly opened and a large man holding a young dark skinned woman by the arm dressed in frilly underthings like the other girls in the brothel entered the office. He escorted her into the room rather roughly making sure to keep her under control. Her hands were bound together in front of her by a set of leather cuffs and those tied through a small metal ring attached to a collar she wore round her neck by a loop of bright chain. Her arms were held in a prayer position and with her hands bound the young woman looked quite helpless as she scanned the room with frightened eyes. She inhaled in ragged breaths through a thick gag as her midnight curly hair practically poured down her back and past her waist, streaks of purple highlighting the locks. Wahkan was about to ask everyone and anyone why they had her tied up and gagged like this when the other door to the office opened quickly and another large man escorting a second young woman with white alabaster skin entered, ushering her just as roughly. She was dressed the same as her female counterpart, the same undergarments and thigh high stockings, and her hands and arms were bound just the same as was the gag. The only difference was where the dark skinned girl had long black hair this girl's was long in the front only with long flowing bangs to her breast held in place with small black bowties by her temples. The rest of her hair in back was short and spiky and as green as the grass in a meadow on a sunny afternoon.

And as soon as she saw the other young woman the green haired one began to scream for her through the gag.

The quiet of the office disappeared as the muffled cries of both the Weavers echoed in the space, muffled screams bouncing off the plaster walls and molding. Each Weaver fought the man holding her firm trying to break free of the stronger hands, jerking their arms and pulling with all the might their legs could make. It was a futile attempt at a tug of war neither young Weaver could win and yet it didn't matter to either one. Both only wanted nothing more than to be with the other, to touch and be held, and they would have fought to the very end to do so. Everyone knew this for a fact because as soon as the pair began to fight to reach each other the crushing emotion of desperation along with the sudden elation of deep sadness being lifted washed over all the men threatening to swamp them each and every one, as if being caught in a tidal wave of empathy. Wahkan felt his heart began to beat fast, his pulse race, and all he wanted to do was to get the pair of Weavers back together. The feeling was so strong it overwhelmed the large man for a minute and he growled. "Why are they tied up? Why are you keeping them apart like this?"

About a half-second after the words were out Carlo was exploding up and out of his throne like chair and pointing a menacing finger at Wahkan, the emotional wave from the Weavers obviously overwhelming the boss of the brothel making it far too easy for him to become angry at the large man. "Hey, do you know where you are? You have any idea who I am or what I can have done to you?"

"Wahkan," John suddenly said drawing everyone's attention to him. Everyone could see the IP was just a hint away from drawing one of those big modified handguns from the holsters sitting low on his hips. The emotional deluge was smashing into everyone like a tempest drawing out the anger from Wahkan and Carlo both, but John was just calm as the water of a river as it slowly flowed by on a sunny afternoon.

"It's not right...they don't understand..." Wahkan growled again with the tip of his fingers on his right hand about to grasp the grip of his gun. The guards all around the office began to surround him as Carlo yelled out across the room.

"You better tell your man here what is what, you understand me John? Or I swear I'll put a bullet in both of you and take-"

"Wahkan," John stated louder cutting off Carlo. His voice never reached above a yell, never became more than stern and yet it drew every eye in the room to him instantly. A calm serenity began to flow through all that looked to the shaman, the peaceful Zen countering the sudden rush of emotions. The anger in Carlo began to ebb amazingly as did the intention to hurt all those around him in Wahkan's eyes. Even the Weavers had stopped fighting to reach each other and stood staring at the man in the black hat with acute attention as he spoke. "Listen to me and be calm... the anger, it's just a side effect, what your feeling isn't you...the Weavers will be fine...trust me."

The large man only nodded and slowly pulled his hand away from the gun's grip as he mumbled a single word over and over only he and John understood. It was an old Lakota word for peace, a mantra Wahkan would say to himself to calm his anger. As he did the emotion in the room stayed high and thick, the desperation and fear still swirling around everyone like an invisible maelstrom continuing with the real threat to bring the meeting to a rather bloody end. John turned to Carlo still holding the man's attention with his words. "It may be a good idea to let the Weavers touch at least. It would certainly help the mood in the room."

Carlo took in a deep breath taking control of his own anger, using the quiet and the strange calm the shaman induced to do what thinking his addled mind could, and then he nodded to the men holding the women. "Let em' go."

As soon as the order was given both Weavers broke free and ran to each other. The dark haired brown skinned one was a couple inches taller than her companion and with their hands and arms bound it only allowed them to hold hands and lean into each other. The desperation and fear that was so strong just moments before was gone now replaced with the joy of love and a contented fulfillment that did just as the shaman had said would happen. Everyone eased, hands loosened and Wahkan actually looked at to the pair now with a small smile as they clung to each other. From the side a small voice spoke up barely audible enough to break the moment it seemed, "how did you know about the empathy?"

John turned and looked to Bentley smiling just enough now to make the left side of his mouth crooked as he answered. "I was told by someone who was once close to the pair about their uniqueness. A side effect of their absorbing energy is both are now empaths...very powerful empaths. It's what also makes the bond between the two so strong, to the point of being unbreakable and making separation impossible for any length of time."

"Who told you what the Weavers could do?" Bentley asked with a shocked whisper. The Magi had just about the worst poker face of anyone Wahkan could remember. John looked about ready to answer the man in the colorful coat when the harsh voice of Carlo cut him off before he could start.

"Yeah, Mr. Shaman, just who have you been talking with about my girls?"

My people believe there is life in everything, from the rocks we walk on to the plants we touch to every animal and being that breathes the very air. There is a life force, an energy, that makes the universe what it is and this essence flows around us, encircling us every second of everyday and there are those among us who can pull this very essence and energy into themselves holding for a brief time before passing it through contact to the ones who can use the energy outwardly, wield it and manipulate it.

Such is the world of the Magi and the Weaver...forever bound together...

No one knows where the first Magi came from or even who the first one was. No one knows if the person was a man or a woman, a child or an adult or elder. Not much is known about the past of the Magi and that's not by accident but design. All the history books tell us is the Magi first appeared that fateful morning on the Western Front, a close third to being the worst morning of my life. The other two I won't be talking about here. There's no other word, sentence, or paragraph devoted to the subject of the history of the Magi in any official capacity. This doesn't mean there's not a story or two floating around, from the myth that the Magi are fallen angels to the one where some strange fairy fly's around touching the special children on the forehead thus 'creating' the Magi. It's all a bunch of bunk, crazy talk, but there never seems to be an end to the fools who dig around trying to find out the origins of the Magi. I've heard if you go asking questions about their history then you'll most certainly be paid a visit by a few members of the Protectorate. They will ask nicely why you're inquiring about the Magi's past and then they will most certainly tell you to stop whatever it is you're doing. The Protectorate does just that, protects the Magi, and in turn the Society protects them on the ground and on the air ships with specially trained Magi Warriors. Both groups are separate and untouchable with everything they do in the light where everyone can see, but back in the dark hidden away from our eyes I'm sure both the Protectorate and the Magi Society are joined at the hip in an odious partnership. And it's the same for any country you visit; the Magi are guarded and in some places revered and some are as crooked as a dog's hind leg. The Society wants their people and their history kept in the shadows for some reason, so much so no one even knows how they are structured or how the Society is run. Some say there's levels a Magi gets promoted too by groups or councils, like rings reaching up to the heavens, and the higher up you go the more powerful the Magi become and these 'Elders' make all the decisions. All I know for sure is by that afternoon we, the Allies on the front, had our own Magi appearing out of the smoke and the fighting in the war got worse...much more than anyone could have dreamt in a terrible nightmare. It was so terrible this magical warfare that after the Great War the Magi Society was formed for one simple task, to seek out and train all magically inclined and capable individuals, and unlike the governments of the advanced countries like the US or France who use Isolationism to keep everyone at arm's length the Society crosses all borders and all in it are considered part of the 'One'...or it use to be from what I've sensed from the Magi I know and talk to. I'm having a hard time seeing all the solidarity of just a couple years ago now, what with the tensions between countries being so bad and all. There used to be no boundary for the Magi, no wall or fence to stop their influence, but I bet those days are disappearing quickly. All I am sure of is if you can use magic then you must register with the Society. There is no choice, go freely or be hunted down and taken in for 'Indoctrination' in chains by the Umbra, the hunters for the Magi and all call the 'Shadows'.

To wield this heavenly energy, this force, a Magi must have the Weaver at his or her side to gift them the magic. No Magi I know of or have heard of can take in the energy from the universe. They can only manipulate it once it has been given to them. Most Magi can only throw the energy as bolts too, like lightning from the fingertips, but there are the few who can do 'more' with the power given by the Weaver. There are a few rare souls called 'Conjurers' who can form the essence into anything they deem. I've only seen one Conjurer and at first the large ball of bright light which she formed and controlled seemed innocent, like a big balloon. Then the energy flowed and changed into the shape of a large Eagle and she sent it flying across a city, blocks and blocks it flew past buildings and people and vehicles and air ships. It finally landed, struck a single man on a balcony setting him on fire and burning him alive as it did. He was a Technoist from what I was told and he may have been a wanted man by the Protectorate. The Conjurer never said why she really killed him and I never had the chance to ask.

Weavers, oh those poor souls, I can't imagine a life being one. What I, and the world for that fact, doesn't know about the

Magi we make up for with the knowledge of what makes the Magi a Magi. The Weaver, the one who can sense and see the life force around us, is born with the gift or curse depending on how you look at it. The ability shows itself at a young age, between 6 and 8, and from that point the life that was a child's can go down two paths. All Weavers, just like Magi, must be registered at the Society when the power manifests and when they are the Magi take them from the families. No one but the Society is allowed to raise a child who has shown the power of being a Weaver because it is too dangerous, too hazardous to the parents and others. A young boy, seven if I remember right, down in Charleston SC was born a Weaver. His folks had no intention of taking him to the Magi or the Society, then one morning he drew in the energy around him and accidentally released it into the door to his bedroom. The man who told me the story choked as he looked at me with a serious expression. The boy was giggling he said to me after getting his voice back, probably laughing at how his old door was glowing like some big night bug when it exploded with enough force to destroy his room. The boy died and his parents never forgave themselves for not getting him registered.

See, a Weaver can pull the energy into themselves from the world around them but once they do the man or woman must release it as soon as they can. A Weaver can't hold the energy in forever, something about the human body not being compatible or such to hold the force for any true length of time, but a Weaver can give the energy to a Magi or infuse an object that can hold it. Now, there are not a lot of things in the world that can hold the energy but there are some crystals and specially crafted jars which can keep a 'charge' for a good while. Things like bedroom doors and such, those can't, and just like that boy in Charleston those things will blow up taking anyone and everything nearby with it when it goes. Suffice to say it depends on the strength of the Weaver and what the object is made of as to how long the force will stay in it because even a crystal can only hold the magic for so long, the energy inside ebbing away back to the ether ever so slowly. A Magi can use the object before that happens though, can absorb the energy from it and use it for whatever they want, just as if the Weaver was standing right there beside them. This became the preferred way for a Magi to fight as the loss of a Weaver leaves a mighty big hole to fill, only so many magical conduits to go around John once said. I know that morning on the front we learned very quickly that once a Magi had no Weaver following behind him or her it left them defenseless and easy targets. A Magi without a Weaver is kind of like a dog without a bone, and that's why the Weaver is so sought after...more of a commodity then a human being. It's why every Weaver wears a collar, placed on them when the Society takes them in, so everyone will know they have been claimed by the Magi.

The second path I spoke of is the child is taken underground, hidden from the outside world and the Society to keep them from being registered. There's a whole Underground infrastructure, I've seen it...the old railroad the slaves who escaped their masters in the South used, and all along it families hide and move in secret always looking over their shoulders for the Umbra, the hunters of the Magi who never have to sleep it seems. And if that wasn't enough to have to worry with constantly there's the market for the sale of Weavers which runs right along that Underground Railroad. If a family runs into an even worse stretch while hiding out a quick sale of a Weaver infused crystal can bring a fair amount of coin while the sale of an actual Weaver can bring in a truckload of gold. I'll let your imagination take you to the dark place a person sold there ends up, I won't be following anytime soon.

Lincoln freed the slaves with the Thirteenth Amendment but no one's come to the aid of the Weavers. The Society and the Government moved swiftly to make a Weaver a human 'with special considerations' and thus in need of 'special attention'. Maybe it's because we can only see them as objects, highly sought after prizes that can bring a nice stack of coin if the opportunity arises? Maybe it's because deep down we fear them so there no compassion in our hearts for them? I wonder why we look on the Magi with awe and the Weaver with a disdain when it's the Gods who can't survive without the ones who pray to them. Whatever the reason the life of *a Weaver is a harsh one, hoarded and sold and taken away from the world to live at another's beck and call.*

If that's not slavery than I don't know what is,

"If I told you Mr. Troisi, you wouldn't believe me."

The man moved around his desk slow, his coat and ascot in perfect place never moving an inch as he walked. Carlo stopped by the large circle table in the room opposite of John and spoke cold and to the point. "Why don't you tell me and I'll decide if I believe it or not."

The shaman looked back without blinking, still smiling, and took a moment to answer with another well thought out response. "The man who contacted your Magi here about the Weavers six months ago, the very same man who hasn't been seen since selling you the pair, he talked to someone. He told a woman he was seeing about the pair and she traded the information to me for some assistance I gave her."

It wasn't a complete lie, as to how he found out about the Weavers, but at the moment with the present company it was better to deceive than to be forthright. John knew it was best to leave the full truth of how he had come to know of the ladies out, cover it with the real truth of why a Protectorate cruiser had ended up being in Brooklyn this morning filled with Marines. All it took was one person talking, the woman who 'befriended' the man who sold the Weavers to Carlo, to speak to the right set of ears at the National Police and the full weight of a devious alliance was about to crash down on the heads of everyone in the brothel. The woman had gone to Protectorate seeking help in finding the man she loved. She knew Carlo had something to do with his disappearance, which was true because he did, and she told them it had to do with those two Weavers he had come across and sold to that mean man Carlo Troisi. It was true, the boss of the brothel had her man killed to keep the Weavers existence a secret and yet if Carlo had just left him alone the woman wouldn't have gone to the police and there would be no Cruiser overhead ready to end this all. Oh the sour taste of irony John thought.

"He talked?" Bentley gasped with shock. John never took his eyes off Carlo as the Magi next to him began to shiver just a little at the news, "Oh no, no, how many others know?"

"Why are you worried so bad Bentley. We've had the pair for months now and the only one who's come asking about them is John here. I think the broad who told John here about my girls didn't talk to all that many people." Carlo sneered while smiling back now.

"You're girls?" Wahkan snarled back without a smile, one of the few now due to the loving emotion of the Weavers flowing over them, not liking how the boss of the brothel referred to the ladies. The inclination in the question was as easy to see and read as the two large modified guns slung low on the man's hips.

"Your damn right, my girls, bought and paid for by me. They're mine!" Carlo pointed out with a growl and a pointed finger at the large man.

John raised an eyebrow at Wahkan signaling his friend silently to calm as he spoke carrying the conversation and negotiation forward. "Well I assume the woman didn't understand what a find her boyfriend Maxwell had come across, the money he could have truly made if he sold the pair in the Underground Markets. As it is she only talked to two men including myself about her lover and his disappearance which makes the chance of someone else knowing about the Weavers very small."

"Yeah, really, well he missed a chance to make some nice coin but then he didn't have his own Magi to tell him just what the pair of Weavers was worth so it was his loss. Now, just what else do you know about my girls?" Carlo asked raising his own eyebrow now mimicking the shaman. Wahkan stood off to the side watching his friend and the boss of the brothel talk with one eye while with the other watched the Weavers closely still trying to remain calm. They were still standing together touching bound hands and the guards just a mere inch or two away. Any opportunity to do a snatch-and-run out the backdoor was out. Hell, he didn't even know where the back door to this place was.

"I know a little more, like I can tell both Weavers grew up in the Society due to the fact both have collars. Their odd hair color is due to the absorption of the energy they take in to gift to a Magi to use, a side effect like the empathy. I know the empathy both possess, which is extremely rare, was used to bind them. It's also why you paid so much for both and why your brothel here is visited frequently by a very rich and exclusive clientele. You keep them apart because when they come together finally and the brothel floods with their emotions-" John explained before the young man leaning up against the wall laughed cutting him off.

"The place explodes, I mean what you felt here was nothing to what happens, and the show those two put on in the back room when their together is wild. Sometimes, if we're lucky, the dark haired one will tie up the green one and spank her!"

"That's enough," Carlo barked at the younger man, a look of embarrassment on the boss of the brothel's face, and for the first time Wahkan noticed the family resemblance between the men, maybe a nephew?

The Magi exhaled loudly and shook his head in obvious frustration at the young man. It wasn't hard to see why John thought as Bentley spoke, "We keep them apart for two days. It is the longest amount of time we can do such a thing before they begin to get too sick."

"And the gags and bounds hands?" Wahkan asked, this time with considerably less anger.

The Magi looked to the guard who had led them in, the one called Michael, and the man took over answering. "When we started to separate them they would yell for each other, cry out all day and night, so we gag them to keep them quiet."

"You know they cry out because it hurts them to be apart, right?" The large friend of the shaman growled and if the guard had been anywhere but his boss's office in the middle of a meeting he might have taken a shot with his pistol at Wahkan from the obvious slight.

"I know we keep their hands bound because the dark haired one accidentally charged the door knob to her room one night and the explosion almost killed her and two of our boys."

The room was quiet again for a moment, the tensions between the guards and Wahkan still strong enough to sense, when the Magi looked to John. "What plans do you have for the Weavers, if I may ask?"

"My plans are my own Mr. Bentley, I am sorry I can't say what those are." John replied and the Magi only nodded slightly, as if disappointed, while the shaman continued on. "Do you know much of their past, the Weavers?"

"No, Maxwell barely knew anything about either short of being called by the man who stumbled upon them one morning in a barn in upstate New York. We do know the one with the green hair is British and she goes by the name Wells. The dark haired one speaks little to us except to ask for her companion. We only know her name is Boles because her companion Wells has said her name out loud...during...while...well you know."

As Bentley spoke, turning a nice dull shade of crimson as he tripped over his words, the shaman locked eyes with the Weavers staring at both equally without flinching or blinking. He already knew the Magi's answer was a lie, young Bentley knew exactly who the Weavers were so there was little reason to listen to the man. The eyes of Wells were bright, youthful, and as brown as the leaves of the tress in autumn. Boles was the stronger of the pair, the more assertive of the two, and her eyes showed it. The brown was deeper and fiercer as she looked back to John. He smiled at her for a moment before speaking knowing what he was about to say would send a ripple through the room and her as well. "Boles there, she's Polynesian, her father and mother turned her over to the Magi because both were afraid if they didn't the others around the village might try and kill her for being a witch."

There was an audible gasp from the Magi. It had to be a little disconcerting to realize someone else knew more about your Weaver than you did. The look in Boles eyes went from that fierce fire to shock in an instant as did the eyes of Wells. One of the guards whispered something just outside the range of making out his words, probably some exclamation as to how the shaman knew this about the dark haired Weaver. Everyone was quiet sifting through shocked and concerned thoughts due to what John had said...how he knew what he knew, that was all but one actually.

"Polynesian huh, funny but she doesn't look like she's from Florida."

The remark from the young man leaning up against the wall playing with the deck of cards still jarred everyone from their silence and deep thinking, like getting punched. Every eye turned to him as every mouth opened and went slack just a bit being stupefied. Michael the guard finally spoke breaking the awkward silence with the most obvious question of the year, "Florida...what...where did that come from?"

"Yeah, Florida...Polynesia's close to Boca Raton, right?" The young man asked looking around the room for support, maybe some help, and finding nothing of the sort from anyone. It was like watching a blind man grope for a glass of water, over and over.

"Polynesian means she's from Hawaii, you know, that big island out in the middle of the Pacific Ocean." Wahkan hissed just as Boles behind him shook her head still wondering how the boy was even allowed here in the same room with all these men.

"Oh, really, well Hawaii and Florida are kind of alike you know...both are tropical right?"

"Angelo," Carlo suddenly snapped bringing everyone's attention to a single point again, him.

"Yeah Uncle," the young man replied and it abruptly became very clear as to how Angelo was where he was in the brothel's organization. The reply also made Carlo wince, an actual grimace of pain, before he answered.

"I need you to be quiet, understand."

"Yea-"

"No," Carlo snapped again holding up a finger silencing Angelo quickly, "not another word or I will make your mother and my sister very unhappy, nod if you understand?"

Angelo looked around the room again; in part to avoid his uncle's hard eyes and partly to see who was staring which was everyone, before turning back to Carlo and nodding slowly just as the boss spoke. "Good, now John, you've seen mine and you obviously know quite a bit about my girls. It's time for you to show me yours and it better be worth my time like I said."

The threat from Carlo was as close to the truth as you could get, right hand of God. If what he was about to do didn't impress the man then John was sure the boss of the brothel here would surely see him shot in the head as well as Wahkan. Yet the shaman felt no fear or worry, his plan had worked perfectly so far and he still had his ace in the hole you might say, one Magi Bentley. See, Carlo had no idea what his mouse of a Magi had been doing with his spare time but he was about to find out. With a slow move, a splendid use of dramatic affect and an even better way of not getting shot, John pulled out of his vest pocket a pouch tied at the top with drawstrings. He held it up for a moment then slowly placed it on the table top before pushing it to the center with a small shove of his hand.

The room was silent as everyone stared at the pouch, some with pure excitement like Bentley and the Weavers behind John while the others were a little lost. What was this, a bag, really? Carlo looked at the pouch for a moment then up to the shaman with a look that was somewhere between incredulity and anger at being mocked. "That's it, a bag? All of this for a bag?"

"Not the bag alone Mr. Troisi, but what's inside the pouch, that's what this has all been about. If you think I'm trying to trick you just ask Bentley here or even better yet look at the Weavers and see how they're reacting. This is, as you say, the very real deal." John responded smiling, holding a hand out to the pair of ladies behind him.

"Oh my...he's right...I can feel the energy from here, it's a real crystal truly infused by Joris himself." Bentley whispered looking to the shaman as Wells only nodded and stepped back away from the table. If any of the men in the room had been paying any attention at all to them, the Weavers, then one might have asked why Wells was acting the way she was. A frightened Weaver should have at least raised a question, but just as John knew would happen all the eyes in the room were on the pouch and nothing else.

"And just what makes a crystal touched by this Joris guy so special, huh?" Carlo asked, the tone in his voice now sounding very skeptical, almost to the point of scoffing at the shaman.

"No Mr. Troisi," Bentley quickly spoke up sensing the suspicion in his employer's voice which in turn raised the panic in his. The Magi was moving quickly to head off Carlo's skepticism, something John had counted on. "What we have here isn't a simple crystal charged by some common Weaver. No sir, what we have here is a rare item, a repository of such power and limitless potential that I cannot put into words how valuable it is."

Maybe the Magi should have tried to put the worth of the crystal in some kind of context the boss of the brothel understood better because Carlo had the expression of a man who believed next to nothing being told to him.

Joris the Misguided...

You know, I've never been one to go for tag along names like 'the Misguided' or 'Daniel the Terrifying'. It's all too much, too damn silly, but if there ever was a more deserving moniker given to a man then 'Misguided' was perfect for Joris. Just like the Magi themselves no one really knows where Joris came from, just that one day he popped up in Finland and began to tour the world with his Magi master Elinor. They say it was quite the contrast between the two; Joris was just like a true Viking standing tall and wide with a long braided strip of dark hair running right down the middle of the cleanly shaved sides of his head, right down his back. Elinor was small Finnish woman with braided blond hair, but she was also a strong Magi and everyone says it was because of her Weaver. Joris was good at doing what a Weaver does, to the point it was unbelievable how strong he was with his ability. He could draw in a seemingly endless amount of the energy, so much that he had to give Elinor little bits of it at a time I've been told. If he had given her all the energy he took in with one push he might have killed the small Magi but I think Elinor could have survived it. She was more than just a simple Magi who threw lightning from the stories I heard, she was a Conjurer and with all the energy Joris gave her Elinor made spectacular creations under her direction. The two were meant to be together people say, maybe they were in love with each other as some have said, which makes what happened next so tragic.

The Magi Society is just that, a group of like-minded individuals all moving toward a single purpose in lock step, no one more important than the other is what they say right? Well, try as you might you'll never rid yourself of all the pettiness and jealousy that comes with a hierarchy. Someone will always covet the spots at the top and the men or women in charge will always have to look over their shoulder. It's the same in the Protectorate, the same with the men who run things in Government, and it's the same in the Magi Society. Anyone who saw Elinor understood she was as smart as she was beautiful and with Joris at her side unstoppable in the climb up the Society's ranks. She was poised to rise right up through those levels of mysterious councils and with Joris and his limitless power Elinor would have been an 'Elder' no doubt.

Would have been if not for the fact someone betrayed her and had her killed, assassinated alone in her room at the Society's home in London. They say it was Joris who found her, had come running screaming her name over and over like a mad man. They had to knock him clean to unconscious to get her body out of his arms, and even after that the Magi had to still pry his hands apart to make him let go of her. Who had Elinor killed? I don't know and if you ask any Magi they won't even mention her name. Whoever had it done had to be high up and as cruel as a jackal to silence any question that might come up? And whoever it was had no idea at what killing Elinor would do, that the act would unleash a monster like no other on the world. The night Joris escaped from the Society he killed four young Magi and one older one. He set their Weavers *free, let them live, and then took off into the dark to hopefully disappear from the world, only that wasn't what Joris had planned. No sir, he had revenge in is heart and death planned for every Magi he could take with him before he was finally done in. Joris blew up the buildings, brought the damn things down by destroying the huge foundations, and cars and the personal air ships of the Magi. He went from London to Dublin to New York and everywhere he went destruction followed with devastating effect on life and property. How he stayed hidden and out of the Umbra's reach I can't even begin to imagine. He had to have had help, some who hid away from prying eyes. The Umbra is trained from day one to hunt down Weavers and Magi, a shadowy group who are exceptional at what they do. The Umbra should have caught Joris long before he made it to Atlanta a year after Elinor's death. They should have stopped him before he killed so many Magi all over the world, but they couldn't and maybe it was justice finally catching up to the Society. In the end no one stopped Joris but himself. He found a non-descript statue in the center of a small town north of the rebuilt city of Atlanta one night. A man working late in a small store remembered seeing Joris, remembered how he poured so much energy into that monument that it glowed as bright as the sun itself and then just stood there. When the statue exploded the force of the blast leveled all the buildings nearby, the local Protectorate had to dig the man out of the wrecked store he was cleaning.*

The boogeyman was gone, all the Magi could rest finally, but then the first crystal Joris left behind showed up. It was so full of energy it knocked out the poor Magi who tried to examine it and this was after months of the crystal being hidden away. The power of Joris, even in death, was beyond what anyone could have imagined or dreamt of what a Weaver could do. Then another crystal surfaced and another and then a jar and another and all were so full of energy it took several Magi to drain them. Joris left little trinkets all along the way to his death, little bombs just ready to explode and the worse part was he knew most would find their way back to the Society. With one last act to finish those who took his Elinor old Joris didn't go quietly into anyone's night. If someone finds a relic of Joris, a crystal or a jar, that someone then must take it to the Society immediately. It's the law of the land and yet just like the Weavers, and anything else for that matter, there's an underground market for anything that Joris might have touched. If you have a Joris infused crystal then you can make some true coin, significantly more than what a Weaver can get you, but you better be quick about the sale because the Umbra is always watching and lurking ready to chase after a piece of Joris

"Do you know how much money comes in when those two girls do that thing they do? I can make triple what I make on a regular night when they get all hot and put out those feelings. The Johns go at it harder and the working girls want it more, it's a win-win for me anyway you look at it. So, tell me, how does a rock touched by this Joris guy match that?"

The question by Carlo went unanswered by the shaman, not because John couldn't answer it but because he just didn't need to. He watched with that small smile as Bentley next to him went in a deep panic speaking in a muddled burst. "Mr. Troisi please, you cannot quantify or set a price on a crystal infused by Joris."

"Then why do I care? If that stone can't make me money the way those two do then we're not talking anymore, understand?" The boss of the brothel asked with a shake of his head.

"Sir, please just imagine for a moment, there are endeavors beyond money-" Bentley tried to explain before getting cut off by Carlo again.

"Money is the only thing that matters here Bentley, the one and only endeavor I care about, understand? I don't see how-"

"Please Mr. Troisi-" Bentley begged to no avail as Carlo wasn't hearing any of it.

"-a rock is going to make me any kind of money like my girls so this whole thing has been a waste of my time."

The room was quiet as Carlo stared at his Magi; hard eyes beat into Bentley until the young man just gave way and nodded. It was time to close my trap John thought just as a rumble rolled through the room, a slight gyration that registered in no one's mind but the shaman's. The cruiser overhead had settled in close to the brothel John thought, the Protectorate and the Society had finally locked in on where the stone might be and it was nothing short of perfect timing for him. "A Joris crystal can fetch triple what your brothel here can make in profit in a year Mr. Troisi, does that sound worth it?" The shaman spoke getting things moving again.

Oh, now that put a new spin on things. Both of Carlo's eyes went wide as he looked to Bentley with a questioning expression. The Magi only nodded quickly seizing on the new chance to get the crystal. The boss of the brothel turned back to John and spoke in a lighter tone now, "triple what I make in a year? How do you know what I make in a year?"

"I'm only guessing at what you might make here with your business Mr. Troisi. I do know what a Joris crystal sells for on the Underground Market, you might even get four times if you find the right buyer and that is just for the one crystal in that pouch on your table. The second one I have to trade is bigger and thus more powerful." John added knowing full well he had his fish hooked and was just reeling him in.

"More powerful," Bentley whispered with his eyes going wide now, from anticipation John could sense.

"That means its more valuable, right?" Carlo asked leaning in just a bit.

"Oh yeah," Wahkan suddenly spoke up drawing everyone's eyes in the room to him, "at least six or seven times what you make here with the Weavers doing their magic. But if you want to make some real coin, you let your Magi here contact some Alchemist or Technoist and you have them make you something special that'll sell for a whole air ship full of money to the right people."

Well that was the end of any need to put a price on the crystal. Carlo was all in now as his face went slack with this new information. He looked over to Bentley who was now clinging to this new turn of events to getting those Joris stones with both hands. "Yes sir, we can do so much with the crystals. I can contact an Alchemist I know and we can create an object that will make you richer than your wildest dream."

And I know just what you would make my dear Magi friend John thought. I know what purpose you have in mind for these stones already and it was quite a foolish path to even try and walk. He was still thinking that when the shaman looked to the boss of the brothel as Carlo spoke, "let me see this stone."

"I would advise against taking the stone out of the pouch Mr. Troisi."

A new sticking point suddenly stopped the happy flow of the moment. Carlo's face squeezed in on its self as he eyed John suspiciously. "And why is that John?"

"Because the Umbra Hounds will know of its precise location in a few minutes and they will have the Protectorate Marines pour down on you from the cruiser that has been slowly circling this neighborhood all morning." John explained. He had a guess the warning would have little to no effect and he was right as Carlo laughed hard after a moment.

"The Protectorate," the man laughed while shaking his head, "I got those jerkoff's in my pocket. Anyways, I got my house protected, plenty of guards with guns. No one's coming into my brothel who isn't invited, understand? Now open that pouch and let me see that stone."

"Then we have a deal Mr. Troisi, both stones for both Weavers?" John asked quickly stopping the boss again as Carlo reached for the pouch. The implication of the question was easy to read, understand. You take the stone from the pouch only when the Weavers are mine and not a second before.

There was a second time when the room was quiet and the mood soured just a bit. Carlo looked to the bag, up to the Weavers, and then back to the bag on the table. He took a minute and then another and another thinking hard over what he was going to do. It didn't help that his Magi was just as nervous about what the boss was going to do.

"Mr. Troisi...what are you going to do?"

Bentley's scared he's going to lose the stone John thought. Well, that wasn't about to happen as John added a little time constraint to the pressure. "I need to see to other important things this morning Mr. Troisi, do we have a deal?"

"You just wait right there...quietly, I'm thinking." Carlo whispered as he looked back up to the Weavers then back to the pouch on the table. You could see the weight on his shoulders and the look on Carlo's face was one of pure calculation. He was running every possible outcome through his mind when Wahkan just added another hundred pounds to the weight on the man's back.

"I told you John, Carlo here would rather have the money in hand than what he could possibly make if he took the stones. He's no gambler."

"I guess your right Wahkan," the shaman sighed beginning to lean over to take the pouch off the table, "I'm sorry to have wasted your morning Mr. Troisi. I hope-"

"Please Mr. Troisi! The things we can do with the stones...if we let them simply walk away!" Bentley practically screamed.

There's a moment when you know a plan you have set in motion will work, has worked, and John had detected that juncture minutes before. Now, he watched as it happened all over again, that pained look in Carlo's eyes shifted as he spat out the words quickly. "You got a deal, both of the girls for both of these stones."

John stopped leaning in and then shifted back to a regular upright stance as he smiled just a little more, "deal, both Weavers for both Joris crystals."

Bentley looked relieved as Carlo quickly snatched the pouch off the table top and began to open the drawstrings. Michael the guard nodded to the door and a man opened it calling out to the hall for someone while he turned back and spoke to John. "I only see one stone, where's the other one?"

"Wahkan will bring it to you after he escorts the Weavers out of the building and on to our air ship."

"Whoa, no one's leaving this room with anyone until Mr. Troisi says it's going to happen." Michael hissed.

The shaman sighed thinking all these stops were only giving the Society and the Protectorate more time to raid this brothel with a force unlike any had seen. Only there was no break this time as Carlo ordered his guard to let everything continue on. "Have Gino walk the big man to the door with the girls." Then John saw it, a small wink to Michael from his boss and the shaman knew the betrayal was set. There was no true deal for the Weavers just as he had assumed, had known. It was all just an act to sell him a big lie. As soon as Carlo had both stones in hand he was going to be shot

John guessed and Wahkan as well, and then both Weavers retrieved forthwith as soon as it was over. Good thing he brought the Umbra in then to keep that from happening.

"What's a Gino?" Wahkan snorted just as the door they came in swung open again and a man as large as him walked in. The floor shook and as everyone turned to look as the sound of machinery echoed in the office. Wahkan looked over an up into what was part man and part machine, the face all flesh except his nose and left cheek and all the way down to the chin where metal took over. The man's jaw and neck was cut right down the middle and John wondered just what else was metal under the suit the man wore, a very large version of what the other guards wore. The shaman instantly noticed Gino's left hand was metal, thin circular metal formed fingers while gears and rods let him open and close the appendage into a fist.

"That is a Gino I presume," John whispered staring at the man in wonder. What kind of pain he must have been in while the doctor and alchemist fused the metal to his body the shaman thought as Michael grinned and slapped the shoulder of his large associate.

"Gino had a small run in with some men who work with another 'Family'. It wasn't pretty what they did to him but thanks to Bentley and one of his alchemist friends we got Gino all fixed up, better than new you could say." Michael extolled as everyone looked on.

"Yeah, better than new..." Wahkan whispered before turning to John with a look of someone who wasn't sure of what was supposed to be coming next. "He's going to walk me to the door."

"Yeah, Gino's going to make sure you come back with the other stone." Michael continued on with a smug grin before chuckling low and menacingly.

Wahkan just stared at John refusing to look anywhere else as he spoke, "and just how is Gino going to do that?"

"Because if you don't come back then I'm going to have Gino tear off the arms and legs of your friend John here, know what I mean?" Michael stated and asked in one breath, that smug tone just biting into Wahkan like a giant gnat.

And speaking of Wahkan, the large man just kept his eyes on John with the unsure look still on his face. The shaman though just nodded back and spoke up reassuring his friend calmly. "Go and take the Weavers to the air ship, we're too close on time to worry now. I'll be fine while you're gone."

"All right," Wahkan answered to the order and turned to the pair of woman. Both were pushed into his arms by the guards and then he was being ushered harshly toward the door of the office. He didn't want to leave John, didn't feel it was right in the least, but

Wahkan had no choice. The Weavers needed to be taken to safety. The first priority John had told him was to get the Weavers out of the building and away from Carlo. Well, he was doing that, and it might just cost him his friend in the process.

John watched his friend leave with the two young women and as the door closed a gasp went up from his side, across the table. The shaman turned to see Carlo and Bentley standing next to each other, shoulder to shoulder, and in the hand of the boss of the brothel rested an oval shaped pure clear crystal that glowed with a bright light from its center, on the inside. A small ripple passed though everyone left in the room, a charge from the crystal and its energy. They know now the shaman thought; the Umbra and the Protectorate will know exactly where the Joris stone is now and in two minutes this brothel is going to be assaulted with more men than anyone could have guessed. That small smile on Carlo's face grew as Bentley gushed while looking at the crystal. Enjoy it you two, because all of this is about to come to a very violent end.

Out in the lobby Wahkan power walked his way to the doors to the foyer practically carrying both of the Weavers. Boles barely got a foot down and Wells just clung to whatever her bound hands could grip as she floated in the air while the trio moved swiftly past the afternoon girls, bumping a few causing them to squeal. Every eye was on them as the large man made for the drapes to the outside and on cue the attendant opened the portal to the foyer.

The man quickly voiced the rehearsed farewell he was to give each 'guest' as they left. It was a quaint but hurried thank you for coming and a have good day, only Wahkan blasted by moving as fast as he could so the words just went out into the empty space. The other attendant didn't even try to say a thing; he just opened the door letting Wahkan go by before he barreled through it. The attendant barely had it closed before he felt the oppressive presence of Gino. The mechanics of his body, the whirring and pinging and hiss of moving parts only added to the uncomfortable mood the half man-half machine brought with him as he stopped at the entrance and watched the large IP from the window.

There should have been sunlight, bright eye-blinding sunlight from the noon day sun but there was just the forbidding dark of a large shadow. The cruiser from before was right overhead, the massive bulk of its body and slope of its side wings throwing the whole block into a semi-dark. Wahkan went from the walk to a dead run, as fast as he could carrying the Weavers. He was so intent on crossing the street that he cut off a car coming at him. The poor man behind the wheel barely hit the brakes in time to stop the automobile as Wells let out a scream through her gag. Boles was screaming something at him as well only her words were more 'mmph' than actual syllables and it wouldn't have mattered one bit to Wahkan. He was just running to get the Weavers to the air ship before what he knew was going to happen actually happened. Damn, he thought, we spent too much time talking in that office and now the Protectorate are right overhead. Damn, he thought one last time as he finally made it across the street and into the empty vacant lot, we wasted too much time. Boles was still trying to talk and Wells was just gasping for breath as the large man came to a stop suddenly halfway into the space before letting the Weavers back down.

"Mmph!" Boles spat, or tried to, as Wahkan pushed her into Wells.

"Sorry, I don't have time get you both all untied and pardon me in advance for the inappropriate touch ladies." He voiced quickly before squatting down.

"Mmph," Boles spat again just as she felt a large hand grab her rump and underside in a tight grip causing her eyes to open as far as the sockets could go. Wells did the same as the thin material of the clothes she had been forced to wear barely held back the man's grope. Then both were being lifted up, clean off the ground upwards toward the sky, and both could only let out a long 'Oooo' as they literally began to fly. What is he doing Boles thought? He's throwing us up into the air with nothing to la-

Her thought was cut short due a rough and impromptu stop, her body and Wells abruptly hitting something hard at the beginning of the fall. Before Boles could garner another thought a hand was grabbing her arm, the skin tough but with a careful grip so as not to hurt her, and dragging her across a wooden deck. Her eyes focused on a pair of work boots and the brown canvas work pants that partially covered them. It was a strange thing to take notice of and remember at the time but there were pockets along the side of the pants. Then she could see Wells being taken along the deck in the same fashion just before a Scottish voice yelled out taking her attention upwards to a man's face.

"GET BACK TO JOHN WAHKAN! THOSE DAMNABLE MARINES ARE STARTING TO DROP!"

He had a very sweet, serene face with long mutton chop sideburns of red hair this man with the thick accent. He knelt between them as Boles watched closely and out of a wide waist belt that had suspenders and about twenty more pockets the man pulled a pair of cutters with some strange tube attached to the handle. She watched him reach for her just as the man who had carried her to...whatever ship this was screamed back from below.

"I CAN SEE THAT WALLY! KEEP AN EYE ON THE LADIES!"

No, don't cut the collar! Boles mind screamed as she realized he was reaching for the leather band around her neck and she began to slide away from the man's hand, her hands trying to reach up to stop him but the chain kept her from reaching his wrist. If I lose my collar...no please, don't cut my collar off! Then another voice yelled out just as Boles realized there was a strong wind ripping at her and pushing down on her body holding her in place.

"DO NOT TOUCH THE COLLARS! JOHN SAID TO LEAVE THE
COLLARS ALONE!"

Boles had only heard the accent once before and she was
suddenly grateful for it once more as it stated exactly what she was
trying to do. The man with the long sideburns only looked at her
and smiled as the gale force wind tore at him. "I won't be touching
your collar lass, no need to worry about that." Then his hand
grabbed the chain that lopped through the collar and with those
strange looking cutters he freed her. With a release of air that
made a small 'whoosh' the sharpened calipers of the tool sliced
through the chain easily and then the man freed the lock for the
cuffs around her hands. With her free the man turned to Wells
doing the same to the chain and cuffs just as Boles pulled the gag
out of her mouth. Then with the same 'whoosh' sound the man
freed Wells then stood back up putting the tool back in his belt
before taking off.

"WHAT'S GOING ON?" Boles screamed out over the
powerful wind but no one answered as she pulled Wells to her in a
hard hug. The smaller Weaver reached up and took the gag out of
her mouth just as the wind, incredibly, picked up in force driving
into them both now, pushing them harder into the wooden deck it
seemed.

"OPEN THE HATCH ZHENG!" The man screamed as he ran
away and the accent from before, the one Boles had barely

remembered, said something so foreign that she had to turn and look. So, with Wells in her arms, the Weaver rolled over just enough to glance back at a strangely dressed man standing up on the raised deck of the air ship she was lying on. The mighty wind that whipped at everything and anything had no effect on him. He was actually shimmering she thought, like he was made of light and not flesh. Then she heard a pop of a door being opened and Boles turned back to see the man called Wally drop down into a slide and disappear into the ship through a hole in the deck where the lid of the raised hatch was up.

On the ground below Wahkan ran away from the side of the air ship, a two hundred foot long wooden Chinese Junk, heading back to get John. The wind from the turbines of the cruiser, the force picking up considerably, tried to slow him but he pushed past it with his powerful legs. He watched in frustration as the Umbra directed Marines of the Protectorate began to drop off the sides of the large metal air ship in units, like ants pouring out of a hole to attack an enemy. This isn't some small squad or just a few soldiers. This is a whole damn Platoon he thought running all out now. They brought a whole damn Platoon to get us. Wahkan saw the marines drop the first ten feet freely, the long green coats they wore flapping in the wind, before the gleaming metal twin-cone shaped packs each wore on their backs kicked on with a loud release of steam and air slowing their decent to the ground. The Marines of the Protectorate, and everyone else for that matter, had long given up on the design of the parachute with its billowing sail for the Descent Packs of the Steam age. One poor soul dropped right in front of Wahkan, the man never noticed the large man due to the helmet he wore with its sides covering his ears, and both started out on the far side of the street from the brothel but only one made it across. As the Protectorate Marine started forward he felt a heavy object slam into the back of his helmet with a loud crack stunning him a moment, just long enough for someone to shove him right into the side of a large truck with enough force to finish knocking him out.

Wahkan ran through the Protectorate Marine right for the brothel. He looked up past the dark green uniform of the man right to the window in the door of Carlo's establishment looking for the man called Gino. He wasn't there, no one was, and Wahkan growled low as he pictured John losing one of his arms to the monster. The thought was cut off quickly when the sound of an explosion followed by shattering glass told him the Protectorate was as good as inside the brothel now.

The Gāi Gōng De Tiānkōng

*That's Chinese for **'The Palace in the Sky'** for all those who don't speak the tongue. It's my home, has been for a while now, ever since I joined up with John after he found me. Before I go into the Tiānkōng and all that she is I guess I should go over just what kind of ships roam the skies of the world these days, from the metal behemoths of the military to those small whips that act as personal craft.*

You know about the military and their crafts, the metal giants that patrol the skies. From a small two barreled gun forward and one aft Frigate to a Cruiser with two three- barrel batteries forward and aft to the mighty Battleship with three massive three-barrel 16 inch batteries forward and four going aft. The Protectorate could easily stand toe-to-toe with any country that comes looking for a fight, on the water or in the skies. Soldiers and Air Shipmen by the hundreds man each one and that's just the regular forces, it doesn't count the ones like the specially trained Marines who drop down off the Air ships. Every country, the Brits and the French and even the Swedish if you can believe it, have a military setup like the States. Everyone has armored and armed flying ships driven by Steam technology and everyone will use them at the drop of a hat if it comes to it.

If slow is your speed then you may prefer the big lazy blimps, the Dirigibles or Zeppelins, which still fly here and there for the express purpose of being nothing but a slow trip from point A to point B. The Zep's are mostly for the rich, the ones who have grown tired of travelling first class on the water in large ships to Europe and abroad. No sir, these folks discovered something new, something more ostentatious, a trip among the clouds is so much more...refined I'd have to guess they would say. There is no third class on a Zeppelin, you either go first or as a worker or you don't go at all. And you better have all your paperwork in place for whenever you get to wherever it is you're going, the guards at the borders never make exceptions and there's always a jail cell open for those who think they're above the rules.

Next are the personal Whips, small crafts like sail boats and schooners that usually have just enough room for the boiler and the turbines and a few people. Some are crazily built things by men and women who scavenge parts from old air ship graveyards and some are very nice and elegant. The Whips never stray too far from land, never go too far, and rarely have any kind of armor or armament. It's a pleasure craft and by all assumption no one would need a large caliber weapon on one...doesn't mean there's not a few who haven't tried and succeeded to put a cannon on one.

Then you have the air craft that don't fit into any kind of a category. I don't mean something like a Bi-plane, no, I'm talking about a craft like the Gāi Gōng De Tiānkōng and the Crescent Moon. Wooden ships that have defied modern design and thus are like strange aberrations crossing the skies, misfits and out of place. The man-of-war used to sail the oceans back long ago, three long decks of long guns dealing devastation with a broadside cannonade large forming large plumes of white gun powder smoke and all the while under the power of the mast and sail. At first the man-of-war was converted to the air ship fleets of every nation, but then were soon passed by and forgotten in favor of steel. A metal ship can take more damage, can hold more men and firepower, and in the end everyone has a metal Frigate or Cruiser because...well because everyone has one. A nation without one would have been naked and asking for trouble. It's the way now, better pack a big gun turret or someone might put you down. The man-of-war was relegated to the history books and the graveyards till one day one was resurrected and its captain proved you can never count out an old dog in any fight. She raised her flag on her man-of-war and let loose her wild spirit on any and every country, refusing to live by anyone's rule of law but her own. Oh yes girls and boys, there's Sky Pirates flying up there the in the skies and one female Captain by the name of Fade is the slyest of them all.

And the strangest of all ships is John's, the Chinese Junk the Gāi Gōng De Tiānkōng. I'm not sure how much of this you're going to believe and how much you'll just toss aside thinking its bull so I'm just going to tell you what there is to tell and you can do with it what you will. The Gāi Gōng De Tiānkōng was built in the year 1405 for the purpose of transporting troops for the grand treasure expedition of Zheng He, only it never made the trip. Zheng left it behind for one reason or another in the yards and another Zheng quickly picked it up, one Zheng Hui the Liànjīn, or Alchemist. Zheng Hui was the greatest alchemist of his time, a favorite of the Emperor, and what he did with the Junk was the proof of his ability. You see, The Gāi Gōng De Tiānkōng flies by means of Alchemy alone, no steam or turbine is used to raise the wooden ship from the ground. No mechanical device or steam tech existed to aid a man to fly back in the day when the Junk was transformed, only the mind of one man and the thaumaturgy he could do gained him the power to fly the skies. It's just the contents of a specially prepared potion painstakingly applied to each and every board that makes up the Tiānkōng. There's no wing or rudder to help it turn or circle, just a large crystal gem embedded into the handle of the rudder board, which through a magic only John and Zheng Hui know of controls the Junk. The crystal also 'hides' the Junk from the eyes of people, like its invisible, that is unless you're actively thinking of it or of Zheng Hui. I'm no Magi, or alchemist or mystic shaman so explaining how this works is beyond my words, but I've seen people walk right by us without blinking with no clue we were there...that was until they walked into the ship. I've seen every type air ship there is and nothing comes close to the Tiānkōng...or Zheng Hui the Alchemist for that matter.

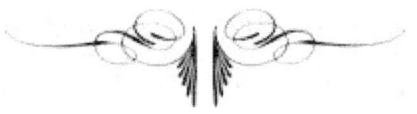

"So, you know a lot about these Weaver people right?"

John turned to the guard called Michael and only nodded. He hadn't forgotten about the threat the man had made, the one where the half-machine man Gino would pull his arms and legs off if Wahkan didn't return. "I know some things, but my guess is your wondering why someone would bind two Weavers as one like Boles and Wells?"

Michael's eyebrow inched up as he nodded once in surprise. "Yeah...how did you know that?"

"I'm really good at guessing," John replied smugly before turning to the happy pair holding the Joris crystal, or one happy and the other beginning to worry. Carlo was a giddy as a child let loose in a candy store with a new dime while Bentley just looked back at him with a pale, kind of sick expression. Yes you, Mr. Magi, your just starting to realize what's about to happen aren't you? John thought as he spoke. "You see you bind two Weavers through a special ritual, something like hand binding only with a mix of alchemy and spiritualism, a special potion made from rare components is even used thus making it more involved. It's very rare when it works because the two Weavers must be more than physically compatible on the surface. The Weavers must be destined to be together I've been told, more than fated sisters or blood brothers. Yet when the binding is successful it's a connection to the very center of the soul for both and it's all done to increase the power of what can be taken in and then given out. Two Weavers working together in unison can make an enormous amount of energy. Some say if you bind the right pair you could even have them absorb more energy than Joris himself to infuse a special crystal for a special purpose."

"A special crystal for a special purpose...what purpose?" The guard Michael asked confused.

Now, knowing what he just said would hit the Magi like a punch to the stomach, John watched as Bentley fought not to throw up while Carlo just stared at the stone ignoring most if not all of the conversation. You have been planning very bad things Mr. Magi and now all your nefariousness has come home the shaman thought as the low rumble rolling through the building grew stronger with each passing second telling John this party was about to come to a very messy end. Is Wahkan across the street by now? He has to be by now the shaman thought again as the young man Angelo crossed the room and stood just behind Michael while speaking up. "Hey, do you think the pair we just gave up could be like that, you know, that special? I mean wouldn't it be just our luck that we traded away our pair of Weavers and they can make those special Joris stones all day long."

And there it was. The cat finally was free of the bag. John smiled more as he watched that sick expression on Bentley's face deepen just a bit more while Carlo next to him finally heard what all the talk that was going on around him. It was time to let the boss of the brothel in on what his Magi had been and was still doing behind his back the shaman decided as he spoke.

"Funny you should say that very thing Angelo, because that's exactly what Bentley was thinking when he learned that Maxwell had suddenly obtained two Weavers, or better yet, when he learned it was the very same two young women rumored to have been bound by an Elder Magi so deeply that their empathic abilities had merged and flowed together leaving them tied to each other forever. It must have felt like fate was playing a cruel twist on Bentley. Your Magi here Angelo, he had heard the stories whispered in the Society about Boles and Wells from those he still talked with after coming here to Mr. Troisi's employment. He heard how strong they were and Bentley thought if the bound pair could infuse gems just as powerful, if not greater, than Joris then he could certainly create something very special with the stones. Only Bentley had a problem, how to get his hands on the Weavers before someone else did. Either that or Maxwell's price for them would surely go up, and it would have, when he learned who they were and what they might be able to do. I can just imagine the torment for Bentley. There they were, Isaac's Weavers...not some story but real flesh and blood and just agonizingly out of reach."

The room went silent. The rumbling from the cruiser kept increasing, silently growing all around them, as the shock Carlo was most certainly feeling numbed him to any stimuli but what the shaman had said. His hands holding the Joris stone lowered ever so slow as he stared back with a slack jaw and eyes as big as two white moons. Time had been against him all morning but John took just a second or two to savor this moment before he carried on.

"It would have ended right there, a fool's wish unanswered, but then Bentley had a sudden idea. He had Mr. Troisi and his money, or better yet the money from the brothel here. My guess is it took one show. One little demonstration of the empathic flood from Boles and Wells to convince your uncle, Angelo, to buy the Weavers on the spot and that was just what Bentley had planned and pushed for from the beginning. 'Oh the money I'm going to make with these girls' Mr. Troisi must have been thinking the whole time sitting there watching them, feeling their lust roll through his body, and all the while from the shadows Bentley had other ideas running through his mind, didn't you my Magi friend?"

"What...what the hell are you saying? What the hell is he saying?" Carlo growled as looked from John to Bentley and back with a quick snap of his neck. The Magi could only shake his head and make small squeaking sounds feeling utterly helpless as he watched his plan come completely undone.

"How many crystals did you have the Weavers make Bentley, huh? Was it more than one, maybe five, or was it somewhere north of twenty five? Instead of telling the man who pays you for your services about the infused gems you gave all of those powerful stones to your collaborator, the alchemist Farzin, didn't you Bentley? Every single crystal and all the while hoping you had found the 'one', the perfect gem to make the 'Philosopher's Stone' from, yet each and every one has crumbled from the alchemist tests, useless and worth nothing now. You should have picked a better partner and alchemist than Farzin because look where the fool has left you now. All that money Mr. Troisi and you could have made selling those infused stones gone because the inept Farzin couldn't convert a single one to that treasured artifact you've long to create my Magi friend, but that was never your plan was it Bentley, to get rich. Money isn't as important to you as it is to Carlo there."

Now the Magi was really sick, breathing hard like he was trying to keep from throwing up his breakfast as John added his last. "That's why you were late to the start of our meeting here, you've been trying to get a hold of Farzin all morning and he hasn't responded to a single call or message you've placed to him...because where the Umbra have him sitting right now there is no phone and no hope of freedom for a very long time."

"WHAT," Carlo roared with flaring neck muscles as he spun looking to the Magi with a vile expression? The fact he had lost money obviously affecting him more than the news of Bentley being involved in a deeper plot with a mysterious alchemist. Losing just a nickel would infuriate the boss of the brothel John gathered and Bentley seemed to understand this as well because right at that moment the Magi began to backpedal like mad to try and get things under his control.

"No Mr. Troisi, I never-"

"YOU STOLE FROM ME? ME, YOU STOLE FROM ME AFTER ALL I HAVE DONE FOR YOU?"

"NO MR. TROISI, I NEVER WOULD-"

Then the screaming out in the brothel's lobby overtook the screaming in the office. Bellows of rage followed by howls and cries that the building was under attack carried through the walls and it ceased the fight going on between the men in a blink. Carlo looked to Michael who had turned back from the sounds outside to stare at his boss who was quickly regretting this meeting. "What the hell is going on out there?"

"I don't know boss," the man responded as the guards in the office began to run out leaving just a token force behind. Well, the plan was working to perfection John thought, maybe not clicking on all cylinders but close enough, as he spoke.

"That would be the Protectorate Marines dropping off the cruiser I warned you about. They're under the direction of the Umbra to seal off the building and prevent any escape. I'm pretty sure the 'Shadows' of the Society had the Marines cut off your escape route out the back to the underground garage next door Mr. Troisi so it might be a good idea to surrender."

"The Umbra...the Shadows are coming for us..." Bentley whispered stumbling over the words like each was a small stone in his mouth. The Magi understood now just how much trouble he was in, or as the locals would put it, how far in the crapper he had fallen.

"What's an Umbra?" Angelo asked looking around hoping to get an answer, but just like before everyone ignored him. Must happen a lot John assumed, being ignored, because it was like second nature to the men in the room to act like Angelo wasn't there with them.

"Why would the Protectorate be coming here? I paid those mooks off for the month!" Carlo screeched reaching into his coat pocket. The building actually shook for a moment and the sound of crashing glass from the lobby meant the time to discuss how all of this had come to pass was just that...past.

"Because the men you paid off are no longer the men in charge I would assume." John winked as he slowly slid his left hand up and behind his back reaching for his knife. No one took notice of his small moves as the screaming and noise out beyond the walls had reached a state of pure calamity.

Carlo didn't take the jest from the shaman well as anyone could see which is why he probably missed the small move John was making. As he shook his head while snarling loud like a bear the boss of the brothel started to pull out the gun he had slowly tried to reach for. He might have been able to surprise the shaman with his attack if not for the fact John was already moving making his own play to get out of the office before the Protectorate Marines took it over. With a vicious knife-hand strike the shaman slammed the edge of his right hand across Michael's throat with a meaty whack crushing the man's larynx. The move was fast, so quick the guard barely had time to do anything except to reach up and grab his throat after the blow and gurgle loudly while trying desperately to breath. John could see everyone else left in the room moving now to strike as his body and mind went into survival and fight mode. He had to get out of the office in one piece and the shaman had every intention of doing just that.

I've held back talking about Alchemists with the Magi and the Weaver because if you had to choose which of the three you'd like to spend a day with the alchemist would probably be number five on the list of three. I'm not saying that every alchemist is some hermit type with a long beard who hasn't showered in oh, say, ten years because they've been locked away in a secret lab somewhere creating a single vial of a some arcane potion that may or may not grow you a tail by accident. I'm just saying that almost all the alchemist I've ever run into meet that distinction with the exception being Zheng Hui and that's because he's a ghost.

It's no secret that alchemist are looked down on, men and women alike who shun the outside world for the inside of some dark and dank laboratory. And it's no secret the alchemist prefer this strange relationship because most have no use for the outside world except when it's time to collect all the different kinds of metals and plants and anything else they may need. Human contact is low on the priority list to the alchemist unless it's to barter a deal, an exchange of some sort that gets them either money to buy more items for their labs or if they're lucky an infused gem from a Weaver. Because that's the grand prize for any alchemist, to obtain duplicitously what they cannot get fairly. By order of the Magi Society and the Protectorate no object charged by a Weaver may be owned or in the possession of an alchemist and there's a damn good reason for that rule.

You see, all alchemists strive for one goal. It's an insatiable ambition that drives them to the brink of madness at times, but then only a deranged individual would find it worth losing one's mind if it meant creating the mythical Philosopher's Stone wouldn't they. The distinction of being the first to make the stone means nothing to the alchemist. The honor of having one's name in history has no real appeal to them. No, it's all about the study, the break through, and not a care is given to anything else. One's reputation or even one's family is nothing compared to possessing the stone, the ultimate source of Alchemical power they say.

The Philosopher's Stone is a myth like I said, it has to be right? I've heard it can do everything from turning water to wine and lead to gold to helping to make the legendary Elixir of Life, the magic potion capable of bringing the dead back from the door of oblivion or extending one's own life. I don't believe a word of it, but not because I don't think the stone exists. I think one day some poor fool may get close to creating it but there's only one man who could have created the Philosopher's Stone in my opinion. He's been dead for a long time and just by chance guides the Junk I live on. Zheng Hui was so knowledgeable of Alchemy and its secrets that the rulers of faraway lands and countries would seek out his mastery of its potential. He was so well adapted to the principles of Alchemy and it's workings that just like poor Elinor the Magi Zheng Hui's enemies set out to ruin him, to destroy his name and his reputation. If Zheng

Hui couldn't or wouldn't make the stone then it can't be made in my
opinion...and maybe people shouldn't even try.

She watched the Protectorate Marines getting in line, ready to drop off the sides of the Cruiser, preparing to fall the short distance before the Descent Packs each wore would turn on slowing their fall. The rails along the forward side of the ship had been removed allowing the Marines to gather in rows and from there to basically just step off the deck into the open air, which was plain crazy to her. Why in the world would you want to jump off a perfectly good air ship simply eluded the mind of Camille and yet here she was watching a large group of young men ready to leap out into nothing but the clear blue without hesitation. The weapons of the Marines gleamed in the sun. Gun barrels had been polished to a high sheen or were just brand new which helped Camille recognize that most of the weapons the men carried were very powerful, so much more than the standard issue a Protectorate Marine would carry, especially a complete Platoon on a training exercise like this one. It was just something to note she thought as the back of her long black and purple bustle-skirt slowly swirled around her long legs from the wind of all the turbines and morning breeze, the front of the skirt held up to her waist by two buckled straps exposing underneath the black pants tucked into dark colored knee high boots with a small heel and lined with silver buttons. The black and dark purple colors of the Umbra seem to heighten Camille's chocolate colored skin, accenting her already timeless beauty. Her long black hair, a mix of braids and wavelets streaked with long lines of amber from her use of Weaver energy, was held back by an ornate hair band making the mane cascade down her back past the purple corset she wore over her black long sleeved blouse. The choker around her neck with the large ivory brooch in the center was the crowning piece to her dress as she stood on the outer bridge deck observing everything closely.

"Are the Umbra sure the Joris Stone is in the brothel? I'd hate to think we wasted our training time on some...mistake." A voice asked condescendingly from behind, the Southern drawl was hard to miss as was the intent of the last part. Camille wondered what bothered the Old Rebel more, the fact she was colored or a woman in charge.

"The stone is down there Admiral. Though how long it's been there I can only guess to due to the fact you're 'honorable' Protectorate Captain in charge of this region was bribed to look the other way and had been for some time now." Camille retorted, the reply meant to set the old Rebel straight, don't throw rocks unless you want one thrown back.

The man, dressed crisply in his blue and grey Air Ship uniform with shoulder insignias gleaming, only walked up and looked over to see the last of the Marines getting ready to start the drop. "I must agree Madame. It was unfortunate for the Captain to choose such a detestable way to end his career with the Protectorate, a waste of a good man and a Protectorate Officer."

"It is I'm sure, but I'm more intrigued by how many Marines are involved in this operation Admiral, being this was just supposed to be a training exercise before I took control." Camille noted finally looking to the Protectorate Naval Officer.

"And why does that bother you Madame?"

The Umbra titled her head just a bit and squinted with contemplation. "It doesn't bother me as much as it just makes me wonder. Why were so many marines being used for a training exercise and in Brooklyn no less? It was quite convenient for such a force, a large elite unit mind you, to be at the ready with such new weapons. These many well trained Protectorate should face little resistance down there, don't you think?"

The Admiral just smiled on and nodded, "I thought the same Madame, about the number of marines and the unit, but according to what I was told there was to be no chance of escape for anyone and thus I was to use all available personnel to ensure that very objective was obtained. And since we were scheduled to train these boys anyway and they were here with all their new-fangled guns, well why not use them all I say."

Camille bit her bottom lip thinking on what the Admiral had said, or better yet disclosed. The Umbra wasn't the paranoid type and yet her mind wouldn't let go of what she watched unfold before her and what her ears took in. The Admiral had been ordered, not by her mind you, to use the whole Platoon to obtain the Joris stone. She wondered just when this directive was given, if the Old Rebel received the order before or after the hounds had picked up the scent of a Joris stone, a crystal no one even knew existed until this morning. The Hounds were specially trained Weavers used by the Umbra and other Protectorate, taught to find certain types of energy. The Hounds had been following the faint trail of Joris energy all morning and it looked as if someone had finally taken the stone out of hiding. She took in a breath ready to continue her questions when a man came up behind the Admiral and spoke up. He was Protectorate, the Captain of the Cruiser actually, which made the Umbra feel just a little more uncomfortable. "Sir, the Hounds confirmed the scent over the Hertzian Wireless. Do we have permission to start the operation?"

"Yes Captain, I would say we do if the Hounds have the scent. Madame, may we proceed?"

"Business before pleasure they say Admiral, you may start." Camille nodded before watching the two men leave her though she wasn't alone long. As the Admiral and Captain nodded to her and then disappeared into the hatch leading to the bridge there leaning up against what the air ship men called the 'bulkhead' was one her fellow Umbra, her second in succession of the conclave. The man's height, at least six foot three, should have precluded him having any possible chance of hiding but Camille knew better. Her second was more than capable of being a 'Shadow' more than any other Umbra she knew of she thought as he quietly walked up smiling.

"You look very lovely this morning. The brooch, as always, is a nice touch." The tall man complimented her in a whisper with a distinct Brooklyn accent, his short black hair held in place against the wind by pomade. His black tail coat looked immaculate over the purple shirt and black tie he wore, which clashed somewhat with the plain black work pants and heavy boots he also wore.

"Thank you Ezio and you look quite handsome." Camille replied with a small smile before turning away to look down at the Deck.

She watched as a large man with an arm full of chevron's denoting his status as the ranking non-commissioned man in charge of the Marine force gave the word to the others. It was time to go, first line over the sides! Camille watched the men begin to drop, stepping right off the side and beginning to fall, and as she watched the first group descend to the street her heart skipped a beat from shock. Down there on the street she saw a large someone running across the road, someone she knew very well, and it made her blood turn cold. He's here Camille thought feeling a tinge of fear, what in the world is Wahkan doing here? Because if he's here than Wallace is here...oh no, that can't be good. What if Wallace gets hurt? Her mind raced for a moment with worry.

"Shall we play our game this morning, or would you prefer to watch that rather large man run across the street?" Ezio asked causing Camille to realize her second had caught her. Ezio was abnormally smart, extremely observant, and as hard to read as the man below who was running headlong into the brothel and probably back to his cohorts.

The lady Umbra only nodded and turned back to watching, it was a sign to Ezio that he should begin and so he did. "You're wondering why there are so many marines being used this morning, why so many for such a small man like Carlo Troisi and his group?"

Well, the game was starting rather slow. He may have overheard my question to the Admiral Camille thought, or Ezio may be trying a different tactic because he saw the way I was looking at Wahkan. You always had to watch her second and which way he started off their special little game of give and take. "And you're wondering why the marines are equipped with the latest armaments, auto-rifles with thermite rounds and heavy guns with explosive shells. Why such a display of weaponry from the marines, especially when confronting a group of men that obviously have nothing better than standard pistols and machine guns?"

She heard a small chuckle and knew they were both even now as Ezio turned to her. Camille looked away from the start of the fight below and up as her second went again. "And your thinking who told our Admiral, such a proper Rebel and Protectorate Officer that he would never disobey a direct order from a superior, to use every marine on the boat when raiding the brothel below? You and I have retrieved Joris stones with just a simple knock on a door in the past, no muss and no fuss. All of this...doesn't it seem like overkill to you? Maybe there's something else down there in the brothel besides the obvious you're starting to consider, something more than the stone which the Protectorate is trying to get?"

Point well-made she thought responding quickly, her eagerness with playing the game taking hold. "Why did a Joris stone suddenly show up here, at this specific brothel, when our hounds assigned here haven't detected a thing in the past? The men who Mr. Troisi answers to have no need, or want for that matter, of a Magi and word is their organization has a standing order to never seek the aid of any of our kind. The Families don't believe in what we do, they call us witches, so why now does one of their ilk have an interest in a Joris stone?"

"Better yet, why chance us, the Umbra, coming to your door looking for said stone when you already have the Protectorate Captain paid to look the other way at all the other nefarious things you do? Why take the risk of facing destruction to get a stone you've been told to never touch by those above your position like you said? Everyone knows the law, even the five Families, and any Joris stone found must be returned or face an unrelenting pursuit and punishment at our hands. So why even take the chance of drawing us and our attention to you thus ending all your other...businesses? What does a man gain from obtaining a stone that will most certainly bring about his demise?"

Another point and it made Camille think for a moment quickly gaining clarity as she stared at her second before continuing on stating a piece of her new found lucidity. "It's because you have a Magi hidden away no one knows about and he needs the stone for some purpose that will hopefully bring you more money than you can count. You've gone against the ones you answer too already with the Magi so why not take the chance on a Joris stone...unless you were tricked into letting the stone find its way into your possession. But why expose the stone knowing we will find it? Why would someone bring the Umbra and the Protectorate to the door of Carlo Troisi and one of the five Families with a Joris stone?"

"Someone who wanted to make sure our raid would give him the necessary time and camouflage to escape with what he came here for. Someone who knew we'd be hunting the stone, following its trail as it moved along the streets, only whoever it was might not have gauged our response properly, in time or personnel." Ezio smiled with a tilt of his head.

"I think this someone knew exactly who, when, and how many would come down on this brothel." Camille whispered turning to look down on the ground below, the clarity brightening in her mind. That's why she saw Wahkan here, why they were all here. John was up to something, the shaman was up-

"And I think I know who that someone is and I am almost as sure that I know why he is here," Ezio abruptly stated causing Camille to look over with wide eyes as her second leaned in. "Greywolf came looking for the one thing we Magi need just as much as the air we breathe...the one pair a certain few in the Society have been searching for."

Oh lord, it's all starting to make sense she thought. "Isaac's Weavers," Camille whispered as that clarity in her mind was as bright as the very sun now.

"Yes, because only the retrieval of a very special pair could produce a swift strike like this, such an overwhelming need to ensure no one gets away."

It made more than perfect sense now Camille thought with a slow inhale. An unregistered Weaver was a dangerous weapon but not so much as to require a whole battalion of marines to capture him or her, yet there was unsubstantiated talk about a special pair bound by one of the Elders. A special pair who had gone missing when their Magi was killed, murdered in his very own mansion just like poor Elinor in her room in London. "Greywolf found Isaac's Weavers. He found them before us, before our Hounds even, but someone else also knew the pair was in the brothel as well. By the star's that's it, that's why there's such a force here and so fast. Someone was going to raid the brothel anyway."

"Exactly, wasn't it very convenient that there were marines already here on board the cruiser armed with the latest weaponry?" Ezio replied with a nod.

"Yes, I agree." Camille whispered back while contemplating what the game had shown her. "John used us, drew us here with the Joris crystal to confuse the ones who had planned on being here anyway. We were the perfect distraction but he wouldn't have known there were so many Marines already onboard."

"Maybe not, or he might have," Ezio stated before leaning in whispering low careful to not be overheard, "it would appear there is a secret cabal in the Protectorate and it may even extend into the Society."

"I agree," was all Camille answered with as her mind ran with the new revelations.

"You know, I think I have some new found respect for the Shaman Greywolf for pulling all this off. Do you think he has the pair already?"

How did her second know all of this, about Isaac's Weavers and this cabal? How did he know it was John? He had to have recognized Wahkan just like she did, and if he did then this 'game' was just a test to see how much she knew or was willing to say she knew. "With the shaman's reputation I would say yes, he has them both already."

"And my lady wins the game," her second whispered one last time before leaning away to look down again. The female Umbra inhaled deeply again trying to organize her thoughts to ask Ezio just how he knew all of this when that plan had to be put away.

"Good morning Miss Camille," A young voice cut in ending Camille's thoughts and the game. The lady Umbra turned to see the new young apprentice Cooper, freshly assigned to her conclave of Magi. He was just a little taller than her, shorter than Ezio, and green and naive to the very bone about the Society. He still believed they, the Society, was a band of one striving toward the future. He'll learn it's quite the opposite Camille thought. The Society was nothing short of a fiefdom, groups of men and women trying to advance their cause or vision with little care for anyone else. These days nothing much was done in the Society except bickering and back room deals, it was all too much like being employed in the Government. The truth was the 'One Grand Society' the Magi were trying to achieve was slowly slipping away, being transformed into that which it was formed to fight...Isolationism.

"Good morning Mr. Cooper," Camille responded stiffly before turning to look down again. She was desperately trying to find Wahkan, or John, because one of them would lead her to Wallace she knew so being courteous at the moment was not a pressing matter.

Cooper looked to Ezio with a confused expression hoping the taller man would help him in understanding why the leader of the conclave was less then enthused this morning. Only the tall Italian man just smiled back, shrugged his shoulders, and went to looking over the side of the rail. The young apprentice sighed and walked over to the other side of Camille to watch what was happening below. All of the marines had dropped by now so the deck was clear. Cooper wasn't sure what his mistress was looking at. "What are we looking for Miss Camille?"

His mistress was about to respond when a loud explosion shook the cruiser, not enough to threaten its flight but more than adequate enough to make it jump a good bit. Camille lost her balance for a moment and fell into her second while Cooper looked over to the bridge door yelling. "What was that? Are we under attack?"

"I would assume so," Camille sighed with frustration as someone on the bridge yelled back to the apprentice.

"Someone just shot at our aft turbines. We'll be fi-"

Whatever the young air ship officer was trying to say was drowned out by a second louder explosion, more light show then fiery death. All at once fireworks ripped and screamed and ricocheted off the metal bulkhead of the air ship blinding everyone and sending the smart ones scurrying for cover. Ezio held onto his mistress and helped her through the hatch to the safety of the interior of the bridge a step behind Cooper. The hatch was barely closed before something large and fast flew right over the top of the cruiser, its shadow darkening the room instantly so close did its fly-over come. Camille looked out the round window right up into the large keel of a wooden man-of-war, a ship she knew very well and which could only mean one thing. An air shipman yelled out what the Umbra had deduced in an instant.

"It's the Crescent Moon! She came right out of the damn sun at us!" The Captain from before screamed in obvious irritation while looking out another large round window.

"FADE, YOU TREACHEROUS WENCH!" The proper old Rebel Admiral yelled at the window as the aft section of the man-of-war filled every port window you could look out of. He had been embarrassed by the surprise attack and no one embarrassed this old Rebel.

"Fade, the Sky Pirate...she's here?" Cooper asked with eyes like tea cup saucers, round and white and full of fear. He turned looking to Camille and Ezio then spun back to the window looking out as the Crescent Moon sped away.

"Well now, this means it's a party!" Ezio laughed and Camille couldn't help but to smile trying to hold back her own giggle.

On the Quarterdeck of the Crescent Moon Fade watched as the distance grew between the Protectorate cruiser and her air ship, gaining altitude with ease from the power of steam driven turbines under her ship. Her long dark red hair flew wildly in the wind behind her, whipped and flipped around as she watched and took in the attack on the Protectorate ship. Her long black jacket was open showing the white shirt she wore underneath along with the black corset. On her right hip bounced the long cutlass she was famous for wielding while on the left was a long knife and stuffed in a bright red sash across her hips was the long pistol made just for her hand by Wally, the Technoist on John Greywolf's ship. A wicked smile played across her lips as she turned to the man standing next to her. Her second was a stout looking man with a long beard, braided down the center, and a head full of hair sticking out from under a skull cap. Fade yelled out with a laugh, "What do you say Mr. Hayes, did the Admiral see us coming?"

"Oh no ma'am, he didn't see a thing, and I'm sure he's letting everyone around him know how much he didn't appreciate the way you said hello one bit."

"Well then," Fade chuckled turning to stare at the cruiser again through her air goggles. The long lenses sat on a frame like regular glasses, Fade hated straps that could get caught in her hair. "I say we let the old Rebel have a taste of our sparklers again. I want to keep the man's attention on me and off the brothel and John."

"Yes ma'am," Mr. Hayes replied with a smile and nod before yelling over the rail to the gun crews below, "Ready the Aft Guns...FIRE!"

The Quarterdeck shook violently as the rear cannons, all five heavy 30 pounders, went off within a hairs breadth of each other. The air filled with smoke from the gunpowder which would have, and did, blind everyone else. Yet Fade had no problem with the smoke as her goggles saw right through the cloud, right to the decks of the Cruiser with ease. And when the metal air ship lit up like the fourth of July from her specially created sparkler shot, well, the sky pirate and her crew rejoiced with all their voices.

"HUZZAH!" Fade screamed loudly watching with childlike glee the cruiser turn and begin to lay chase after her. "Here she come's my crew. Let's show the Protectorate how true Sky Pirates fly and fight."

"Sir, we can't leave the Marines down there on the street!" A young officer loudly demanded at the Admiral on the chaotic bridge of the Cruiser, who never flinched when he fired back.

"That is Fade up there, a wanted criminal, a Sky Pirate who we have been ordered to arrest on sight and as such we will capture her!"

"But the marines' si-" the officer tried one last time only to have the full wrath of the old Rebel hit him with a full broadside.

"Get off of my bridge Lieutenant; get off of it right NOW! Full power to the turbines, wings to twenty percent climb! I want that wench in my hands gentlemen, and I want her NOW!"

Camille only watched quietly as the bridge of the cruiser became a cacophony of different voices screaming out new orders, acknowledging others, and even other airship men giving out direction and distance the Crescent Moon. She looked at the hatch entrance to the bridge thinking of Wallace as she felt the world turn on its axis, the cruiser moving now to begin its pursuit of Fade. Please, just go and get out here Wallace...don't let them catch you my sweet Camille thought one last before looking back to the organized chaos that was the bridge aboard a Protectorate command.

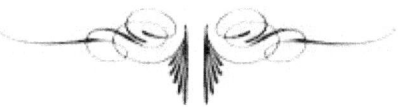

There are two very important ladies to our little group, two besides Wells and Boles, and I guess it's time I introduce them to you.

Captain Fade the Sky Pirate, no last name because let's face it, the woman doesn't need one.

If you took the confidence of Wild Bill, mixed in the cunning of Butch Cassidy and the daring of Jesse James then you'd have half of the Sky Pirate Captain. You'd still have to add the skill of Lord Nelson with a ship and the ruthlessness of Edward Teach when it comes to meeting ones enemies on the battlefield to equal Fade. There hasn't been a woman quite like Fade and I can tell you right now every Government of most every nation sure as hell doesn't want another one like her anytime soon. She is wild and untamed, a bad combination for a woman in this day and age. There's either a warrant or a bounty or just a bunch of hostile feelings following the lady around wherever she goes. Yes, she's a Pirate and yes she robs air trains and supply stations but its only because she needs to in order to survive and when Jesse James did it no one seemed to care, right?

I know Fade ran away from home at an early age from talking with her. She chose to grow up on the streets away from her father and his ways and being on her own taught Fade how to survive and who to trust. I think if I had to compare her to anyone it might be Anne Bonny or Mary Read, the famous female Pirates from the Caribbean. And yet, Fade is more than both of them. She has a crew of men and women who are loyal to the bone for her and it's not out of fear. That time when she was young growing up on the street, it taught her how to be a leader among the masses. You can send a soldier off to be an Officer, doesn't mean that soldier learns how to lead others or have other people follow. Not a one in her crew fears her because just like it is with Wally and me concerning John, those in her crew are drawn to her and stay to follow because you know that's where you were meant to be. They will fight and die for her because in the end you know she would do the same for you, to her very last breath. Fade has never used a lash on a man or woman in her crew that I have heard of and there was only one uprising from a woman which she quelled quickly with her cutlass.

No, Fade has no equal in the skies when she commands and leads. She has few equals in physical combat and no fear of anyone. She has only one weakness and out of respect for the lady I will never tell what that weakness is...

And then there is Camille Brousseau, the youngest Magi man or woman to head a conclave of the Society's hunters, the Umbra. Rumor says she's family to the grand lady Marie Laveau, the longtime Voodoo Queen of New Orleans before her death, but she's never admitted such to me and I think it's just other Magi trying to slow her ascent through the Society with lies. Camille is one of the smartest people I have ever met and due to the color of her skin one of the most compassionate I think. Maybe being looked down on because she's black makes her see the world differently? Being an IP I've met prejudice and I have felt such an overwhelming anger for someone thinking of me as less than human. A consuming anger that threatened to tear me apart from the inside making my sight far too short to see anything but the bad, but for Camille she only sees the good of this world even though it has never shown her anything but animosity.

She was accepted into the Society at the age of eight and by twelve she had impressed her teachers and Elders so much with her skill that invites were passed around to come and see her when she worked. It was no surprise I've been told when she was accepted into the Umbra and just a year later given charge of a conclave. Like Fade, Camille was born and bred to lead and in the Society that is a quality the Magi Elders never miss when looking for those who would take their place and thus be in control of the future of the magical ones. And just like Fade, Camille has only one weakness and just like Fade I will never ever tell anyone about it. I respect the lady too much to do her any kind of harm...

Just what in the name of the Great Spirit was going on here? Wahkan thought quickly as he sprinted across the street.

The Protectorate Marine's standard issue weapon used to the bolt action 1903 by Springfield, but that was before the Technoist at the weapon company entered the picture and started to modify and convert everything for them. Now most marines were given the M1 by Springfield, a specially designed lightweight rifle fed by a mag of cartridges from the top, equipped with an array of long scopes for better accuracy and other attachments improving handling and the distance a man could engage the enemy with. These marines this morning though, they weren't carrying the standard Springfield's. Wahkan had noticed when they were dropping down that each marine was carrying the new modified auto-rifles by Browning and Williams, the ones with the new types of ammunition, the HS310. A marine issued the Browning and Williams HS310 could fire a standard thirty caliber bullet or an armor piercing round or even one tipped with thermite to burn through anything the bullet hit and he could fire in a greater number than the M1 because the auto-rifle held a twenty round box clip fed from the bottom. And then there were those scopes and other attachments on the auto-rifles that provided long range sight and arc lights to throw back the dark. No, Wahkan thought, these marines didn't come to mess around. They came to quickly suppress any resistance and do that with little effort.

One of the marines stopped on the sidewalk, squared his body to the entrance of the brothel, and aimed a very large rifle at the doors. It was one of the new heavy guns from Thompson, a three barrel auto-repeating monstrosity that fired modified explosive 12 gauge shotgun shells, one at a time or all three at once. It was devastation in an easy carry form, if you could handle the weight of the gun that is, which was three times that of the Browning and Williams HS310 and the fact it was like carrying a 2X2 box around with a fat awkward stock on a strap under your shoulder didn't help. You had to be pretty big to handle the kick of the beast if you fired all three shells at once, which this marine was and did. The doors to the brothel might as well have been made of paper because the only thing left after the marine discharged his heavy gun was splinters and aftermath. The blast made the muscled man step back a couple of feet from the kick as well as everyone on the sidewalk was deaf for a moment which gave Wahkan the advantage. He fired his first round from the modified Colt Peacemaker in his left hand and the round grazed the shoulder of one marine slamming into the side of a car that the occupant had abandoned when all the shooting started. The thin metal around the engine compartment popped as the round went in, the marines positioned ready to make entry all turned and spotted Wahkan, but then the front of the car exploded knocking every one of them flat. Wally and his patented two stage bullet, after impact a chemical reaction would kick in heating up everything around it to red hot. The round wasn't as hot or as messy as thermite, but it was hot enough to cause the gas in that engine to explode and in turn make a nice improvised bomb that cleared the immediate area...with the exception of the man using the heavy gun.

Wahkan never slowed or stopped after taking out the marines by the car, just turned both of his Peacemakers right at the heavy gunner and fired. Before the man could bring the large rifle up both rounds hit the Thompson, one struck the stock breaking it while the other hit the beast in its mechanical heart, the ejector. The marine stumbled back from the impacts and that was all Wahkan needed as he ran right into the man hitting him with a hard muscled shoulder before scooping him up with a snap. The IP pushed his legs again and using the marine like a battering ram Wahkan went through what was left of the first set of doors and then through the next pair like a runaway train. The expensive wood the doors were made of exploded as the pair of large men went through, debris flying outward all over the lobby. Wahkan came to a stop and dropped the heavy gunner, who crumpled onto the marble floor with a moan, while taking a look around in shock. The marines had come with their new guns ready to put any resistance down, only it looked like Carlo had every intention of keeping what was his...his. At present the lobby was nothing but a shooting range, the marines on one end and Carlo's men on the other. Whoever thought the brothel was lightly defended had made a huge mistake in the reconnaissance department Wahkan thought as he ducked and found cover. Carlo's men had their own Technoist modified weapons and they were just as ready to use them as the marines were with theirs. Thompson 45 Caliber machine guns with twin round magazines laid down a withering fire of explosive tipped bullets on the marines that quickly destroyed what cover there was, tables exploded and lounges shredded in puffs of feathers.

Ok, this is going to be harder than I had anticipated Wahkan thought as he watched the marines' fire back with their thermite rounds. Raging fires began to break out all along the back wall and that grand staircase he and John had passed on the way to the back rooms was quickly catching and burning. Great job Carlo, Wahkan sighed thinking, build everything out of wood so the place can go up like a box of matches. He turned ready to make a dash down the side to the back rooms to find John when he spotted a marine looking at him, a familiar face he had just been itching to punch a fist through.

"Devlin!"

The marine looked up from his cover behind a column and upon seeing the large IP growled and spat, "Wahkan!"

Oh yeah, this fight inside the brothel just got good while on the Gāi Gōng De Tiānkōng...

Boles held tight to Wells as the wind from the large turbine fans of the Cruiser overhead poured down on them, crushing them against the deck of the air ship. The under-garments she wore ripped from the force of the wind and yet she never relinquished her hold on her precious Wells, and the green haired Weaver held on just as tight. Then Boles saw the man called Wally pop back up from inside the ship through the open hatch and he was holding the weirdest looking thing in his hands. It looked like a rifle but with a really big barrel, like someone had merged a large pipe with the rest of the gun, and in between where the front hand went and where the back hand held the grip was a large rotating oblong wheel. Boles looked on in awe as Wally dragged out a long tube from inside the ship which was attached to the top of the butt end of the rifle, the part that goes up on your shoulder, she didn't know what they called that piece. She watched through the high wind as Wally got the rifle in position on his shoulder just as the shimmering man behind on the Quarterdeck screamed out.

"WHAT ARE YOU DOING WALLACE?"

"I'M JUST GONNA GET THAT FAT LASS OVER US TO MOVE ZHENG!" The man yelled while pointing the business end of the large barrel at one of the turbine fans on the Cruiser. He pushed a sliding bar on the side of the grip and Boles could see the rifle wiggle with some kind of force as she heard him yell out. "COME ON DARLIN', MOVE FOR OLD WALLACE, JUST A LITTLE SHIMMY TO THE LEFT FOR ME SWEETHEART'!"

Then the rifle made a great 'whoosh' sound, like his cutters, along with a loud pop and Boles barely caught sight of a long metal tube being launched out of the large barrel. Wally jerked from the force the rifle made when he fired it and Boles heard a second 'whoosh' and she started to realize the tube that ran out the back was attached to something inside the ship and whatever that thing was it was powering the rifle. The metal tube the rifle fired went upwards, raced right for the turbine fan with the power from the rifle, but then just a few feet short the power of the wind from the giant fan stalled the tube. It hovered for a split second before it exploded with a fiery blast that shook everything. Boles and Wells screamed as the Cruiser's fan squealed and shuddered for a moment from the blast and before any of the three could think Wally let loose with two more rounds screaming all the while.

"I SAID MOVE YOU FAT BOTTOMED PIECE O'-"

One and then another blast shook the Cruiser and amazingly the turbine fan started to make a metal-on-metal screeching noise. The protective ring the fan sat in, bent from the three straight explosions, grabbed and pinched the blades of the whirling machine just a bit here and there. Yet it wasn't enough to stop the turbine, the cruiser sat right where it had settled in for the raid, right over the Junk. Wallace looked ready to unleash a hellish barrage into the belly of the beast per se, but then a shadow swept over the cruiser and the loud sounds of an air ship moving fast rumbled and shook everything around the Tiānkōng. Wallace let out a whoop when above him the sounds of fireworks crackled and popped by the hundreds, it told him exactly who had come to their aid.

"IT IS FADE! SHE IS ATTACKING THE CRUISER WALLACE!"

Boles dared a look up to see the cruiser begin to move finally, the turbine fans roaring even louder and with more force. Boles held onto Wells even as the wind tore the green haired Weaver from the embrace she was using to keep her precious one close, all her strength just to hold onto her companion wasn't enough suddenly.

"I CAN SEE THAT ZHENG, JUST GET US OVER BY THE BROTHEL! JOHN AND WAHKAN WILL NEED A HAND I'M SURE!" Wally yelled back. The Junk suddenly leapt to life lifting fast, rising high into the air so quickly Boles felt her stomach roll with the abrupt and dynamic change. Then, as the ship rose above the buildings on either side, it swung viciously round and dropped back down setting itself lengthwise across the front of the brothel. Whoever's driving this ship is really good Boles thought just before the ship unexpectedly listed, the right side dropping considerably lower than the left, exposing the deck to the front of the building. The move was so out of the normal it took Boles by surprise and she lost her grip on Wells, her companion's body sliding away from her grasp. The dark haired Weaver barely had the time to reach up and grab a hand hold of the stout and short wood post that probably served as a mast for the Junk at one time.

"WELLS," she yelled as she watched her love scream while sliding all the way, downward across the deck till she reached the rail where her feet stopped her from going over the side and onto the street below. "WELLS,"

"I'M FINE! I'M FINE BOLES!" Wells screamed back looking back up with of all things a smile, which quickly faded when the bullets began to slam into the deck all around her.

I've met Technoist and I've met Steam Engineers, men and women from both sides who thought they were the cream on top of the coffee with whatever it was they did, but not a one could match Wally. The man is simply a genius when it comes to anything mechanical, a savant when it comes to Steam Tech, and if you tell him I said that I'll beat you to death. We need to keep the man grounded please and from tearing everything apart on the air ship just to put it back together.

Wallace Amos McAndrew was born in a small village in Kinross-Shire, Scotland in 1900. The exact location of his family is a secret now. After John found Wally, after what the Felton's had done to him we all swore to never tell anyone where the new homestead is. It would do no good getting Wally's parents killed.

Suffice to say he had a fine childhood; his mother took care of the

house while his father worked. It wasn't till he was six that his true

calling showed, the fact little Wally could take most anything apart

and then put it back together. His curiosity to see how things

worked was never quenched, every time he was able to pull

something apart and put it back together just made Wally more

inquisitive about other things mechanical. The only thing that

stopped him was his size, some bolts and nuts he wasn't strong

enough to turn yet, and that's where his brother Innes came in to

help. The two were inseparable, always seen around the village

together, and everyone knew the McAndrew brothers well.

Everyone also knew about Wally and his gift and soon people were

bringing the boy things to fix, objects and devices like watches and

clocks right up to large machinery from farms. It became a game,

quick go out and search for something in your field or attic,

something so torn up that the McAndrew boy could never fix it in a

thousand years.

Only Wally fixed everything those villagers found, everything

from the watches to machines to old rust bucket wagons and carts.

Wally and Innes, at the age of 9 and 12 respectively, were the toast

of Kinross-Shire, then the youngest McAndrew really started to

shine. He built a boiler with his own hands, his own nine year old

hands mind you, and his steam tech was better than any found anywhere in Kinross, and then he improved it using his own design making it better than any in Scotland. The McAndrew house was flooded with electricity from a homemade turbine/generator Wally built, something he read about in a newspaper a friend had dropped off at the house one afternoon and he decided impishly to make better. You see, that's the real magic that is Wallace McAndrew, he started to make modifications and adjustments to all sorts of stuff mechanical and made it better. By the time he was 15 Wallace had built a scary reputation, a Technoist and Steam Engineer like no other, and like all men with a reputation it isn't long before someone comes looking to see just how good you truly are.

In Wallace's case it was the British government. In 1914 he was 'asked' to appear in Edinburgh to meet some of His Majesty's engineers. So Wally's father drove him down and there in a room in a county building Wallace met what was considered the best Great Britain had to offer. These were hand-picked Technoist and Steam Engineers. They had come looking to put this whole rumor of a Scottish boy and his ability with machines to rest. They had pictures of his boiler at the family home and other creations but not a one put stock in the photos. It all had to be fake, a joke played on the Scots and the Brits alike they all hissed. Then they talked to Wally and he explained why this pipe was here and why this box was there and all that disbelief came to an end. In less than an hour he had silenced every one of the hand-picked experts, not a one could argue with the boiler design or the talent of 15 year old Wallace McAndrew. As the experts left the room in awe a lady entered and that's when Wally should have run for the doors and all the way back to Kinross.

To make this story short she worked for the Royal Guards, the British version of our Protectorate, and before Wally knew it he was working for them building all sorts of weapons or improving on what was already around. It was just before the Great War and it's safe to say some of the things Wally made found their ways to the battlefields. After the war Wallace left the RG, his mind and heart wanted nothing more than peace, and he almost found it. He settled back down in Kinross with his brother Innes and went about his business of just working with his hands and it was a quiet existence. That was till Wally's reputation came calling once again. A man by the name of Felton and his brothers found out about Wallace and his talent, his knack for making weapons, and they decided it might be worthwhile to sell a few of Wally's weapons only they were told no by Innes, his brother was done with making weapons.

The Felton's didn't like the answer much and came back fighting. The family Felton kidnapped Wallace in 1925 when he went into town with his brother. They murdered Innes at a store they were in, and held Wally captive for an entire year. What they did to Wally, the torture and things, I'll never understand and I'll *never forget what the Scotsman has let slip when he talks about those dread days. The Felton's got nothing for the act, not one weapon or design or even a doodle did Wally give them. It was all for naught. Somehow Wally escaped the bastards and we found him in Dublin, barely alive in a shack that people used to store old broken turbines. He was damn near gone from madness. John healed him, brought his mind back from the dark where he had retreated, and even though he still carries the scars Wally thinks little of the Felton's and for that I am relieved...*

While the lobby had descended into a bloody pitched battle with both sides fighting tooth and nail the back office was the opposite. After John had incapacitated the guard Michael with his knife hand everyone made a move for their weapons, the two guards by Carlo pulling out standard 45 automatics while the other two drew long nosed 38's. The only two who didn't have a gun were the shaman and Angelo, the latter deciding for some insane reason to reach out and grab John by the waistcoat. Only John countered quickly slamming his right hand up and into the young man's arm letting the sound of the appendage snapping echo just briefly. The men lined up their gun sights on the shaman, but with a pull of that same broken arm John spun poor Angelo right in front of him and in between the guards and their weapons. The young nephew of the boss barely had time to yell from the pain in his arm before he felt the cold steel of the shaman's knife puncture his side just over his hip causing him to scream out for his family.

"Ah, Uncle!"

"Shut up Angelo," the boss of the brothel yelled out as he pointed the snub nosed 38 at his nephew's back along with his other guards. Then his arm swung and with a snap his gun was just an inch from Bentley's forehead, the sweet spot right above and between the eyes. "You brought the heat down on me? After all I've given you!"

"No Mr. Troisi," the Magi whispered holding up his hands in the usual surrendering fashion, "I didn't mean for any of this to happen...but I can fix it. Please, let me fix it."

Carlo just shook his head hissing low, "you can't fix this Bentley. It's too late to fix now, it's too far gone."

"Mr. Troisi please, I didn't bring the Protectorate here to your door. It was John Greywolf."

The shaman kept an eye out over the shoulder of Angelo watching closely the two guards and Carlo. To his right Michael was coughing, still trying to get a breath in past his broken throat as John spoke. "Yes, I brought the Umbra with me, following my Joris stone, because I knew you had no true intention to let me walk away with Boles and Wells in a trade. Yet the Protectorate already had plans to raid you Carlo. The men who had Isaac killed, they did it to obtain the Weavers Boles and Wells, only both escaped before these men could find them and unfortunately for the pair they ran into Maxwell who turned them over to you and now what was Isaac's fate will be yours. These men will kill everyone in this brothel if needed to take the Weavers from you Carlo. The death of an innocent in this plot of theirs, even one as black as you, is nothing to them."

The gun pointed at Bentley's head lowered slowly, just like before as the boss of the brothel let the words sink in. John shook his head as he continued on. "You and Bentley were expendable the moment the lady friend of Maxwell talked and told everyone about you two and the deal you made for the Weavers. Don Masseria won't be coming to help you either Carlo and neither will Mr. Luciano because someone from the Protectorate already visited both last night offering them a choice, their necks or yours', and both decided against you."

"They turned their backs on me...no...You're lying to me, about everything." Carlo whispered bringing his gun back to pointing at Angelo's back, hoping to get just one chance at shooting the shaman.

"No I'm not Carlo and you know in your heart, right this very moment, I'm not lying. I knew the crystal would be too much for your Magi Bentley, with his own plans an all, to resist which is how I was able to walk into your brothel with my weapons, the same Magi who has been secretly working behind your back this whole time. He's been using your money and your 'girls' to further his own schemes. No Carlo, you knew the penalty for working with this traitor of a Magi when Masseria said not to and because of that decision you are dead. The Protectorate has come and you have nowhere to run, nowhere to hide. I don't see the marines making many arrests today, just cleaning up."

Bentley turned and looked to the shaman with a confused expression, as if he needed the extra help muddling his thoughts in the middle of the situation. "You came here to rescue the Weavers before the Protectorate could take them in a raid...and you brought the Umbra as well so you would have a distraction? How did you know all of this?"

If there was to be an answer to the Magi's question no one would ever know. John abruptly gave the knife a small jerk when he felt Angelo try to step away and the sudden pain spike caused the young man to freeze and scream again. "UNCLE,"

"SHUT UP ANGELO," Carlo bellowed back. His gun was shaking from the anger that was flowing through his body. The boss of the brothel had been played by everyone in the room it seemed, but none as well the man in a big black hat. The shaman had embarrassed the boss of the brothel and that was just too much to take.

"Your uncle isn't coming to help you Angelo. He's starting to realize just how much he was betrayed by his own people and that anger ripping into his stomach won't let him feel any kind of compassion for you. So in a second I'm going to pull out my knife and when I do you better duck because your uncle and his men are going to shoot you in the back if you don't." John whispered feeling the opportunity to exit the office was just about to occur and he didn't want to miss it.

"What," Angelo whispered back shaking from shock now?

Again there was no answer from John, just a second or two of silence as he stared at Carlo and the boss of the brothel glared back eyeing him down the barrel of his gun. Then the door the shaman had come through originally when all this started blew open from a blast, maybe a stray explosive round got away from someone in the lobby? Whatever it was and whoever was responsible the shaman didn't care. When the others in the room moved to cover their eyes and ears from the blast John did exactly what he told Angelo he would do. He pulled his knife free from the young man's side before spinning and bolting for the other exit to the room. Just as Carlo and the guards recovered and brought their guns back to bear on the shaman Angelo did what John had told him to do and dropped to the floor covering up. When the boss and his boys opened up sending bullets flying at John they missed Angelo by just inches while creating a winding trail of holes along the wall behind the shaman, who never slowed a step as he reached the door with that trail following close on his backside. John blew through wooden obstacle with his shoulder knocking the jamb off the wall and sending the lock tumbling down the hall as the portal swung outward viciously, the edge of the door catching an incoming guard of Carlo's flush against the wall knocking him out as well. I'm out of the office John thought fleeing down the hall back to the lobby, just not out the woods yet.

In the office Carlo growled and started to go around the table to follow the shaman. He was going to thoroughly enjoy shooting the man, over and over and over and over again. Hell, he was going to reload six or seven times and when he was done shooting the shaman that many times he was going to reload another six or seven times more and do it all over again. Yet just as Carlo started to move around the table, from what was left of the entrance that had just blown open, several Marines flooded the room. The boss of the brothel stopped and stood still staring at all the rifles pointed at him, so many large black barrels, and what John said just minutes ago came back. Damn, he had been dead all this time and never knew it. The marines all fired at the same time, the bullets ripping and tearing into Carlo and his guards till they were dead on the floor.

No one moved to help or finish off poor Angelo as he lay still and quiet on the floor. In the end when it was all over Angelo was one of the few to survive the raid and the only one from that day Luciano took in. Over the years as he rose in the ranks of the 'Family' he never forgot the day John Greywolf stabbed him and by doing so saved his life from his crazy uncle. After the marines finished off Carlo one soldier came across the cowering ball that was Bentley, curled up and crying in a corner. He was taken rather forcefully by the marines, hauled off to never be seen again, just like his partner Farzin.

The lobby was gone, any and everything that may have been opulent and garish just that morning was now in pieces or so full of holes you could easily see tomorrow morning coming when you looked through it. And yet Carlo's men hung in against the Protectorate Marines trading armor piercing round for explosive round. And in the midst of the chaos, ignoring every exploding round and ear shrieking ricochet that popped around them, Wahkan ran right at the Marine Sergeant named Devlin, an old enemy from his past who had once been a friend. As the pair rushed screaming warrior cries at each other the marines gained a slight advantage on the brothel guards. A grenade tossed with perfect angle and power crossed the lobby and bounced once before disappearing down the hall to the back offices. A second before Wahkan and Devlin slammed into each other like a pair of large angry bulls the accurately thrown bomb went off shaking the building with the blast. Even before the rumbling of the explosion had stopped shaking everything a group of soldiers poured down the hall and into the back of the brothel leaving the rest of the marine platoon to fight the guards in the lobby.

"Climb Moon, get me back up into the sky my ship!" Fade whispered as she looked back to see the Protectorate cruiser was closing and doing so fast. The old Rebel wasn't about to make this easy she knew instinctively and that just made Fade smile a little more. "Come on old man, come and let us see if you can catch me!"

To her left her second Mr. Hayes stood watching the same cruiser make up ground on the Crescent Moon The cruiser had bigger boilers to push more fans so it was going to catch them before the Pirate ship could make good an escape, and it was going to do it easily. He watched as the large gun turrets began to twist and turn; all six barrels swinging round to get a bearing on the stern of the man-of-war. "Captain, I think the Admiral wants to make sure he gets to slap the cuffs on you personally."

"Yes, it looks that way doesn't it Mr. Hayes." Fade replied before turning away from watching the cruiser's pursuit of her. She looked skyward and forward to where the Moon was flying to when she spotted what she knew would be coming along. The large silvery zeppelin gleamed in the noon day sun, like a long metal barrel just lazily floating along with the clouds. Fade smiled and ordered her helmswoman with confidence. "Too bad there's never going to be a man to lock me up. Take us right for the blimp Talia, right for the middle of it!"

"The blimp Captain, right for the middle you say?" Talia yelled back questioning the sanity of the direction just for a moment.

"That's the order, fly right at that big fat balloon. If the Admiral wants to shoot me he better be a damn good shot." Fade finished turning back to watch the cruiser. She felt the Crescent Moon turn slightly to line up with the Zeppelin and she grinned again before issuing her next order. "Cut the steam to the turbines by a quarter Mr. Hayes."

"You want to cut the steam Captain?" Mr. Hayes quickly asked feeling just a little stunned. "You actually mean to slow us down?"

"That's right Mr. Hayes, if that old Rebel wants to put me in irons so bad let's give him a chance to do just that!" Fade answered with a chuckle never looking to her second. A moment later the command was heeded, she knew this because the rumble of the deck under her feet lessened just a little. There wasn't a thing that happened on Fade's ship that she didn't know about in an instant.

Even a mutiny by some fool once went nowhere right after a word was uttered about it.

"Mother, is that air ship coming at us?"

The question by little Alastair was a genuine inquiry filled with concern, unlike the other thousand he had asked while traveling across the country from San Francisco. His mother Audrina looked out the large windows of the zeppelin at what had been unfolding for the last few minutes and found it hard to speak. Her dress from Paris, one of the latest in Victorian fashion mind you, made a slight ruffling sound as she looked to her husband Roger. The man was very smart, became very rich from being very smart, and thus would obviously understand easier just what was going on. "Is that air ship really coming at us darling?"

"From all that I see my dear, I would have to say yes, that old air ship is coming right for us." Roger replied calmly dressed in his long coat and top hat. They had come to the dining deck of the zeppelin to have an early lunch so when they docked in Manhattan the family could disembark and make their way to their penthouse in uptown without stopping. Only now, looking at the large man-of-war as it sped toward them, being anywhere but the dining deck would be fortuitous the lady thought.

"Should we head back to the state room Roger?"

Audrina's husband just shook his head as the other passengers on the deck began to take notice of the fast approaching air ship and the fact it was coming right for them. Well-dressed men and women began to crowd the windows to see, and the moment it registered what could and was about to happen some cried out and others yelled for the Captain of the zeppelin to change course. Roger knew it was useless to scream for the blimp to change course, these things take minutes and minutes to make the slightest of turns. No, changing the way we're going won't work and neither will heading back to our room Roger thought as he answered his lovely wife with a calm but hollow response.

"No darling, there is nowhere that would be safe on the zeppelin if that air ship hits us."

Camille stood at the back of the bridge holding onto a piece of some machinery that aided the Protectorate cruiser in some fashion, just what that was though she had no clue. When it came to the everyday operation of a Protectorate Air Ship she was so not the one you would ever want to ask a question of. All she knew was this thing hummed with power and was part of the very ship, which meant whatever this thing was it had to be stable enough to keep her upright. She felt the deck under her feet rumble with the thrust of the turbines, the fans on the underside keeping cruiser aloft and the ones aft and on the wings propelling it forward. We could catch her Camille thought, but if I know Fade she's already planning something the Umbra was considering when that something popped up right then and there.

"Sir, Fade is flying right for that zeppelin. I'd swear she was going to ram it sir, but now it looks like she's slowing down as well." Someone yelled out above the din that was the communication on the bridge.

She's not going to ram the zeppelin Camille thought to herself. Fade is just using it to keep you fools from using those damn giant guns on her. And funny, the Umbra leader wasn't the only one who had figured out the Sky Pirate's ploy. "We can't shoot at her now sir. If we hit that zeppelin with one of our shells..." the Captain stated while looking out a new long glass that shined without a single scratch.

"I know Captain. I'm not blind or stupid. If we miss the Crescent Moon we'll certainly hit the zeppelin and if we do hit her damn ship it'll fall into the Brooklyn neighborhood below and kill who knows how many innocents. A loss I am more than willing to accept being that it is Brooklyn and Fade and all, but unfortunately it is an action I am sure the Protectorate command will most certainly not tolerate." The Admiral spat in frustration watching intently as the cruiser reeled in the Crescent Moon.

"Now there's the old South talking!" Ezio laughed drawing a hard look from the Admiral and a multitude of grins from the others. The Admiral was a Mississippi Rebel through and through and he was not afraid to show it when he deemed it necessary Camille smiled.

"Ah," Wells screamed as a number of bullets hit the deck all around her, which being at the angle she was only made it all the worse. She slid down crouching on the rail and leaning against the deck trying to avoid getting shot while up above her Boles had stopped yelling for her. The green haired Weaver dared a quick look up to see if her companion was all right. She saw Boles was still hanging on the post but was now trying to cover up as whoever had been shooting at her was now shooting at the dark haired Weaver. "BOLES,"

"GET DOWN LASSIES," Wally ordered the Weavers in a strong voice drawing Wells attention to him. He was standing half in and half out of the hatch using the lean of the ship's deck to balance. With the strange rifle in his hand Wells watched as he pulled with the hand holding the front grip twice making a loud ratcheting sound as he pointed the weapon at the brothel. The large circular wheel in the middle of the rifle spun exactly twice and stopped just as Wally pushed down on the slider switch on the rear grip. What is he doing Wells was thinking when he pulled the trigger and the rifle fired. That loud 'whoosh' happened again and this time a small round object like a ball shot out. Wally kept firing sending more and more of the round objects flying out, through broken windows in the buildings front facade and down on the street. Wells closed her eyes getting ready for the upcoming explosion, just like before, only there was just a strange popping noise and the Scotsman yelling loudly.

"BREATHE THAT YO BUNCH OF BOWFIN DOBBERS!"

What was he saying? Boles thought lost in the words she had never heard before, but Wells knew exactly what the Scotsman had called the men on the street and none of it was very nice. Then she saw smoke begin to drift up from the street and float out the windows Wally had fired the small round projectiles through. A scent, strong and severely potent, hit Wells nose and she immediately tried to recoil because it was so strong and harsh, unpleasant wouldn't even begin to describe it. What is that smell? She thought reaching up to cover her nose with her hand as she heard coughing and wheezing from the poor souls down on the street who were totally immersed in this stuff. Then Wally ratcheted the front part of the rifle again and the wheel spun once again. This time the rifle shot out tubes again, but unlike the ones from before these had small spikes along the body. Wells saw one hit the wall by the window and stick solid, then another and another in a rough circle. A moment later each one literally popped, not explode, just popped with enough force to bring a section of the brick wall down, and with all them 'popping' it created a huge hole in the side of the brothel on the second floor.

"THERE'S THE DOOR BROTHER JOHN," Wally yelled out before ratcheting the rifle one last time, 'NOW GET YOUR ARSE ON THE BOAT!"

Wells lay as flat as she could against the deck of the ship with her hand over her mouth and nose while strangely enough hoping for the same thing. Whoever the man was who got her and Boles out of that place, away from that evil man, she wanted him to get to safety so she could thank him. Even if she and Boles was his now, his property, it didn't matter. At least they were away from that Magi and the young one who use to watch them when they-

Bullets slammed into the deck again above her head and the Weaver knew the ones in the building were firing at the air ship blindly. Wells tried to duck even more realizing all the Scotsman's attacks had gotten more than just a look from the bad men. It had brought on a full attack, for just a second or two before ending abruptly. It was quiet then, the shooting had stopped, just long enough for a high pitched scream to echo out breaking the quiet, the shrill sound so familiar to Wells she knew instantly who it was and as she looked up the deck she knew her beloved Boles had been struck by a round. Wells knew it as soon as her side erupted in fiery pain.

"BOLES,"

The punch to his face was solid but because Devlin was off balance it wasn't even enough to make Wahkan blink. He shrugged off the blow with a growl, "I see you still like to slap like a girl. Who taught you how to punch Devlin, your sister?"

Wahkan countered with a powerful blow to the sergeant's body lifting the marine's feet free of the marble floor for a moment, actually bunny hopping the man for a split second. The large IP landed another punch, a quick strike to the marine's ribs once again, but this time the man was ready. Devlin went with the punch sliding back just enough to have it strike soft before reaching up and grabbing a fist full of Wahkan's shirt a split second before landing a nasty head-butt that sounded like a hammer hitting concrete. The world spun wickedly to the right for a moment as Wahkan felt Devlin push him back while sneering, "And you still can't take a shot to the chin!"

The effect of the head-butt was short lived as Wahkan pushed the pain away with a quick shake of his head. Oh, it was going to take more than a head butt to drop him, especially if he was going up against Devlin. They had history this son-of-a-bitch Devlin and him Wahkan thought, and I'm going to end it right here. The large IP squeezed his hand into a fist and spat, "you killed my friend."

"And you killed my brother,"

"I had too, he was hurting innocent people-." Wahkan said shaking his head before getting cut off.

"Just like you were doing, and yet he was the only one who died, so I'm going to beat you to death for what you did to him." Devlin hissed. What little hair on the marine's head which wasn't close cropped was disheveled adding to the sinister look the large man gave the IP, adding a new level of viciousness to the fight. Wahkan though just ignored the words shaking his head one last time, the last time the pair would exchange anything coming close to a pleasantry. Devlin took in a deep breath getting ready to let out a loud warrior scream again, a bellow of pure rage. Only a second blast at the end the lobby caught both of the combatant's attention. Wahkan turned and looked to see a larger man then himself running right through the shooting, past the flying debris ignoring bullets and all the damage he was taking and the IP instantly recognized who it was.

"Aw crap," Wahkan whispered as he watched a marine step in front of the larger man trying to stop him only to get hit with a metal backhand that sent the smaller man flying over a table top, "its Gino."

"What the hell is a 'Gino'?" Devlin asked as a second marine fell to the half-man-half-machine from a hard front kick.

"One of Carlo's boys...he wants to kill me." Wahkan sighed, as if the fact the thing running at them was more of a nuisance than a threat. The large IP reached down and picked up a table leg holding it like a club taking a deep breath. Gino was coming at them like a tank, just a few feet away now.

"Really, well, he can stand in line. I get first dibs," Devlin shot back reaching down and picking up the busted heavy gun by the barrels. There was no intention to shoot Gino, and anyway, Devlin was more of hands on type of soldier. When the larger half-man-half-machine finally reached the pair a moment later Devlin went to work swinging his club right at Gino's head and as what was left of the heavy gun came swinging for its intended target, like Babe Ruth swinging for the fences at Yankee Stadium, Wahkan swung his used-to-be-a-nice-table-leg club at the same time at the half-man-half-machine's chest. Both attacks though came to the same conclusion, a barrage that missed pitifully.

The heavy gun slammed into the metal hand that replaced the flesh one Gino lost and came to an instantaneous stop a few inches from his metal face. The table leg met the same fate, crashing and splintering into a hundred pieces against Gino's upraised arm. The block left Wahkan wondering again just how much of the large man was metal and just how much was flesh, along with a six inch stump in his hands. Then Gino snarled low and the rumble, along with the impressive failure of their attacks, caused both men to whisper at the same time.

"Aw crap,"

The large marine Devlin started to back pedal, he had to find a gun, any kind of a gun, because he was dead sure he was going to have to shoot this...'Gino' or whatever it was to stop him. As he did the half-man-half-machine reached out and grabbed Wahkan by the waistcoat with a quick snap of his human hand, a lot faster than the IP thought Gino could move, and with a toss that seemed far too easy Carlo's man threw Wahkan across the room right at Devlin. The marine heard his name wailed and looked up from his search just in time to see the large object about to hit him was his old enemy Wahkan. There was a heavy thump as the IP slammed back first into the marine's chest, and then both crunching into one of the last marble columns left standing in the lobby. The large stone post may have been hit a few times during all the shooting and stood tall still, but against the combined weight of both Wahkan and Devlin it had no chance. The white marble post finally broke and fell down in large and medium sized chunks as both men collapsed to the floor with it.

"Damn that hurt," Wahkan coughed before Devlin was pushing him away.

"Get Off Me!" The large marine grumbled.

Gino stalked right after his prey without a second's hesitation. He knew he had both men dead to rights. Neither man was going to live past lunch. So ready was the half-man-half-machine to kill that he barely noticed the two small round objects land and bounce in from the street. He was a step from getting to the large brown man first, just a step, but then the man rolled in one direction and the marine rolled in the other just a second before those damn round objects popped and began to release some type of smoke. A second later Gino stopped cold as the worst, foulest, odor hit his nostrils like being punched. It was one of the few human things Gino had left. His sense of smell had survived the hit on him by the other 'Family' and then the melding of metal to his crushed body. As silly as it sounds he cherished the ability to smell, it became so important to keeping his humanity somewhat because he lost everything else from eating normal food to the feeling in most of his body. When you're turned into a monster to save your life then the smallest of things that made you a man once have weight and importance.

Only now it seemed his sense of smell wasn't helping at all. All three men began to choke and gag and cough from the fumes. Wahkan stayed low trying to get away from Wally's gas bomb and as he did he saw John suddenly jump up and over the banister of the grand staircase using a marine's face like a rung on a ladder. The shaman was heading up to the other floors to get out obviously, so it was probably the best time for me to get the hell out of here as well Wahkan thought. He got up and found his modified Peacemakers a few feet away just as Gino went to take an awkward swipe at him, an easy attack to duck. The large man slid over grabbing his guns off the floor and rolled over firing one into Gino's leg and the other at Devlin.

Please let his legs be flesh, please oh please no metal Wahkan thought as the bullet struck the half-man-half-machine just above his knee. Gino let out a howl of pain and dropped to his knees grabbing the area where the bullet entered. Something finally went right Wahkan thought as he fired his second round just a couple of inches away from Devlin's head. The bullet hit with a ricochet 'ping' sending the large marine scrambling for new cover. As he ducked behind what was left of a lounge chair Devlin found an HS310 left behind by one of his comrades. He picked up the rifle, gripped it hard into his shoulder, and popped up ready to shoot Wahkan ignoring the need to look down the round reticle of the attached long glass. It didn't make Devlin happy what he was about to do. He didn't want to give the IP the opportunity to die before he had a chance to beat him like a dog, but when he saw the lobby was empty of any sign of Wahkan and the wounded Gino, well, Devlin only screamed as loud in anger as his throat and lungs would allow.

Some would say it's strange how we all ended up at John's side. Wally and Zheng...Camille and Fade...me. We all showed up at different times and from different paths and yet everyone found the shaman. John doesn't trust easy, befriends people even less, but those who can truly call him a friend have found a peace when doing so.

After the war was over I left the Protectorate. I had as much Army life as I could stand, as much fighting as I could take. I went home and thought I would live a quiet life, just rejoin my people and never look back. I have never been more wrong with an assumption in my life than I was on that day. Returning to a normal life or any semblance of one wasn't in the cards for me. Between the nightmares and the way the others looked at me, having fought for the white man in his war wasn't a popular thing to do in an IP's eyes, I fell into a dark I never knew could exist. I tried to find my own way out, tried to climb out with my own hands you could say because I've never been one to ask for any kind of help from anyone. I was too deep though, too lost and under the thumb of...something too strong to let me go. I committed awful things while I was gone, awful and malicious, and I would still be doing each and every one if it wasn't for John coming to lead me out of the dark. I never asked for his help and yet there he was, like some holy man offering me the chance at redemption. I snatched at that chance to see the light again, but I damn near tossed it all away just a month later.

Yes, I killed Devlin's brother and a few others. I had no choice. I couldn't let the man walk away from what he had done, let him escape the jailer because no matter how much Devlin denies it his brother was evil. For killing him John could have abandon me and washed his hands of me right then and there and for a time I wish he had. I didn't want to see what I had done. I couldn't stand to see what my hands had done, and yet John just told me if I wanted he would help me. I haven't looked back from that day and its why my home is on the flying Junk. If John needs me then that's where I want to be...where I need to be. I'm not some sidekick or follower...I'm a friend.

The hall wasn't like the one he had come down to enter the back office. There were no other doors to other smaller offices or work areas. This was nothing but a plain white passage way with a 90 degree turn at the end John started to run down toward. It's the back way in. No one comes this way but the guards so no need to show off for anyone the shaman thought as he ran. The abrupt sound of gunfire told him the marines had found Carlo and a summary execution has been performed on the spot. Did they get Bentley too? John didn't think a dead Magi would be accepted by the superiors running this 'operation' so Bentley was probably spared. He reached the end of the hall and turned left without stopping racing for the door back to the lobby, which from what

John could hear was still under attack. There were loud bangs from explosions and the screech of ricochets bouncing off marble, but just a few feet from the door it blew inward from a kick and a pair of marines ran in, right at John.

Well, hopefully these were the only two.

The shaman spun the knife in his right hand so the spine ran along the side of his forearm with the blade out. The first Marine saw him almost at once and began to point his modified HS310 at him, but John just kept running at the soldier. The second marine behind the first spotted John a half-second later and screamed out for him to freeze. "Stop, Protectorate Marine!"

John ducked at his waist slightly lowering his upper body just as the first marine got his rifle lined up with where he used to be and fired. The large round from the weapon passed over the shaman's shoulder whizzing by his left ear and before the soldier could take a second try at shooting the man in the black hat John lashed out at the first Marine. He brought the knife up with all his might, yet controlled and tight, while his left hand grabbed the young man's forward hand on the rifle covering it with his. As the knife's razor sharp blade cut clean through the Marine's coat and shirt, right to the flesh and muscle of the man's arm, the shaman's hand squeezed and pushed the barrel of the rifle into the wall keeping the weapon under control for the moment making it one less thing to worry about. The injured man abruptly yelled out in pain from the slash while John kept moving, spinning into him pinning him against the wall, and then kicking with all his strength backwards into the second marine's stomach. The strike caught the man perfectly in his stomach about an inch above his liver, the force sending him back where he came from, out into the lobby.

Whatever training the marines gave their young men it surely was based on grit because even injured the young man John pinned tried to fight back with one arm. He tried to push on the shaman and get his weapon free. It only drew a quick hit to the back of his head with the butt of the knife, a special creation from Wally for John and the shaman's only weapon he ever carried. The blow finished the fight rendering the man unconscious and thus his body limp and falling to the floor. A round from someone in the lobby fight struck the door frame splintering it in a shower of pieces behind John and he knew it was now or never for getting out of here. He turned and ran for the exit, to the spot where the second marine was getting up to a kneeling position after landing from being kicked in the stomach. The soldier looked up to see the man in the black hat one last time, or better yet the sole of his strange boot because that's exactly what hit his face as the shaman used him to scale the banister in a leap. All at once his nose broke and two of his front teeth popped out, which thankfully the marine never felt as the kick knocked him cold a microsecond before the strike landed square.

The shaman went over the rail and was halfway up the stairs in a blink. It might have been a good thing except John was now totally out in the open and with both the guards of the brothel and the Protectorate Marines still shooting at each other the situation was less than ideal. Never mind the stairs were on fire as well as all the drapes and everything else that was flammable caught and blazed. The smoke was getting thick as he ran up to the second floor taking two steps at a time and all the while feeling round after round skim and skip past his body. Then one of Carlo's men stepped out from behind the cover he had been hiding behind and John had to react.

"What do we do when we catch her sir?"

The Captain's question was a valid one and in any other circumstance at any other time the Admiral would have smiled with a pure vile glee while answering, but this wasn't such a time and he couldn't find the words to speak. The cruiser was going to catch the Crescent Moon, before or after it passed the Zeppelin, and when it did the Admiral would have finally caught the wicked Fade. He should have answered that question with one exulted breath and yet he couldn't, not yet for some reason.

"Sir...what do we do when we catch her?"

There was something wrong the Old Rebel thought. She was running right at the zeppelin, slow and sluggish. What the hell was that woman up to? She only had two choices, go around or over the blimp because it was too late to try and go under. Fade had gotten too close to the slow moving ship to try and risk going beneath it at her present speed. The masts on the man-of-war were too tall to try a sudden move like that. And yet Fade wasn't some deckhand at the helm, no, she chose this track and as such the Old Rebel better move to cut her off he thought.

"Fade will be on the zeppelin in a minute sir, we should have her shortly after." The Captain stated with a grin just as the Admiral finally responded.

"Tell engineering I want all the power our boilers can provide, all the speed we can make, and I want it right now!"

Everyone on the bridge stopped talking and calling out information. They looked to the Captain as the man nodded, "yes sir, all the speed we can make." No one knew what the Admiral was thinking; why he would order more speed if they were already going to catch the Crescent Moon. And yet no one questioned the venerable Old Rebel because, well, he was the Old Rebel for God's sake. The Captain looked back at the venerable Protectorate Officer and knew partially what he was doing increasing the speed of the cruiser. He was doing more than pressing the matter, he closing the envelope for any chance of escape for Fade.

"Captain, the Admiral just picked up his speed. He's closing in on us fast!" A sailor called out, his eye locked to the long glass he was using to watch the cruiser. The metal air ship just kept growing and growing in his eye piece and the sailor was feeling just a little antsy for it.

She heard her sailor's direction; his words mixing with mental numbers which she calculated quickly keeping a tally in her head of just how close this gambit was going to be. Fade stood next to Talia at the wheel as she stared at the large zeppelin her Crescent Moon flew toward. Wally's special air goggles magnified at a touch of a button on the side and Fade clicked it once to see the scared faces of the officers on the bridge running to and fro trying to decide what to do. That old blimp creeped slower than a snail so trying to go up or down wasn't going to work and neither was trying to turn. Fade clicked the button again and she heard a small whir from her glasses as her view returned to normal.

"Captain," Mr. Hayes suddenly spoke up from behind her with a voice just tinged with concern, "begging your pardon, but we're getting very close to the blimp."

Those numbers she kept a tally of in her head told her not yet, just a moment more. "I know Mr. Hayes, and I plan on getting just a little closer."

"Closer Captain," Talia whined keeping the helm straight?

Then the numbers clicked, the tally evening itself out, and Fade leaned over yelling into a large circular mouth piece by the side of the helm. "Cut the steam to one quarter NOW!"

Everyone standing on the quarterdeck, and the main deck below, heard the order and knew at once what was going to happen. The Crescent Moon needed just short of forty-five percent, a little over a quarter ahead, of steam to keep her bulk in the air. Anything short of that and she was heading down to make a landing, rough or soft only mattered as to how fast the turbines beneath her spun. At first nothing seemed to happen, the Moon just kept on flying right for the zeppelin, and then the man-of-war shuddered hard as the sound of the turbines suddenly lessened. Then the Moon dropped and began to fall almost, level as could be with her wings set for straight flight, right for the Brooklyn neighborhood below.

"There she goes!" The air ship man standing next to the windows called out as he watched the man-of-war start to drop like a rock.

"I knew it...I knew it!" The Old Rebel hissed as the Captain next to him only whispered in disbelief.

"She's going to try and go under, that close and she's going to try a stunt like that!"

"It's no stunt Captain," The Admiral sneered while turning back to the bridge, "wings up 10 degrees! Get the ship over that blimp before she gets under it!"

Back in the rear of the bridge, all forgotten about now, Camille and her Umbra stood watching the air ship battle unfold. Mr. Cooper though wasn't as sure of what was happening as his Mistress and her second were. His youth was most certainly showing. "What's happening now?"

"Fade has the advantage, that's what happening." Ezio answered smiling broadly still.

"Falling out the sky is an advantage," Cooper retorted quickly.

"She cut the steam to her turbines, which is why she's falling," Camille answered this time just as she had to lean back into the bulkhead as the cruiser abruptly climbed higher into the sky, "as soon as she puts the steam back on she'll have the advantage."

"How,"

"Well, think Mr. Cooper, where is a Protectorate Air Ship most vulnerable?" Ezio asked just as the Admiral ordered wings to level.

It only took a second for the young Umbra to realize what was transpiring and just what the Sky Pirate was trying to succeed in doing. "She'll shoot us right out the sky. There's nothing to stop her from destroying the turbines under us."

"Not unless the Admiral turns the cruiser in the right direction, if he moves with Fade, shadows her and stays on top while dropping altitude, then this is all for nothing. She won't have a shot; Fade's man-of-war has no way to shoot straight up." Camille told her young apprentice and when he squinted with confusion she sighed and continued on. "The Moon can't list far enough over to give her a shot at the bottom of this air ship if we stay on top."

"And if the Admiral guesses wrong?" Cooper asked quickly. Camille assumed her apprentice knew the answer to the question, anyone would, it was just the boy was too young and afraid to face the answer yet. Ezio though, standing beside her and holding onto the same stanchion as his mistress to keep from falling down, had no problem stating the obvious.

"Oh it will be just like you stated Mr. Cooper. Fade will shoot us right out of the sky."

"Then go under the blimp just like Fade is doing!" The young apprentice blurted out, as if all the years of flying air ships in combat on the bridge at the moment didn't exist. Camille only shook her head at her young Magi as Ezio answered.

"We're going too fast to dive under the blimp now, it's why Fade slowed. She lured the Admiral to speed up thus cutting off that option for him and all the while making it possible for her to turn the tables on him."

The look on Mr. Cooper's face told Camille he fully understood now. Below her at that very same moment on the bridge of the zeppelin that same look was on another Captain's face. Henry Claskill was the second youngest captain in the Eastern Sky Zeppelin Service, the youngest being just a year younger than his 30 years. He had been a pilot with the Royal Guard Air Wing during the Great War giving aid to the British side as it held off the German air machine. After seeing too many men die needlessly on too many missions over foreign soil Henry decided a life at the helm of a zeppelin as it crossed the States was the best thing for him. He loved flying and this way, floating along without care, could never be mistaken for the stressful aerial dog fighting where it was kill or be killed.

It was the perfect thing for his worn soul...that was till today. Now he stood on the bridge of his zeppelin watching in horror as the large air ships that had been speeding right for him split going in different directions. The man-of-war was by far in the worse position of the two. The cruiser was at full speed and was going high so it would clear them with ease, but the man-of-war was going slow and dropping just as lethargically. Its masts would never clear the fuselage of the zeppelin. The tall wooden spires of the man-of-war would certainly grab the long metal tube hanging from the dirigible and drag both of them down to the ground. Henry stood looking on in fear as the bow of the ship passed below, so close he could see people running to and fro on the teak deck. Then the first mast, the fore-mast, as it passed so close he saw the very tip top of the pole. One of his officers behind him whispered a prayer to the lord savior above to spare them all and Henry added his own silent petition to it as the main-mast, the tallest of the three, came right for them, the top of it dead-even with the window he looked out of.

Carlo's guard had every intention of killing him, which was amazing because the smoke made seeing anyone clearly almost impossible. John though caught just a glimpse of that purpose in the man's face before he was shot dead, a bullet from a Protectorate Marine ending him short of doing anything. As the guard crumpled to the floor the shaman bolted past the body reaching the second landing just as the building shook, though not from an explosion. The shaman heard Wally's voice above every other sound telling him to get back to the Tiānkōng, something about a door being open now. Another guard came running out of the smoke at John swinging the butt of his tommy gun at his head. The blow could have crushed his skull, if he was still there, but right before impact John ducked. With two quick slashes from his knife across the man's legs the shaman dropped the guard watching the man bounce then slide down the marble steps to the lobby below.

It was time to go and John wasted not a second as he ran in the direction the guard had come from. The upper floors of the brothel were just like any other hotel, open long halls with the entrance to a room every ten feet or so. As he reached the corner and turned left to make an exit from the building down the hall John noticed the long balcony was full of people, from the working women trying to just find a safe place to hide to a guard going hand to hand with a Protectorate Marine. Everyone was either fighting or lying on the floor in heap and all were in his way. Damn, this isn't going to easy John thought before he spotted the telltale green smoke from Wally's special steam launcher rounds just a second before he caught sight of the poor people coughing like mad while trying to escape from the gas. Even better, now it's going to stink like crazy the shaman thought as his eyes saw the large opening at the end of the madness, a large opening in the brick wall to the outside. Then a bullet stuck the wall behind him and the shaman just took off in a dead sprint for the end of the balcony and the opening.

The first few people never felt him run by. There was just a quick brush of the shoulder and then the man in the black hat was gone in a rush. Then a marine was trying to push some frightened woman over the side and John had to slow a little just as the

Protectorate spotted him. The man let go of the lady and started to try and raise his rifle at the rushing attacker, but the shaman was still too fast. Before the rifle was even half way up John brought his knife around in a quick slash to the man's cheek a second before delivering a stomp to his knee breaking the joint with a loud crack that echoed. Suddenly a second marine appeared to John's right, running straight out of a room he had been standing in. The soldier tried to grab the man in the black hat reaching for him with his hands but John was again just a little quicker letting go of the first marine's rifle and spinning back away from the other's lunge. The second marine slammed into the rail and almost went over catching himself in mid flip just in time...that was till John kicked him hard in his stomach and the poor man went the rest of the way over with a yodeling yelp all the way down. The shaman looked over to the first marine who was now holding his face with one hand and his knee with the other before he turned in a full circle and kept running for daylight. The woman the first marine had tried to throw over the rail before his comrade had made the leap unceremoniously watched as her savoir ran away, the eagle feather spinning crazily from the back of his hat, and then she heard the Protectorate moan. She found a boot, one of the other girls must have run right out if it, and started to just beat the man senseless. No one was going to throw her over some balcony like a piece of trash.

He ran past two more girls who were busy kicking and slapping another marine as the shaman slid his knife back into its sheath then John saw the girl from before, the one from Carlo's office with the long brown curly hair. She stumbled out of a room coughing and gagging from Wally's concoction right in the path of his escape. Bullets started to hit all around her, plinking and screeching, and the girl just danced in a circle screaming loudly. Her white calf high boots clicked on the marble loudly as she jumped from foot to foot, the sunlight pouring through the huge opening in the wall and hazy smoke made her look strangely like an angel. She looked up to see the man from Carlo's office running right at her, yeah, sprinting like a convict fleeing a Protectorate police men...which is what he was doing essentially. Her mouth went just as wide as her eyes as she realized the man in the black hat had no intention of stopping. Nope, he wasn't even going to turn and miss her. The lady started to scream a second before John bent at the waist enough to scoop her up and then both were out the hole Wally had created, leaping out into the sun with the lady on his shoulder wailing.

"OH MY GAWWWWWWDDDDDD!"

Wahkan ran out past the busted frame of the doors to the sidewalk covering his nose and mouth from the noxious fumes. Damn Wally, you didn't have to make the smoke bombs smell so damn bad, did you? He looked up to see the Tiānkōng sitting awkwardly in the street, then back to the lobby. John was in there somewhere, but he was busy getting out so that's exactly what the large man decided he was going to do. Some marine who had been hurt from the exploding car just moments before yelled and pointed his rifle at the large IP. Thank the Great Spirit the man was still shaken because he missed Wahkan by about a foot or so.

"Damn that was close, too close for me!" Wahkan hissed running for the Tiānkōng. There on the starboard side of the Junk, the side lowest to the ground, was the break in the rail where one would come aboard. The large man ran right for it using the hood of a car as a ladder to jump up and grab the ship. Wahkan was just pulling himself up when he saw John come leaping out of the building from the second floor like some damn bird, and he had a girl over his shoulder too. He started to laugh, that was till he saw the dark haired weaver lying on the deck of the ship in her own blood.

"GET DOWN!"

Roger yelled the order as loud as he could as he pulled his wife Audrina and his little Alastair down to the floor of the dining deck. The old air ship had suddenly started to drop obviously intending to go under them while a large Protectorate cruiser was roaring over them at the same time. Roger had watched in horror

as the fore mast of the man-of-war came right for the long tube

that was and would be for the next hour at least his home. The

stout mast passed right under them, close enough for someone on

the bridge to reach out a window and touch it for God's sake. Now

though, the main mast was coming and this pole was taller the first

one, by a good ten feet or so. He held Audrina and his son in a hard

hug as the last of the air ship he watched in terror dropped out of

view from the window before falling to the floor, the last image in

his mind was the main mast about to crash into the bottom of the

large gondola square on. All around them the other passengers

yelled and screamed while going to the floor to keep from being

thrown down when they were struck.

"BRACE YOURSELVES!" Henry Claskill, Captain of the

zeppelin called the 'Zephyr', yelled to the bridge crew.

Oh God, it's going to hit us and tear us free from the riggings

the captain's mind screamed. He spread his legs to absorb the force

of the impact and leaned up against the helm choosing the only

thing in the room that give him a sturdy base to hang on to. Henry

could picture it all in his mind, how it was all going to end. The mast

would hit them just below the window, the wooden pole would

tear into the thin metal that made up the gondola, and as the man-

of-war began to drag the long metal tube the rigging holding it to

the blimp would just snap from the force. The gondola wouldn't come down in one piece but in pieces, the bridge and the kitchen and part of the dining deck would fall first into Brooklyn below. What was left, if the blimp didn't get some tear in its side and deflate, would float along aimlessly at the winds mercy till someone or something brought what was left of the zeppelin to the ground.

Henry had just enough time, a second or two, to think all of this wouldn't have happened if it wasn't for that damn Protectorate cruiser going over the top of them. The damn turbines on the bottom of that metal behemoth just pushed the blimp downward, right down on top of the fool flying that old air ship. Then the one man of his crew who had stayed by the windows to keep watch screamed out the mast was right there, it was going to hit them. Henry clenched every muscle in his body as his heart beat so damn hard it rang in his ears, and then a loud metallic shriek echoed all around the bridge and the deck under him abruptly shifted backwards, lurching and jumping. He grabbed the pedestal of the ship's wheel while watching the air man who had been standing there go flying across the bridge. The loud whine of rope rigging being stretched to the breaking point filled the air next as the shriek of protesting metal lessened, and then everything went silent. Henry could feel the gondola sway and twist, the blimp literally bouncing in the sky from the combination of the turbine blast from above and the collision with the man-of-war's main mast. Henry turned and ran to the opposite side of the bridge and helped the air man that had been thrown up off the floor as he watched both of the air ships speed away, the cruiser above turning abruptly to starboard while the man-of-war sped up amazingly. Damn, we were nothing but a bump in the road to them he thought.

"GIVE ME ALL THE STEAM YOU HAVE DOWN THERE BOYS! GET US BACK IN THE AIR!" Fade screamed into the tube that went down below decks to the rooms that held the boilers. She gave the command just as the bow started to cross the zeppelin's path and it wasn't a moment too soon because the Moon was close to falling too fast. The man-of-war didn't shudder this time as the steam sent the turbines spinning at an unbelievable speed, it actually convulsed and roiled. The deck hopped and danced under her feet as the Moon leapt forward like a giant horse biting at the bit to run, the hull humming with the new thrust of power. With the burst of speed she was right under the cruiser now, what the Crescent Moon lacked in power she more than made up for in agility and quickness.

Her gamble had paid off for the moment, though it almost it hadn't. That Old Rebel had sped up so much that both ships crossed the path of the blimp at the same time and his downdraft had almost sent the that big bag of air right down on top of her. As it was the main mast had only ripped a nice gash in the underside of the zeppelin's gondola instead of tearing it down, the blimp was still airborne at least, and with her turbines and fans at full power the

Crescent Moon was ready to fight. Fade looked upward to see that big old metal belly of the Protectorate Cruiser and she smiled from ear to ear. Whichever way you turn, whichever way you run, I'm going to hurt you old man. "Mr. Hayes, get the gun crews to the ready! Load the cannons with scatter shot, no exploding rounds!"

"YOU HEARD THE CAPTAIN, GET TO YOUR GUNS!" Her second screamed out as Fade watched the cruiser closely. On the main deck below, and the two below the main, the men and women in Fade's crew ran to their assigned cannons, large cast iron thirty pound rolling long guns. When the Captain came across the Moon the old warship still had all three gun decks fully set with one hundred cannons still operational, fifty per broadside. Every cannon still used gun powder and fuse, Fade had steadfastly refused to modify a single one. These beasts were born to roar she had smiled with a gleam in her eye, so let's leave them to do just that, and now those crews raced to fill each long guns throat with special round shot.

The bridge of the cruiser looked like it had slipped into a form of organized panic with the Protectorate officers and air men screaming out information. Camille leaned back against the metal stanchion she was using as a brace after looking away from her second and watched wondering when Fade would end this little skirmish. The Captain stood by the Admiral yelling out the door to the bridge's foredeck at the air men standing there. "WHERE'S FADE?"

"SHE'S RIGHT BELOW US SIR!"

She's below me, right underneath us the Admiral thought quickly as he turned to the door and barked out his order. "IS SHE TURNING?"

"NO SIR, SHE'S STAY-WAIT, SHE'S GOING TO PORT!" The air men yelled out suddenly and the Old Rebel turned to the helm on hearing the change.

"HARD TO PORT!"

Fade looked up at the belly of the beast and laughed, all it took was one little twitch and she had the Admiral jumping like a frog on a lily pad in a pond. "Swing us back starboard Talia! Get ready on the wings, down fifteen degrees on the port and up ten on the starboard when I give the word."

"Aye Captain," Her helmswomen acknowledge spinning the ship's wheel. The man to her left stood at the ready on the switches which controlled the wings and the flaps which controlled if the air ship climbed or descended.

"SHE"S GOING BACK TO STARBOARD SIR!" The other air men standing on the opposite bridge foredeck called out.

"Damn," the Admiral spat looking to the helmsmen with an angry eye, "hard to starboard, down on the wings ten degrees. I'll force her out of the sky!"

"Not this day you won't," Camille whispered with a cold eye to the Admiral before looking to Ezio and Cooper, "hold on to something, Fade's going to fire all those guns of hers in a second or two."

"How do you know that?" Cooper asked quickly in a voice that was an octave higher than it should have been and filled with fear.

Ezio chuckled and shook his head, "because the Sky Pirate beat us to being the one to shoot first." The young Umbra looked to his elder Magi with a confused eye, and then like Camille had foretold Fade fired most of her cannons.

"Back to port Talia...set the wings now!" Fade ordered with a shout. Her helmswomen spun the ships wheel again sending the Moon back to port just as the man to her left set the wings as commanded. Almost at once the man-of-war began to turn and as it did the air ship rolled onto its port side jutting the starboard right up into the sky. The list was as far as the Moon could go, as much as Fade dared, because any farther and the turbines underneath her would stop providing the precious lift needed to keep aloft. Just like a ship on the sea, list too far and you'll roll and sink like a lead weight...but Fade knew her Moon and she knew how far her ship could go. As the man-of-war twisted the gun crews all reacted swiftly setting the cannons into their berths before the list became too much to move the cannons. The round flared ends of the long guns barrels popped out the many open portals ready to fire when told too.

Henry Claskill watched the two air ships maneuver from the bridge of the zeppelin and as it all unfolded in front of him it looked too familiar. It was just like his days with the Royal Guard in the war, dog fighting with the Germans, no...It was exactly like that. They were doing the 'S' maneuver, and the cruiser was setup perfectly now for a kill shot as the quicker smaller ship cut a hard turn setting itself up for the perfect pass, just off its aft section. He stared in disbelief knowing full well when the smaller man-of-war crossed under the aft of the cruiser the air ship would attack, and it did with a spectacular show. Mr. Hayes held onto the starboard rail looking right up into the sun almost and waited, time moving so slow it felt like it was going backwards. The belly of the cruiser approached growing in size as it did and he knew the Admiral was trying to force the Moon out of the sky. Good luck with that you old-

"Mr. Hayes," Fade suddenly yelled from behind.

-Rebel you. "Yes Captain?"

The cruiser was almost overhead, a few yards just past the starboard side now as Fade gave the order, "kick that Old Rebel in his ass when we fly by."

The large wing of the Protectorate ship was just close to passing the bow of the Moon as Mr. Hayes howled. "FIRE YOUR GUNS!"

It wasn't all at once, not a full uncontrolled broadside, but each cannon firing separately with a precision that comes from doing a task over and over, which was exactly how Fade's gun crews had trained and attacked. The first three long guns in the first row on all three decks fired just as the cruiser's large wing passed over, the cannon roaring and sending its payload straight and true. The scatter shot started out as a regular cannon shot, the large ball spinning and flying, but then halfway to the cruiser the metallic skin of the ball broke and ten smaller ones inside sprang forth. The larger than baseball sized shots raced and hit the wing of the cruiser tearing into the metal, ripping and shredding the mechanical gears inside. Then, one after the other with the same perfect precision, each row of cannons fired into the air ship above them. As Fade passed under the cruiser standing on the quarterdeck she howled with joy watching the turbines and fans meant to keep the large air ship aloft explode and fall apart, the whole aft end of the cruiser was ablaze and smoking in seconds. Her cannons had most certainly roared and her magnificent crew had mortally wounded the beast, the coup-de-grace given by the last row of guns. The tall rudder was shredded with holes as the scatter shot struck just before Fade turned to the helm.

"Swing us back in line with the cruiser Talia, set the wings for level flight."

"Aye Captain," both barked as the Moon rolled back over to level while also swinging back to follow the cruiser now.

Each and every blast of the cannonade was felt, the bridge going up and then down so viciously that it looked like the men and women were jumping. The Admiral barely held onto the pedestal of the ship's wheel as the cruiser convulsed and bucked throwing anyone and everything not tied down around like loose change in your pocket. Camille had readied herself for the reaction the ship would make and yet she still was tossed head and right shoulder first into the stanchion she had been leaning on. The world spun and she was sure the floor was going to make a very violent appearance, only the hands of her second saved Camille from hitting the deck. He grabbed her by the waist and pulled her into him just as the ship shook again almost sending both to the deck. Explosions, distant and numerous, rattled the cruiser over and over as she held onto Ezio.

"There go a bunch of our turbines!" Her second stated loudly just as alarms started to go off on the ship from its various areas.

Then it was over, the attack that is. There were no more loud blasts of cannon fire, no more violent convulsions of the ship being struck by cannonade though the cruiser was shaking as bad as an old Model T on a dirt road Camille thought. She got her feet under her just as the air man on the foredeck out by the bridge screamed out. "The Crescent Moon is behind us, coming up on the port side!"

"She's going to finish us off!" Cooper wailed looking around terrified.

"We're already done for Mr. Cooper. Fade's just going to make sure the Old Rebel knows who did it."

She expected to see damage, but when Camille looked back to the fantail of the cruiser after getting outside she had to smile just a little. There wasn't a scratch to the top side of the cruiser, but her underside was a billowing a smoke trail that was beginning to obscure the sight of the city below. Camille could see flames from the damaged and broken turbines on the fantail all the way up to amidships, bright orange fans of flames. We can't stay aloft like this...we're going to crash right in the middle of the borough she abruptly thought and the concern from the realization wiped the smile right from her face. Down there on the streets and in the houses were thousands of innocent people who could and would die if the cruiser crashed into their neighborhoods. The Umbra looked up to see the Crescent Moon closing in on the side of the Protectorate air ship a second before she heard the Admiral yell out an order.

"Shut down all the turbines aft of amidships! Divert all the steam to the forward fans! We have to keep the ship up as long as possible!"

She turned and looked into the bridge just as the damaged cruiser shuddered and dropped closer to the ground with a sudden jolt. On the Moon Fade was quiet while her crew hollered and yelled in joy watching their nemesis burn and fall slowly toward the ground, her goggles zoomed in on an unsettling sight. She had hoped to catch the Old Rebel coming out of the bridge to shake a fist at her for beating him yet again only it wasn't the Admiral who popped out to check on the damage to the cruiser. Fade's blood ran cold as she pressed the button on the goggles and the image in the glasses enlarged. It was her friend, her dearest besides John Greywolf.

"Oh God no," She whispered as she watched Camille look toward the fantail of the ship before turning to look back at bridge, "no, no...What is she doing on that damn ship?"

"What is it Captain?" Mr. Hayes asked and from the sound of his voice he was a little worried about what Fade had seen.

"It's Camille, she's on that cruiser."

"Miss Camille...she's aboard the ship too...why?" Mr. Hayes asked now truly worried.

Fade leaned into the rail letting her hips brace her against the wood rail as she did, "get my personal whip ready to fly Mr. Hayes."

"Yes Captain, are you going to get Miss Camille?"

"No, you are, after that Old Rebel gets the cruiser down your going to get her."

"Me ma'am?" Mr. Hayes snorted just a little taken aback.

The Captain only nodded as she kept her eyes on the cruiser knowing full well the Admiral had a plan to get the ship on the ground safely. She had to grudgingly admit the man was a good air ship officer, just a little greedy and thus slightly out of control when it came to trying to capture her.

The pair hung in the air for the slightest of moments, like a string of bright baubles hanging from the ears of a Hollywood starlet, and all the while the lady was screaming her head off. John saw the Tiānkōng and Wally standing half-in-half-out of the hatch and steered his body for his friend and engineer. He could have made the jump easily but with the extra weight on his shoulder the shaman found himself dropping faster than he was ready for. Wally thankfully saw this as well and reached out with his hand and forearm just as John hit the deck with his feet, the padding on his moccasins deadening the sound of his landing. His hand slapped high onto Wally's forearm grabbing into the muscled appendage just as he felt the engineer do the same squeezing to get a solid hold. With his other hand Wally braced the lady's landing keeping her head from bouncing off the deck of the Tiānkōng.

"Damn, it's good to see you Wally!" John chuckled as he laid the lady on the deck, her body now shaking in shock from the jump out the window. "Go Zheng, get us out of here!"

"Always glad to be of service to you my brother!" The Scotsman laughed before looking down to the lady on the deck smiling as the Tiānkōng began to move silently lifting on the morning air. "And a good morning to you lass, hope nothing was broken or hurt in all the commotion?"

"What...who?" She asked backed stuttering just a bit looking around nervously. Where did this air ship come from? She hadn't seen it before, not even when she was trying to get out of the room when all that smelly smoke was everywhere.

The Tiānkōng sailed above the buildings and began to climb quickly free of the cramped confines of the street. Zheng placed a hand over the large crystal in the rudder board and the Tiānkōng responded quickly to his silent mental commands as the ghost steered the air ship away from the neighborhood. John stood up leaving the lady sitting on the deck as Wally did the same. The shaman scanned aft looking for Wahkan and the Weavers and he spotted both just as his friend screamed out. "JOHN, SHE'S DYING!"

In a flash the shaman took off running toward the spot by the third mast where he saw the stocking covered legs of Boles, Wahkan by her side and next to him the hysterical form of Wells crying out as he came up. "OH BLESSED SPIRITS NO, PLEASE NO!"

Her dark skin looked grey now, dull and slightly cold to the touch as John knelt by Boles side and put a hand on the side of her neck, just down from Wahkan's hand which cradled the Weaver's head gingerly. Her pulse was slow, her heartbeat feeling sluggish in his palm. He looked down her body to see a wound from a round, probably from one of Carlo's guards, had hit her right side where the lower part of her liver would be. She's bleeding to death inside and out he knew instinctively just as Wahkan spoke. "Save her John, you have to save her please."

As he looked up into the eyes of his friend John could see the worry there, the fear that can consume a woman or man with the snap of a finger. Behind Wahkan he watched Wally take Wells into a hug and pull her away as the ghost forever at the helm of the Tiānkōng spoke. "You must not let her die John. Her spirit and the other one...we cannot lose them."

The shaman stared at the alchemist then down to see Boles gasp for air trying to form a word and talk. She's trying to tell me to help Wells, to not let her love see her die John thought quickly as a small tear ran down the dark haired Weaver's cheek. She knows she's dying and all she's thinking about is her companion, her Wells. "SAVE HER PLEASE!" The green haired weaver begged clinging to Wally sobbing so hard her body literally jerked.

No Boles, you will not leave your heart alone in this world John thought as he reached down with his left hand and put the palm over the wound pressing down slightly. Boles jerked and gasped from the sudden hurt the embrace brought as her eyes locked with John's and his words reached past the terror and pain of dying. "Remember the walks you took with your mother on the beach Boles back in Hawaii, those long walks when you were young and she would laugh as you ran and played in the tide. Remember the moment you saw you're Wells the first time, that moment when your soul yearned to meld with hers. Remember all the times of your young life when you were the happiest Boles, when you were alive the most, and cling to them now as hard as your heart can. Choose to live now Boles, live because you want to, because you have to."

Wahkan sat there perfectly still holding Boles head gently in his hand, tenderly with an affection he never knew he could feel for someone, for a person he had never met. He watched her eyes intently as Boles nodded and then gasped again as a surge of energy rolled through her body. The fire in the wound from the bullet passing through her side began to subside as a strange glow enveloped the hand of the shaman while he started to chant words Boles had never heard before. From behind them Wells inhaled slow and deep as she stared mesmerized at the sight, the green hue around the hand of the man who had come to take her away from that horrible place. She watched as her love, her Boles, twitched and spasm from the strange energy she was feeling from the man in the black hat, an energy clearly helping the Weaver. Wells could see it easily, with each contraction of a leg or arm the color of Boles skin became stronger and deeper in color. He's saving her Wells thought joyfully as the despair she felt was pushed back out of her heart.

"Oh my God...he's really healing her." The woman who flew out of the second floor on John's shoulder whispered with disbelief while entranced by what was taking place on the deck of the ship. If she hadn't been standing there, frozen to the spot she had stopped after walking up, at that exact moment watching it all with wide eyed amazement she wouldn't have believed it if you told her.

The Admiral felt every shudder and shake of the cruiser and it was like being stabbed in the heart each and every time the ship twitched. He had been out dueled, out witted, and beaten like a fresh Protectorate cadet. It was the second time Fade had delivered the equivalent of a slap to the face of the Old Rebel and he was getting very tired of the lashing by the Sky Pirate. Yet that was all secondary now, he had to get his ship down in one piece and away from the neighborhoods below. The Admiral held up his personal old long glass, a present gifted to him by the Supreme Commander of the Protectorate, and looked out of the forward window to the horizon. The Captain from the ship looked in the same direction with a new set of binoculars complete with the upgrade to the lenses. The man pushed a button on the side and the whir of mechanics sounded as the glasses began to zoom in on the same thing the Admiral was looking at and as soon as the Captain realized what it was he spoke up, cheerfully actually because the damaged cruiser was pointing right in the same direction.

"Sir, it's the-"

"Yes Captain," the Old Rebel broke in still looking through his long glass noting the location was growing closer with each passing minute as did the ground beneath the ship, "it's the Brooklyn Naval Yards we departed from this morning. Do I have all the steam going to my forward turbines?"

"Yes sir, engineering shut off all the valves and pipes going aft. They had to due to the damage from the attack." The Captain replied turning to watch his commander, a second of reluctance for what he was about to ask pushed aside. "Do we send the crew to the escape baskets sir?"

The Old Rebel just shook his head, "No Captain, by the time the men get to the baskets we'll either be on the ground at the Yards or crashed into some neighborhood. Helmsman, how are my wings?"

"Set for level flight Admiral, but the starboard wing has failed. I can't control the flaps and the rudder is sluggish. The ships wheel feels loose and ready to give."

"Well then, it's a good thing we're pointing in the general direction we need to go and won't have to turn." The Admiral replied drawing a small snort from Ezio in the back. At first the Old Rebel had every intention of seeing the tall Umbra shot, but much like everything else these days that would have been frowned upon by the Protectorate Command. Now though he smiled as the tall man at least wasn't grinding on all of his nerves at once and the retort was slightly funny. "Captain, get the Yards on the wireless transmitter and tell them to prepare for our...arrival."

"Yes sir," The Captain nodded then turned to another officer and gave him the order.

Another explosion preceded a buck of the cruiser which preceded another loss of altitude from the air ship. The cruiser was now just feet above the houses that it flew over and pieces of what was left of the aft turbines fell onto the street and structures below.

Thankfully nothing was catching on fire...yet Camille thought as she stepped back onto the bridge and with wobbly steps crossed to her second. "What's happening?"

"The Admiral is making for the naval yards and hopefully a safe landing. It's the only choice we have if we don't want to crash into the people below. We can't steer and we're barely staying aloft." Ezio answered and the response brought out a quick stab from the youngest Umbra.

"We wouldn't be in this predicament if Fade hadn't shown up!" Cooper snapped.

The opinion was filled with fear and thus had little to no actual basis or thinking. Camille sighed leaning up against the same stanchion she had before and looked her young Magi in the eye. "Blaming Fade for being Fade is like blaming the Old Rebel over there for being the Old Rebel or blaming night for having to follow day."

Cooper looked instantly confused and Ezio chuckled at the young man. "Just hang onto anything that won't break free and I'll tell you what it means when we land...or crash...whichever one we end up doing here in a minute."

"Sir, I don't think we're going to clear the last row of houses!" The Captain suddenly called out turning and gripping the pedestal yet again while looking out the windows. The cruiser was barely staying up and the last row of houses before getting to the open space of the Yards loomed as the remaining hurdle to get over. The Admiral though just stood ramrod straight staring at the piers and air docks up in the distance like it was oasis in the middle of a desert, willing the steel air ship to stay aloft. The cruiser was so close now, just one last set of houses to clear and they could make the piers and water. It wasn't ideal, not by any consideration, to land in the water with an air ship. The water would cause untold damage to the turbine blades and mechanics if the damaged cruiser sat at the pier berth for any length of time, but hitting the water was better than the ground. The Old Rebel knew from the way his ship was limping it would never make a controlled landing in a suspended air dock. The ship wouldn't make it through the doors being unable to steer.

Then the last houses passed under the bow of the damaged cruiser and everyone held their breathes hoping not to feel or hear any kind of noise other than the last throes of the air ship as it fought to reach the Yards. Camille somehow pushed every other sound, the beating of her heart and even the thoughts in her head away. All she focused on was the quiet that she had she achieved, no more noises please. No more crashing. A long minute went by, drug by like someone dragging a sack full of lead bars. Then Camille started to smile as deep down she knew the cruiser was past the houses now, had to be, just as the sound of metal screeching and popping started to grow. Oh what in the blue tempest was this new issue now the Umbra asked herself looking around?

Fade leaned over the rail of the quarterdeck a little farther and hissed as she watched the last foot of the cruiser nip the edge of the roof of the last house. Sparks and pieces of rudder flew at the hit and that's when the Sky Pirate grasped the scene fully. The bow was higher and not from an angle like it should have been due to the aft turbines being gone, but because the cruiser was literally bending in half right at the amidships. With all the steam pushing the forward turbines to keep the air ship up the aft was now just dead weight and as such was pulling and ripping the cruiser apart, in half right down the middle. "Oh would you please," she whispered as her second stood by her side looking on as well.

"Maybe we were too good in our aim Captain?"

"I think so Mr. Hayes, but for now all we can hope for is that Old Rebel knows how to get his ship down on solid ground." Fade replied watching the Protectorate air ship stagger and begin to descend toward the ground.

What luck the Admiral didn't have in the fight with Fade he was finding in spades at the moment, because there was just one open berth at the Yards and thankfully the cruiser was pointed right at it. The sound of metal giving way under the stress of being pulled by a force greater than it could sustain echoed now all around the bridge. The Captain came back stating they had permission to land at the berth, which was nice the Old Rebel thought because they were going to hit that berth no matter if they had permission or not. Just as Fade had run through numbers in her head before cutting power to her turbines to slip below the zeppelin the Admiral was doing the same as he watched the fences of the yard pass beneath the cruiser. They were now maybe twenty to twenty five feet off the ground and losing altitude with each second. The cruiser would make the berth, he knew it, just how hard the landing would be though, now that was the real question he was trying to answer.

"Admiral, the hull is breaking." Someone yelled out but the Old Rebel just stared hard out the windows at the fast approaching berth.

The keel will hold, everything else might come apart but the backbone of the air ship will hold the Admiral told himself as he ordered his helm. "Take us down to half ahead, down 5 degrees on the port wing! Everyone, brace yourselves for a hard landing!"

"Aye sir," the helm responded just as the Admiral turned to the Captain.

"Captain, I want you to pull out your gun and shoot me directly in my heart a second before we land."

"Sir," the Captain asked back with shock.

"I'm a Naval Officer from the great state of Mississippi about to crash land in Brooklyn New York, I can think of nothing worse to live with." The Old Rebel snapped and the remark only made Ezio start to laugh uncontrollably in the back. Everyone turned to look at the tall Umbra just a moment before others began to laugh as well. Even the Admiral had to laugh. It was all he really could do just before the cruiser dropped in altitude so fast everyone felt it and a new noise became thunderous on the bridge.

The sound of the metal hull ripping disappeared as the aft section of the cruiser hit the ground from the drop in altitude and began to drag. What was left of the rudder and the damaged turbines broke away bouncing and skipping along the ground and with just forty yards to go to the water the Admiral gave one last order, "All Stop!"

With no power to the turbines the cruiser fell the last ten feet out of the air, but with the momentum and inertia of the fall the air ship hit the water and not the ground. The weight of the cruiser displaced so much water the pier was swamped and it slipped beneath the wave it created, a shack at the quay wall meant to house guards disappeared as did some of the pier itself. Then the cruiser popped up, like a cork righting itself, and the sound of alarms took over. On the bridge Camille held on to Ezio, who held her, with one hand and the stanchion with the other while looking around, even with the landing in the water the sudden stop had been hard on the personnel on the bridge with most getting thrown about like rag dolls...once again. The Admiral and the Captain stood back up from behind the ship's wheel while everyone else slowly got to their feet.

"We're alive...we made it!" Cooper called out quickly with a laugh.

"It looks that way," Camille whispered staring at the Admiral who only shook his head at the sight of the excited young man. He clearly didn't understand the ramifications of what just occurred, the pain to one's honor and ego the Admiral and Camille thought silently.

The Sky Pirate captain watched with a small smile and somewhat light heart as the cruiser crashed with perfect control by the pier. The celebration was short lived though as she spun away from the rail and looked to her helm. "Take us into the clouds and back out over Manhattan, all-ahead three-quarters on the turbines."

"Yes Captain,"

"Mr. Hayes, get my whip airborne and get Miss Camille, bring her back to the ship." Fade ordered just as she passed her second. The man nodded and she gave him a quick addendum to her order, "take her to my quarters and then make her take off every piece of clothing she's wearing."

"Um, take her clothes Captain?" The second asked with a stutter taken back just a bit a second time.

"You heard me, everything she has on including her stockings...naked as the day she was born Mr. Hayes." Fade stated before quickly disappearing down the steps off the deck. Her second stood there wide eyed wondering just how he was going to do what his captain wanted, and why his captain wanted to do it in the first place. When Talia started to giggle at the helm Mr. Hayes looked over with a snap and a growl which only made her snort suddenly trying to stop chuckling.

The Protectorate Marines pushed any and all onlookers and looky-loos out the area fast and with a demeanor that said it was best to keep moving or face a nasty fate for sticking around. It was nothing new for the Protectorate to 'Protect' via a heavy hand and it was the same here as Devlin looked up at the sky, searching with intensity for an air ship some called a story but he knew to be true. There were tales of an old Junk that was invisible to all it passed by unless you were thinking about it and at the moment he was sure thinking of it. He knew it had to be close because he knew Wahkan rode on it and right now all he wanted was that big IP standing in front of him again. All he wanted to do was stomp-

"How do we look Sergeant?" A Protectorate Marine Office asked standing next to Devlin. He was the Commander of the Weapons Platoon and thus the head man on the ground.

The large sergeant turned to his superior and answered stoically. "We secured the brothel, the prostitutes are being held in the north part of the lobby and what's left of Carlo's men in the south, sir."

"The perimeter?"

"Being secured at the moment sir, we had some local Protectorate Police show up and help out." Devlin answered again and when the Commander's face soured he continued on explaining the uninvited guests. "The locals are here just for support, they're not in the loop and we're keeping a close eye on anyone not in the Platoon sir, no one's going to get too close to the real reason we're here."

The Commander looked out to the street and then back to his sergeant and whispered. "Good, keep it under control. Do we have the pair we came for secured?"

Devlin sighed again and shook his head, "we've gone room to room sweeping for any stray people and haven't found the pair yet. We'll start looking for any secret rooms next, the pair couldn't have escaped us sir."

The Commander was about to order his sergeant to carry on when a corporeal ran up breathing heavy, as if he just ran down from the 5th floor. "Sirs, Sergeant Murphy inside told me to come out here and give you a sit rep."

"Go ahead corporeal," The Commandeer acknowledged with a nod.

"Some of the prostitutes inside were overheard talking. They said a pair of girls who were kept out of sight of everyone else got carried out by a large IP just minutes before we started the operation." The young corporeal relayed. He stood quietly watching his Commander look to Sergeant Devlin and whisper while the large man just closed his eyes and bit his bottom lip in frustration.

"Someone got here before us?" The Commander asked confused and the sergeant's response being other than what he had expected only added to the confusion.

"Wahkan...that son-of-a-bitch,"

"You know this IP? Is he working for someone?" The Commander asked quickly.

Before Devlin could answer though the corporeal spoke up, "the IP wasn't alone according to the girls. There was a man with the IP, white hair and a custom leather waistcoat wearing a black hat with a beaded band and an Eagle feather hanging from the back."

"He wasn't alone? Oh that's just perfect." The Commander asked back before reaching up and wiping the corners of his mouth like he was trying to get rid of a bad taste. Maybe he was as he replied, "this just got very serious gentlemen. I have to pass this up to the ones who sent us so get ready to answer a lot of questions with nothing but the truth. We try to cover this up and we'll be as dead as Carlo before the day is done."

"Yes sir," the sergeant and corporal replied. As soon as the Commander was gone Devlin went back to looking in the sky for the Junk, for his old enemy, while the corporal looked with him but the young soldier was never really sure what he was supposed to be looking for.

When the round had struck her side Boles felt a pain so harsh and overwhelming she could barely breathe for a minute. She gasped for air fighting the sudden agony as her side burned and her hand felt wet where the palm pressed against the spot. Boles looked up to see the air ship moving now through the sky flying away from that dark place where she had been brought six months ago and even with the pain she felt a ray of happiness touch her heart. They were free of that man and his awful nephew, free of all the guards who treated her and Wells like they were nothing more than objects.

"BOLES,"

The dark haired Weaver turned toward the sound of her name and saw her beautiful Wells calling out for her. Oh my love, don't come over here. Please, I don't want you to see me like this Boles thought just as the sound of loud footsteps crashing on the wood deck caused her to look up and see the large Native man running at her. He was the one in the room, the one who took us out of that place. She blinked slowly then as she felt her body loosing heat, growing colder as something wet spread out beneath and under her on the deck, and then he was there when she opened her eyes. He was holding her head in his hand with a gentle touch and there was Wells by his side and both were screaming.

"JOHN, SHE'S DYING,"

"OH BLESSED SPIRITS NO, PLEASE NO!"

More running, more footsteps...Boles heard it all as she looked up into the large man's eyes and saw the fear there, the concern for her. Please, she wanted to say as the other man with the black hat from the room appeared at her side, please don't let Wells see me die. She felt so tired now, so very tired and it was so cold. Please don't let my heart see me like this Boles tried to say looking to the man in the black hat and he knew, he understood what she was trying to tell him. Even though the words wouldn't come, wouldn't form on her tongue, Boles could tell the man understood her intention about Wells. Then he was touching her, putting a hand to the wound on her side and the pain spiked from the contact. Boles gasped as she locked eyes with the man, his grey eyes commanding her as much as his words, just like that moment in room when spoke and everyone had to listen to him. It was like that now, as if she couldn't turn away as he told her to cling to life with every bit of strength she had. Boles tried to answer him, to say yes she would fight for her Wells, and then the strange energy washed over her body just like the waves did back on Hawaii when she walked on the beach with her mother.

How did he know about that, my fondest memory? I only told Isaac and it was just once Boles thought just before the pain in her side exploded again. It was like time was rolling backwards, these last minutes retreating to the point where she had been shot and the moment before, only the Weaver knew that couldn't possible. So what was happening to her Boles wanted to ask as her legs and arms began to twitch uncontrollably? This energy in me, it's making me jump, like being gently shocked over and over. Time was lost to Boles, especially now with what was happening to her. Was it a minute or an hour? She couldn't tell until it suddenly stopped, the feeling of being shocked and the pain.

He saved me...he saved me. Boles looked up to him as the strange man continued to sing with those strange words. Had he been singing this whole time? He must have been singing, had to have, and I just missed it she smiled as the sudden need to sleep took her. I need to rest. I'm so tired I can't stay...awake...where am

I? Boles thought as the dark crept in and began to drag her down into a deep slumber. Her last memory would be looking over to see Wells, a small smile on her sweet face and to her left was the large IP holding her head in his hand. He looked so handsome...so...relieved. The dark finally pulled her under and Boles was fast asleep, the fear and pain of dying lost in the final plunge.

"Boles," Wells asked slowly reaching down to touch her love. Wally had let her go once the shaman had finished and now the Weaver only wanted to ensure her heart this wasn't some dream. The words the man in the black hat had chanted changed abruptly in mid-stream becoming a song it almost sounded like to the green haired Weaver, and then Boles was asleep. Wells stepped over needing, wanting to know her love would be fine now and when her hand touched Boles the feeling was warm and Wells knew instantly everything was safe now.

As she did John shifted and slid away with a small sway to his movements, away from Boles while breathing deep. Wahkan looked up to see his friend and knew the shaman was weak now; the drain on his energy had to be massive to heal a wound like that. The IP looked to see Wells looking up to him before turning back to John and speaking. "John, are you okay brother?"

"I'm fine Wahkan...and so is Boles. We need to get her below and in bed though so she can rest." John said smiling while getting to his feet. Wally had walked over once Wells was calm to lend a hand to the shaman as a high pitched voice broke in.

"Oh my God...you really healed her...you saved her life!"

Everyone turned to see the woman who John had carried out the window when he jumped standing there looking at them in awe. Her mouth moved in small twitches as she pointed to Boles and spoke in a faraway voice. "She was dying...and you healed her...you saved her!"

John shook his head causing the Eagle feather to twist in the growing wind again, "I only gave her the help to live miss, Boles chose on her own to forestall death today."

"What does that mean?" She asked looking at the group and when she realized they were all looking back and her flimsy undergarments barely covered her body in certain spots, well hands began to move and cover quickly. "Who are you guys?"

The three men looked to each other with questioning looks, as if explaining who they were wasn't as simple as putting it all in words, then back to the lady with those same looks. Wells knelt watching it all while holding Boles hand in one of hers as the other rested on Wahkan's thigh. When there was no answer the woman's eyes grew a little wider, if it was possible, and she gasped covering herself even more as she spoke in pure fear. "Oh no, your white slavers aren't you? You're going to strip the three of us naked, tie and gag us, and then sell us to the highest bidder!" She screamed clutching at her body harder.

There was an awkward silence on the deck suddenly, the three men staring at the terrified woman with the same confused expressions while she looked back scared half-to-death. No one said a word, only looked on with fear and shock, and then the palpable moment was broken when a voice spoke up from the woman's side, the shimmering form of Zheng appearing out of thin air. "That is very detailed...how long have you had this fantasy of being tied up?"

"When did we decide to become white slavers?" Wally abruptly asked John after turning to him, the confused look still on his face. The woman gave a small squeal and jump from the ghost's sudden appearance as the men kept talking.

"When did we decide to pick up an extra passenger, that's what I'd like to know? I thought the plan was to get Boles and Wells out only." Wahkan asked looking from Wally to John.

"I had no choice," John replied to both before looking to the lady, "she was blocking the exit Wally made for me."

The engineer only nodded in acknowledgement with a chuckle as Wahkan shook his head. He felt the hand on his thigh squeeze a little and he turned to see Wells looking at him with a tinge of worry in her eyes. "Are you hit, are you hurt?" he asked quickly with concern.

"No, I'm fine...are we safe now, Boles and I...really safe?"

The IP only nodded with a grin and a small chuckle which made Wells smile as well just a little as the lady looked at the group again and asked. "So you're not white slavers and you're not going to tie us up?"

"Again, how long have you had this fantasy?" Zheng asked making the lady jump just a bit again.

"Frankly Madame," the shaman replied with a sigh and a tip of his hat after Zheng finished, "I'm too tired to even wrestle you to the deck. Now if you'll excuse us, we need to get Boles to a comfortable place so she can rest."

"The room next to Wahkan's should be good, nice and quiet and I can adjust the radiator easily if the ladies get cold." Wally offered and the proposal was quickly agreed to by some with a nod.

Wahkan didn't even acknowledge the offer though. He just began to move as Wells watched the big man put Boles hands in her lap with a tender touch before easily picking her up in his arms. He's must be so strong Wells thought as she rose eagerly from her kneeling position and followed the man who followed the one they all called John. As they walked inside the door to the interior of the Junk the man in the black hat called back to the man with the thick sideburns. "Wally, why don't you get the lady on the deck there a blanket to cover up with and then ask her where she wants us to drop her off?"

"I'll do just that," the man smiled as Wells looked back just once before disappearing down into the ship. He looked so sweet she thought, which was crazy right because just a minute ago she was watching Boles die on the deck of the ship and crying in fear. Wally nodded to Wells then reached into a chest by the door and pulled out a large grey blanket that he held out to lady with a wink. "Here you go lass, now where would you like us to drop you off?"

"Umm," the lady hummed pulling the blanket around her shoulder while looking at Wally with a lost expression, "anywhere uptown would be fine...are you sure-"

"No ma'am, we won't be tying you up today," Wally remarked with a shake of his head before turning back to Zheng who appeared at the rudder board by the jewel once again, "take us uptown Zheng, maybe by the Museum of Natural History. Is that all right lass?"

"Yeah...yeah...that'll be fine." The lady whispered as the engineer smiled brightly.

"Perfect, I just love the Museum."

Wells kept up with Wahkan, never more than a step behind with her hand on his back the entire way. She didn't keep track of the direction or where they were going. She didn't even notice that the stairs they took made a switchback making a quick 180 degree turn and led them back toward the bow of the ship. So lost in the happiness of seeing Boles saved and being safe Wells paid little attention to where she was or where she was going. All she knew was there was a long hall they were walking down passing an opening first that led into a room that looked like a kitchen with the quick glance she took, then they passed another door before finally stopping by a second one. John opened it then stepped back letting Wahkan enter carrying a sleeping Boles who was now snoring ever so pleasantly while lying against the large man's chest. Wells followed the pair in and noticed a quaint state room complete with a bed and night stand, a chest at the foot of the bed, and a small writing table. Actually, with the exception of staying with Isaac, Wells had never been in a room this nice.

She stood back just enough to let Wahkan put Boles in the bed laying her gently on the mattress and her head on the pillow. The Weaver slid in and took a quick seat on the edge of the bed gripping her love's hand in hers, staring at Boles taking in the relaxed look on her love's face with joy. Wells sighed feeling a tear roll down her face before turning to look at the large IP. "We're really safe?" She asked again still not believing what had just happened this morning.

"Yes Wells, you're safe now." The man they called John spoke up entering the room holding two robes in his hand. He walked over and put the garments down on the edge of the bed before standing up. "You might want to get out of those clothes when we leave, doesn't seem right to stay in what Carlo made you wear."

"It doesn't, does it?" She whispered back reaching up with her freehand to wipe away a tear. John turned and walked out leaving just Wahkan and the large man spoke quickly before leaving as well.

"The kitchen is just down the hall. We have food if you get hungry and water or coffee if you're thirsty. If you need anything else just holler and we'll get it for you." Then he was gone, out the door with it closing behind. Wells looked around the room for a moment taking in small unsteady breaths before finally crying. She turned back to Boles and John's words came back amazingly bringing a certainty to her and her emotions. It wasn't right to stay dressed like this she decided with that certainty, in these clothes of that old terrible life back in that pit. Wells inhaled deeply and used the influx of energy the breath brought to take hold of her world. She leaned over and opened the night stand drawer looking for something specific, but it wasn't there so she closed the bin and looked around the room. When her eyes caught sight of the writing table Wells knew what she needed was in there, had to be, and the shiny pair of scissors glowed like a star from heaven when she saw them in the drawer she had opened. The Weaver went back to the bed and began to cut the flimsy underclothes off Boles removing the bloody top and bloomers then the boots and stockings. She threw all the clothes in a pile on the floor then swiftly added hers to the lump, even tossing the silly hair ties on her bangs, before taking the blanket on the bed and covering her Boles. The last things were the leather cuffs around each of their wrists, the ones the men in the brothel used to secure them. Those, the Weaver tossed in the center of the pile silently cursing the things existence with a hiss trying not to disturb Boles, who was so fast asleep it looked like she might rest soundly through one of the engineer's exploding bombs.

There, it was done, that old terrible life was gone now Wells thought as she picked up a robe and slipped it on. No looking back, no thinking back on those days and nights locked in the dark room when she would cry for Boles feeling so torn her very soul ached. She sat back on the bed leaning up against the headboard and looked down on her beautiful love, her Boles. A knock at the door brought her attention up and when the portal opened after a second the engineer with the sweet serene face popped in smiling warmly.

"Don't mean to bother lass. I just wanted to make sure the temp in the room is to your liking."

"Yes, it's fine," Wells replied smiling back as the engineer stepped in and pointed out a switch on the wall. It looked like it might slide up and down as he spoke and demonstrated just that fact.

"If it gets a little dark for you just push the switch up and the lights will brighten, kind of like the wick on an old gas lamp. Um, I take it you might want to be getting rid of those old clothes?" Wally asked pointing to the pile on the floor. It was as if the Technoist knew the vileness the pile represented and the memories it brought on.

"Please," Wells simply said and without a hesitation. Wally walked over and picked up the pile getting everything tucked under one arm and the boots in one hand. It was then she noticed he was wearing a hat now. It looked like one her old master Isaac had in a closet. He called it a bowler and the funny part was the hat looked better on Wally than it ever did on Isaac. On the brim of the bowler sat a pair goggles and as he begin to leave giving a tip of the hat to her a small wink of light bounced off the glass of the specs. Then he was gone as well and the room was silent with the exception of the sound of Boles snoring.

Her eyes started to burn, not like before with the strange gas that came from the round objects the rifle fired at Wally's direction, but from just being worn. Wells closed her eyes to rest them, for nothing more than just a minute, and amazingly she slipped right into a slumber next to Boles. The events of the morning, all of it from being taken away to watching John save her love...it all had finally come to take payment. Wells breathed deep and slept with her Boles, together finally after so long of being forced apart.

The shaman watched the woman run down the alley toward the street and wondered if she was really going to run out in the street in nothing but her unmentionables and a blanket. It would be ridiculously easy to catch a cab dressed in a blanket and little else, which also worried John just a bit. The mean streets of Manhattan, even the Upper East Side, were not the best place to be running around dressed in your underthings. Still, she had taken off like being shot out of a canon once her feet hit the ground so she must have had some kind of plan. The Tiānkōng lifted into the sky silently without stirring even a look from one single passerby heading to the clouds that were starting to build. As it did the deck angled just a bit and when John looked back he saw Wally and Wahkan walking up, a small sack in the hands of the Technoist.

"The ladies are sleeping now, resting after the morning's events."

"Is that their clothes?" Wahkan asked pointing to the bag in the engineer's hand. Wally only nodded as John took over.

"Good, toss it over the side onto the roof of a building when you get the chance. If we're lucky everything gets burned in the belly of some boiler and none are the wiser."

Wally just nodded then looked around noting all the small holes in the deck and chipped wood from the bullets that hit the

Tiānkōng. "I'll get to work on repairs right after I drop the sack over the side."

"We'll help Wally. By the way what the hell did you put in those gas grenades?" Wahkan remarked with raised eyebrows.

"You like the new and improved ones, eh?"

"Like them? People on the ground were throwing up all over the place." Wahkan shot back shaking his head with a small grin. "And that doesn't include the ones who were blind while throwing up all over the place."

The Technoist did a small dancing jig toward the rail while cackling loudly, "I knew it, adding all those new spices to me mix would bring down the hoose!"

Wahkan looked on with a shocked smile then turned to John who only chuckled while shaking his head before starting to remove his waistcoat. The trio went to work on fixing all the damage the marines and Carlo's guards did to the Tiānkōng as the air ship cruised along through the sky passing air trains hauling long lines of cars and zeppelins carrying long gleaming gondolas filled with the rich taking a long slow ride to anywhere.

So I guess the time has come to tell you about my friend and brother warrior, John.

He doesn't talk much about his past and what he does say is usually so cryptic it takes me half a day to break it down to where I understand it. I know he was born in the South, maybe Tennessee or Georgia, orphaned at birth and left to die until he was taken in by a lady with no name. I know from the talks we've had the elderly woman from Peru who raised him only went by the name 'Grandmother'. She was the one who trained him and three others in the tradition of Shamanism. I know he has two sisters and a brother, four souls all the same age and all left to die at birth till 'Grandmother' took them in.

From there I know John was taught to read and write like all of us along with learning Shamanism and the tenets within, but for a reason he has never said my brother was also taught the ancient Martial Art of Takenouchi-ryu. The art is considered by many to be the perfection of unarmed combat, jujutsu, and John has mastered it to the point of making his hands and feet as much a weapon as the knife he carries on his back. I've seen him use a sword and a pole to such a devastating effect it leaves no doubt of his prowess with either, but to this day I have never seen my brother pick up a gun. He has never made a long range attack with Wally's steam powered launcher or one of my modified Colts. He's never fired a gun I think. John is one of the last men I know who prefer pugilism over high powered munitions. I could never do it like my brother, fight that way in close quarter with patience and skill, and trust me

I've been in enough fist fights to know I'd rather run you down under my boots then flip you over my shoulder. Also, my Colts have pulled and kept my big fat butt out of more fires than I can tell you about, and I'll add, the more distance I have between myself and an adversary the better I feel. John though, he fights in that sacred and cramped three foot space that exist among us all, revels in it. The closer the fight the better for my brother, and woe to anyone who by choice or fault let's him get that close because you'll regret it before you can blink.

The real magic, no pun intended though it was a great spot for one, is John's Shamanism, the only 'Shaman' I have ever seen by the way. Yes, we IP have elders we call 'Medicine Men' and 'Medicine Women' who commune with the spirits of the land to divine what action we should take to better our tribe's path. Sometimes our Elders even channel the spirits through dance letting the spirits take them and use them, but we do not call them 'Shamans'. And I can say safely I've never known an Elder like John. To tell it like he does, John simply 'travels' to distant worlds via the astral conduit, past the veil that separates ours and these other realms. He talks once there with those who have departed from this middle plane we exist on, those like Zheng Hui, and he gathers information. Ghosts...spirits...names really never seem to explain it well enough, do they? I talked with Zheng after deciding to follow John, after he saved me, and what he told me might be called 'pure fantasy', except for the fact the ghost is here standing on the deck of the Tiānkōng when his physical body died some 400 years ago. John found him wandering the greyness that is Purgatory, only it's not really Purgatory he's told me before, like I said you have to break down the things he tells you. He talked with Zheng, just a small conversation, and the alchemist told me he thought nothing of the meeting as he continued to wander on aimlessly...that was till John came back later. And John returned again and again to talk with the alchemist until the pair had developed a friendship, a bond, and Zheng made his play to gain entry back to our world. The alchemist agreed to tell the young shaman where he had hidden his famed air ship in exchange for the chance to be its helmsman once more, a chance to fly his Tiānkōng among the clouds again. It was a gamble for Zheng to give up the secret hiding spot of his famed air ship. John could have taken the ship and never returned to let the alchemist decide his fate, but my brother did. He came back and honored Zheng's request and now the ghost is tied to the Tiānkōng, forever bound to its decks and walls and forever thankful to John for giving him the chance to return to the skies and fly his precious Junk once more.

And journeying isn't the only power John gained from his Shamanism, as you know now he can heal most wounds with a touch and words, and the energy he uses to do this comes from the same source as that which a Weaver pulls from around them.

That's right, John uses 'natural' magic, energy from Mother Earth and Father Sky, a direct draw from nature and all that surrounds him. I said earlier how a Magi had to have a Weaver give them the energy to wield; well John doesn't need a Weaver because John isn't a Magi. He doesn't throw lightning or create with his energy. He heals with a touch and more from some of the tales I have heard but never seen.

I know it sounds folksy but there are parts of John's past that I don't know but wish too and on those nights when we sit on the forecastle of the Tiānkōng and talk I listen for any chance to learn more about him, my brother.

Night fell quietly on all in Brooklyn, and all were certainly happy for it. After having a full battle in the sky that almost had a Protectorate cruiser dropping on their heads and along with that 'Hotel' being raided, well a little peace and quiet was most certainly needed. Over dinners people discussed and argued about what just happened, why it occurred, and just what the hell was a Protectorate cruiser doing running around the skies here in Brooklyn? Some answers were close to the real truth, but more were so fantastical it bordered on severe paranoia...or did it.

As soon as the cruiser was back on the ground or in the water if you need to be exacting, Ezio and Camille made a quick exit with Cooper just a few steps behind. It was easy to blend in and thus exit the ship, which was just what Camille needed to do once she spotted the small whip circling the yards. She was first off the gangway bypassing men and equipment being rushed onto the ship to fight the fires and tend to any wounded. She looked back once to see her second following and Mr. Cooper right there as well, but then the tall man gave a simple small nod before spinning to confront the young apprentice Umbra. Camille wasn't sure if her second was acting on the promise he made earlier to explain what she had said to Mr. Cooper, or if her second knew where she was headed and thus was giving her the necessary space to do so. If Ezio did know who she was meeting with and he was keeping it a secret then she was risking more than just her own skin now in this subterfuge. Still, Camille used the distraction to perfection making a quick escape of the Naval Yards disappearing into the neighborhoods of Brooklyn with fast steps.

She moved with a purpose down the streets which had become crowded with onlookers trying to decipher and figure out just what had happened in this usual sleepy community. Camille walked right to an alley way darting down the cramped passage to pop out on another street which she crossed just as fast. Down another alley and then finally stepping out on another empty lane filled with tall brownstone homes. Camille looked right then left before turning right and heading up toward Manhattan and the bridge that allowed everyone access back and forth from Brooklyn. She made it only a few feet when the sound of turbine fans echoed and small dust devils began to form and spin on the street. She stopped and turned looking to the sky as she did and there, floating down just as easy as a bird coming in for a landing was the same whip which had been circling the yards. Camille knew who the personal craft belonged to and she knew by stepping on to it she was violating every rule the Society had passed about certain actions, befriending certain individuals.

It doesn't matter she thought as the ship hovered and a small step ladder folded out to allow her quick access, and that is what Camille did. She never hesitated for a second as she strode up the ladder and onto the ship, much like the first day she had met Fade the decision to go and meet with the Sky Pirate was easy to choose. No one other than Camille herself would deem who was appropriate to meet with and befriend she decided as the ladder was barely pulled in before the whip took off heading into the skies. The Umbra leader stepped down into the cockpit where a familiar face stood holding onto the ships wheel, though in the past he had looked better.

"Are you all right Mr. Hayes?" She asked as the whip began to speed and gain altitude.

The man, Fade's second, only looked straight forward refusing to make eye contact for the moment. "I'm fine ma'am, are you all right? You didn't get hurt with the battle and all?"

"I wasn't hurt Mr. Hayes...and Fade, she wasn't hurt I hope?"

"Oh no ma'am," the second stated quickly as he steered the whip around an air hauler and then by a slow moving zeppelin, "our Captain is as right as the rain that falls. She was worried more about you, about hurting you during the battle?"

Camille only smiled thinking she had the same worry for her dear friend during the fight, "then get us to the Moon Mr. Hayes, as quick as you can." She turned and faced the wind letting it flow over her making her long hair fly and her clothes ripple.

Fade's second didn't mention what would, was supposed to, happen when they rejoined the Crescent Moon. Oh how he was going to be embarrassed when he asked for her clothes.

How long she slept Wells wasn't sure. All she knew the bed was empty next to her when she stirred to wake and the spot should have been occupied. The green hared Weaver sat up quickly noting the room was darker now it seemed, but not enough to hide the brown skin of Boles who was busy slipping a robe on over her naked form. Wells stood up off the bed quickly while whispering, "What are you doing?"

"Where are we?" Her companion asked back with a quick inquiry of her own.

Wells pulled her robe tight around her and whispered, "An air ship, the man who...took us, we're on his ship."

"There's no scar," Boles suddenly said holding the robe open and looking down to her flank area, "and there should be one. What did he do to me?"

The tone of her love's voice sounded astonished but also accusatory on the edge and Wells walked over quickly shaking her head worried. "I don't know what he did. There was a bit of strange energy, some I've never felt before, and then you were safe. The wound...the bleeding...it was all gone."

Boles took Wells hand and placed it over the spot where there should have been an ugly scar, a hole made from a very large bullet. Only as Wells hand slid across the dark soft skin there was nothing, not even a blemish as Boles spoke. "It's like there was never even a wound my heart...no damage or anything."

"I don't understand either my soul...but I won't feel scared or suspicious of what he did, I can't. He saved you Boles and for that I will always be indebted to him."

The remark was only meant to state the grateful feeling Wells felt for having the one she loved saved by a man who could have let her die. Yet, the words only brought a swift rebuke from the dark haired Weaver. "He saved me because a dead Weaver brings in no coin, remember my heart, we're nothing more than a payday to people."

"Not to these men," Wells whispered, tried to counter the feeling the distrust and simmering anger swimming over her as Boles empathy came alive. In truth, one wouldn't need to be an empath to feel the emotion of Well's companion, it was very easy to see all one needed to recognize in her eyes. Yet it had little effect at first on Boles who used her mistrust like a shield.

"All men and women see us that way Wells. We ended up in the hands of those last men because of another man and woman who only saw money!"

"I know Boles, but these men...they are different. We're not bound, not forced to be apart. We can leave this room and go where we please on the ship." Wells countered while using her own empathic power to send her love to Boles. She hoped to negate and diffuse this wave of emotion from the one she cared so much for and in silence the two skirmished for control of the moment. Wells didn't want to confront her Boles and the dark haired Weaver wanted no lot in a fight this night. So both sighed and looked at each other with small smiles before Boles, still holding her heart's hand whispered. "Do you know where the kitchen is? I'm very thirsty."

It was done, the senseless fight, and Wells was glad for this. The reason for the altercation wasn't resolved by any stretch of the imagination, but at least for now an amicable peace had been reached with her precious Boles. She nodded and took the lead heading for the door to the room. When she turned the small ornate knob Wells half expected it to be locked, these last months there hadn't been a single door that gave when she opened it. Every gateway had been a locked portal, every egress but this one because when she gave the metal opener a turn the door popped open on command. Wells just smiled a little more as she stepped out into the hall noting that she never realized there was a rug which ran down the middle of the passage, a long red one with an elegant and elaborate border. It looks...foreign Wells thought as Boles whispered behind her.

"Do you feel that, the strange energy that's emanating from everywhere? It is so...nice, like being touched with a gentle summer wind on the beach."

When the green haired Weaver looked up she noticed Boles had reached out and was slowly tracing her fingers along a random board, one of the many which made up the wall. Wells had most certainly taken notice of the strange energy which flowed out of everything it seemed on this ship, from the ceiling to the wall to the floor they treaded on. "Yes, I felt it after I reached the room, though I didn't pay much attention to it at the time."

"Why is that?" Boles turned and grinned. Her smile was so beautiful Wells thought, the kind of smile that makes your heart jump and skip with joy when you see it. The kind of smile that makes you swoon when you know you'll see it every day from that moment on.

"Because you were hurt...mortally," Wells giggled as Boles made her equally beautiful 'oops' face which made her giggle more. The fact her love had almost died seemed to be of little importance as the pair, hand in hand, quietly stepped down the hall toward the open door Wells remembered was the entrance to the kitchen. With each step their feet tingled from the strange energy that flowed from everywhere, their fingers tickled by it as they touched the walls just before they arrived at the entrance to the kitchen. Boles smiled as her nose picked up the scent of food, but more importantly was the smell of coffee, dark and aromatic. Oh how she had longed for the taste of coffee again, being denied the sweet brew these last months at the evil place just added to the pain she had been put through. Only as she was about to enter the kitchen her ears picked up sounds coming down the stairs from outside. Wells heard it too and before Boles could stop her the smaller Weaver silently and quickly went up the stairs to find the ones making the noise.

The pair went up the stairs all the way to the top step at the turn and then past the turn and then crawling up to the last step before reaching the top. Wells hazily remembered the entrance to the interior of the Junk, and as she sat on the steps looking out past the open door she could see all the way down to the bow. Only she didn't need too because just before midway to the center, about 20 feet away, sat the two men who she had seen this morning. There was the one with the bowler and serene face surrounded by those long sideburns sitting on a crate with what looked like a banjo in his lap. He was playing it with a quick paced tune, his fingers danced on the neck and picked the strings effortlessly by the bridge, while across from him the large man who had carried them to the ship sat on two crates stacked together. He was playing a harmonica keeping up with the banjo's tune easily, the sounds of the two instruments mixing perfectly. They must play together a lot Wells thought as Boles sat next to her and watched just as intensely. Both of the men had their shirts off and both were focusing on nothing but the music, so much so they never heard the whispers between the two Weavers.

"What song are they playing?" Boles asked slightly mesmerized giving her heart's hand a small squeeze as she did.

"I don't know, but I've heard music like that before. I heard it when I was in and around London with the Society." Wells whispered back with her eyes locked on the pair.

The pair continued to watch and neither realized at first there was a man missing, that was till a sound from below broke into their vigil of the men on the deck. Boles and Wells both gave a small yelp turning to see what the noise was then turned back quickly to the men on the deck when they realized the music had stopped. Their eyes opened wide and large when they saw both Wally and Wahkan staring back then with a small laugh both broke and ran down the steps back into the ship making enough noise to tell everyone around they had been hiding. Neither saw the smile on the men's faces or heard what they said.

"Kind of childlike, isn't it?" Wally chuckled low.

"Kind of nice really considering," Wahkan replied with the same chuckle. Both sat their looking at the entrance for a moment before the large man turned to the engineer and spoke. "Now everything would be even better if I could get you to stop stepping all over my entrance to the song."

Wally turned back and with a mock air of importance responded, "Well if you learned how to play that damn whistle I might not have to carry you through the song you dobber."

There was a moment of silence with the only sound being the wind blowing across the deck, and then both men chuckled and Wally gave off a quick count down before playing his banjo again. Wahkan joined right in and the catchy tune the Weavers had been intrigued by floated along on the night breeze. On the deck above them, by the large crystal embedded in the rudder handle at his usual station, Zhantee listened and smiled. This was his place, his spot in this world, and he had no regrets of giving up paradise for it.

Both of the Weavers tried to be quiet as they ran down the steps, their bare feet made little to no sound, but it was the giggling that gave up their presence. It was their mirth that made it hard to hide their passing and both were still happily trotting along as they stepped into the kitchen without looking. All the joy though came to a quick stop, as abrupt as turning off Wally's light switch, as both Boles and Wells spotted the third man from the morning, the one with the black hat. Only now the hat was missing and he was just like the pair on the deck above, sans a shirt, standing in the kitchen staring back. His long white hair flowed down his back Wells noted as they stood on the other side of a long table and benches that served as the eating area for the crew. A long table like that, for just three people, seemed a little dreary Boles thought as the man smiled.

"I thought I heard you two up and about."

At first the Weavers only stood and stared at John, their eyes taking him in. They're scared, still full of mistrust and suspicion the shaman thought as he picked up a cup off the small rack that held them and turned to the large elaborate machine of Wally's creation that sat on the wooden counter. He twisted a small valve here, cranked a turn of a wheel there, and the sound of steam flowing through the large metal box signaled all would be ready in a minute. John turned and noted the Weavers had slowly stepped into the kitchen further, slowly crept down the table and begun the process of approaching him cautiously.

"Would you like some coffee? I think it's a favorite of yours, isn't Boles?" The shaman offered with a small smile holding the cup under a spout.

"Yes, we would." Wells answered quickly, the intoxicating smell of the brew reaching her nose and obviously helping her to decide to take a chance on the man. Boles though looked at her hard for a moment, a questioning look most give when someone does something the other wants no part of.

John only smiled and pushed a lever to the side allowing the magic elixir from Wally's special machine to pour forth. As he did the Weavers approached the last few feet to stand by him, both watching the cup fill and each noticing the many tattoos on his body. There were the ones around each wrist, weaving lines that seemed to have no end and no beginning, and then there were the ones on each pectoral. The left one was an Eagle and the right one a Wolf. Wells stepped out from Boles shadow just a bit and spotted the large one that took up most of his back and inhaled slowly at the design. It looked was a large mix, an amalgamation of a wolf's head and a bear's breaking a set of chains and coming forth from the man's very insides. John suddenly spoke and Wells looked away from that spectacular tattoo and back to his grey eyes.

"There not the traditional markings a shaman might have, but then again I am not a very traditional type of shaman. You like your coffee black, right Boles, no milk or sugar?"

"Yes, no milk or sugar," Wells answered for her love which drew another questioning look from the dark haired Weaver.

That smile on John's face grew just a smidge as the scene between the two Weavers was quite comical. The shaman handed the cup of dark brew to Boles and she took it after eyeing it for a moment, that distrust in her heart still causing a pause to all her moves. She took a sip and the effect was immediate, the tightness in her shoulder muscles and neck faded and a small smile appeared just at the corners of her mouth. John picked up another cup and spoke as he took a step to the left, "And you like your coffee like your tea right Wells, milk and a spoon of sugar?"

The green haired Weaver gasped and locked eyes with John as Boles beside her did the same looking over the top of her cup. The shaman opened the door to another large metal box with pipes and levers and valves coming out of it. As the box was opened wisps of what looked like fog slipped out as he reached in to grab something. The Weavers felt the cold from the machine slither out wrapping around their bare feet. "Hmm, we're almost out of milk. We'll have to stop for some soon." John remarked to the room and no one special before pouring a small amount of white liquid into the cup from a glass bottle.

"What is that? How does it make everything cold?" Boles asked with the curiosity in her voice telling John silently the mistrust was slowly starting to disappear with her.

"Wally built it after reading a newspaper article about some Swedish men who invented what they call a 'Refrigerator'. There's some trick with a coil and heat dispersion with the steam that travels through it, all kind of technical and not what I do best. It took Wally a few tries to perfect it, froze everything solid like a stone at first, but now he's got it working perfectly. We can keep meat and other perishables in here for a time, keeps us from having to go to the store so much. My name is John by the way, sorry for not being courteous beforehand." The shaman stated pouring a spoonful of sugar in the cup next. He moved back to the elaborate coffee machine and opened the same lever pouring the brew into the cup filling it.

He did it perfectly, just the right amount of sugar and milk to coffee Wells thought as she took the mug from the shaman. How did he know that, all of this, how does he know all about us she asked herself as she took a sip. The light taste was heaven to Wells, the hot liquid flowing down her throat creating a divine sensation she hadn't experienced since...well since the death of her old Magi Isaac. As she took another sip Boles next to her spoke while John poured a third cup of coffee for himself.

"When do you want to check us?"

The question brought the happy moment to a stark end for Wells, the sweet taste of the coffee fleeing with the onset of reality. It was what every Weaver who was 'given' a new Magi had to do. It was degrading and humiliating. She looked up to John dreading the words she knew was coming, and yet when he spoke he shocked them both yet once more.

"'Check you', what does that mean?" John asked sipping from his cup.

"You own us now, that man...at that place this morning...he traded us to you so we belong to you now." Boles answered coldly, the tension in her muscles from before coming back. She stood tall, ready for to face the music you might say the shaman thought as he responded.

"Ah, and due to that...fact, in the past you have been 'checked' by your new...owner for a lack of a better term."

Wells only nodded slowly as Boles breathed deep, that tension gaining strength again, turning her neck into a steel girder almost. "We usually come in and stand without clothes, turn around so you can look for any...things you do not like."

John nodded and sipped his coffee again, "Oh, really, that seems a little barbaric."

"It is, so very humiliating." Wells added with a small whisper.

The shaman lowered his cup down to his chest letting his arm hang easy as he shook his head. "I won't be 'checking' either of you my friends. I have never owned any man or woman in my past and I don't plan on starting now. You two can sleep easy tonight and all others knowing as long as your here on our ship you will never have to endure that practice again."

The Weavers stood there in the kitchen staring back at the man with eyes wide. No one, and that was never, had said something like this to them. Even Isaac, when he took them as his Weavers checked them over, made sure there were no scars or festering wounds or abnormalities. Just like any trade where property is being exchanged the merchandise must be inspected, only this wasn't the case this time. The shock was easy for John to see and he stepped forward getting close to both of the Weavers.

"You don't want to...check us?" Boles whispered lost, confused, and utterly relieved.

"No," John stated looking down into the dark brown eyes of the Weaver, "because I do not 'own' you and I never will. You are free now Boles, you and Wells, and as such you can leave the Tiānkōng at any time you wish."

"We're...free...you mean...free?" Wells whispered in disbelief. It couldn't be true, a Weaver without a Magi...no, that wasn't possible. Weavers were never just allowed to go free. The Society would never let that happen. If a Magi was killed or died by natural circumstances then his or her Weaver was taken back to the Society and turned over to a new Magi, it was and always had been done this way. Boles next to her spoke up as John only nodded to her question.

"We can't be...free...Weavers can't be without a Magi."

"Will you two are, as of this morning you two have no master." John nodded before taking a sip of his coffee.

'Oh glory be' Wells thought trying to take in what the man had just said, trying to comprehend the whole prospect of it. No more standing naked in front of someone being looked over like a piece of meat...no more being ordered to infuse things or pass energy to a Magi...no more nightmares of being a slave. Then John said something that made her heart stop, almost instantly and completely.

"You can even take your collars off, if you wished?" The statement, meant to be nothing more than an assurance of their freedom, sent a shockwave through both Weavers.

Wells reached up and grabbed her collar so quick she came close to spilling her coffee as she gasped for breath. "No, please no! If you take our collars...the Umbra will come...they will come for us..."

"No my heart, I won't let them take you or me, I won't let that happen!" Boles interjected reaching over and taking her love's hand in hers. She turned quickly back to John and he could see the fear in her eyes now, all the strength from before, all the tension and defiance in her muscles gone in a flash at the mere mention of removing the collars. "Please, don't take our collars. If you do the Umbra will come and they will take us away. They will take us and separate-"

"No Boles, calm down...that will not happen."

"Us...we'll...be taken...away." The dark haired Weaver said slowly, her voice slowing as a calm force from out of nowhere took hold of her soul. It was just like that morning when the back room threatened to descend into anger and fighting but before it could a serene feeling swept along and eased everyone around, this was that same calm again, coming from him. The terror from just the moment before faded under the presence of this new peace, the fear swept away as she stared back into John's grey eyes and felt that serenity ease her to a safe place.

"No Boles, no Umbra will find you I promise. You don't have to take the collars off. You can leave them on for as long as you want."

"We can...leave them on?" Wells asked feeling her own heart beat return to normal again. The peace she felt from John settling her soul back to a grounded state.

The shaman only nodded and looked down, "Yes, and you may leave the Tiānkōng anytime you wish like I said. I only ask for one thing, one simple bargain."

"What is that?" Boles inquired quickly.

"You allow me to obtain you new clothes to wear before you depart. It would seem less than chivalrous of me to let you leave wearing just robes and nothing else."

'What was that' was exactly the thought that came to Boles? First he won't check them like everyone else has done and it was because he was letting them go free, which NO ONE ever does with a Weaver. She turned to look at Wells who had an expression on her face that was somewhere between confused and utterly traumatized. She looked back to John and swallowed hard, "why would you do that?"

"Why not," the shaman replied with a wink before putting his hand out to shake, "but I do require a handshake for the bargain. As a shaman and a gentleman I must ask that all barters be agreed upon by both parties."

The Weavers stared at the appendage lost for a moment still, a handshake? Was this man for real? Then Boles slowly reached out and took the hand in hers, the shaman's grasp practically swallowing her small palm. She shook it and looked up at John with incredulity as he nodded and turned to go leaving the kitchen in quiet. The pair stood there in silence holding their steaming cups of coffee trying to desperately comprehend what just had occurred. After a minute or two Boles shook her head and led Wells back to their room where she shut the door before going to sit on the bed. Wells watched her move, knew her love was trying hard to think, and as much as she hated to break that concentration she did just that by walking over and sitting down by her on the bed. The pair sat in quiet at first drinking from the cups of coffee in sips, but then Wells whispered what her heart and mind raced with.

"We're free Boles,"

"Do you think that's true my heart? Do you think we're really free?" Boles asked back shaking her head. The rebellious spirit Boles showed so prominently just moments before was mired now, slowly sinking in the ominous feeling of the unknown. From her earliest memories Boles had been in the care of someone, owned outright at times, be it by the Society or a Magi. Now, she was free, but what did that mean really? Could she truly walk off this ship and out into the world and be...free...was a Weaver ever truly free?

Wells again sensed the despair her love was feeling, the confusion and uncertainty of what lie ahead for both of them. She put her cup on the nightstand and then did the same with Boles cup before sitting so close to her love Wells was almost in her lap. Her right leg was tucked into her body in front and it touched Boles right leg, which was a mirror of Wells position, and the left leg which dangled off the side of the bed wrapped around Boles leg lovingly. She leaned into her very soul wrapping her arms around her Boles while looking up and whispering, "I don't know about tomorrow and if you asked me I say I don't care. I know I have you now my soul, in my arms, and these men haven't tried to stop that. John, he means us no harm and neither does the one called Wally...and strangely I think the one called Wahkan, he cares for us."

"And how do you know all of this my heart?" Boles asked leaning down and nuzzling her love's nose with her own, her whisper filled with affection and devotion.

"I don't feel fear from them. I feel only compassion and a need to protect, some fatherly and some amorously. May we speak of this later though my soul?"

"Later?" Boles asked already sensing the want in her partner's voice and feelings.

"Yes my only one," Wells growled suddenly using the name for Boles when she wanted to be claimed and taken by the one she loved, "I only want to be yours tonight and let the morrow be what it will be."

The overture of the request set Boles blood to boil, memories and images of being with Wells flooded her brain driving her desire to a level she couldn't contain. Boles gasped as her hand slid up between the folds of Wells robe, slid along the soft hot flesh there gliding over the breast of the green haired Weaver seductively. And all the while she kissed Wells, devoured her heart's kiss with her own, their tongues dancing between them as they began to meld. Her fingers found the hard pink flesh on the tip of Wells breast and squeezed it drawing out a long moan from the smaller Weaver. Then Boles reached up and slowly running her hand up first to caress the face of her love as they continued to kiss, her fingers sensually stroking the soft skin of the cheek. She drew her fingers back at the moment when she broke from the kiss and Boles only smiled with all he want showing in the grin. Her hand travelled down from Wells face to slowly wrap her index around the ring on her heart's collar. Boles growled low just as her Wells had done a moment before as she pulled on the collar drawing her love's face down her body toward her breasts.

"Prove it me my heart, show me your devotion."

"Yes...yessssss," Wells whispered as she gave herself over to Boles. It was one their games, just one of their ways of sharing, and for both it was all driven by the moment. Some nights Wells wanted to be controlled and then loosed by the one she loved with all her heart, a fantasy that was one of Wells strongest cravings, while some nights she just wanted to be loved gently. Boles knew which and played along giving her Wells whatever she wanted. Wells pulled open her love's robe and with the help of being directed she began to kiss and nibble on the soft flesh of Boles breast. The touch was like throwing fuel on an already raging fire and the ecstasy felt by both quickly spread out across the ship like a wave. The heat and lust from the pair, the very emotions they felt, swept across the decks of the Junk due their empathy and it was impossible to miss.

Before, his fingers had danced over the frets with ease on the banjo as he played each lick. Now Wally could barely hold the instrument. He suddenly only wanted to be in bed with one Camille Brousseau and he was finding it very difficult to think of anything else. He kept trying to pick and do the right runs on the frets to keep the tune going only Wally couldn't stop picturing Camille. He could see her beneath him just as easy as he could see Wahkan sitting in front of him, her back to his chest as he thrust with his hips and she pressed backwards with hers into him letting his-

"Oh Great Spirit, are you-"

"Yes," Wally answered cutting off Wahkan before swallowing hard, "umm...are you-"

"I almost bit right through my harmonica!" Wahkan shot back just before swallowing hard himself.

"I see...Brother John wasn't telling tales when he said these two could do...this."

Wahkan put his harmonica in his pants pocket with a shaky hand nodding just once. "With those two on board, we may never get a night's peace."

"I see," Wally repeated setting the banjo on the rail before standing up gingerly shaking his right leg, "well if you'll excuse me good sir...I'm going to go below and stick my loins in the refrigerator to hopefully cool everything down."

"Yeah...okay...I'm going have Zheng fly us by a lake somewhere so I can jump in." Wahkan replied breathing deep while refusing to get up. He wasn't even sure if he could stand up at the moment or what might happen if he tried. All Wahkan was sure of was he didn't want to look like Wally, walking down the deck with a limp from a very stiff leg.

His personal whip was larger than the average one, longer and grander than the usual single mast sailboat. Ezio had come into some money from an investment, you might say, and said money had been used to secretly purchase a large two mast whip for his travel. Ezio loved his whip. It was his sanctuary from all the harshness of the day and the growing political pettiness of the Society. He kept the whip hidden very well, no one knew of its existence, even his dear friend and Mistress Camille. As he walked toward the private hangars in New Jersey where he had docked it well away from any prying eyes the tall Umbra began to think on the day's final events. When he saw the small whip circling the Yards and how Camille was following it he knew instantly Fade had come to fetch her. Was the Sky Pirate on the whip? Ezio doubted it but with the way his friend was moving so quickly to reach the whip he knew Camille needed to see Fade. So he had turned and blocked Mr. Cooper from following, given her just enough time to slip off the damaged cruiser and into the crowd and disappear.

Fade, of all people to befriend and hold in your heart Camille. Oh what the Society will do to you if they ever discover that relationship my friend Ezio thought as he quickly stepped up and onto his ship. Two men stood ready by the cockpit as the lights on the air field blazed behind him from the open hangar doors. "Are we ready to leave gentlemen?" He asked quickly.

"Yes sir, all provisions have been taken aboard including water and fuel for the boilers." The man to the left replied just as quickly.

"And our guest, have all the arrangements been made?"

"Yes sir, she arrived an hour ago and is waiting below for you." The man to the right responded.

Ezio nodded with a smile before giving the order to fly. When the man on the right asked for a destination the tall Umbra only told him he would provide that information later. Then Ezio ducked and disappeared into the bowels of the air ship through the companionway. He turned back and shut the entrance then spun back and went the rest of the way down into the converted cabin. The state room Ezio entered wasn't as opulent as Carlo's brothel, but then it wasn't far behind the place either. There were thick rugs over deep dark hardwood floors, two long couches facing each other, and on the far wall by the entrance to the bedroom and shower in back was a full bar. The tall Umbra's head was just an inch or two from touching the ceiling as he walked over to the bar and pulled out two long flute glasses. Just as he opened a small door and pulled out an ice bucket containing a nice bottle of champagne a woman dressed in a thick robe and drying her hair with a towel appeared out of the back. He smiled as he looked to her and spoke.

"Good evening my angel, my Alice, I see you've cleaned up."

"Don't even 'Good evening' me Ezio," the woman snapped pulling the towel down. The long flowing curly brown hair from before, a custom made wig, was gone revealing shoulder length blond hair that held just enough of a lovely shade of red to tinge the mane perfectly. Gone also were the flimsy underclothes she had worn while 'working' in the brothel. "Do you know what I have been through these last months for you?"

All right, she was upset, and she had every right to be Ezio quickly decided. He nodded profusely as he poured the champagne. "I know my sweet, I know, but understand every bit of information you sent to me was crucial and essential."

"Essential to what exactly, what are you working on?" The lady asked eyeing Ezio with hard eyes.

"To discovering something very detestable," Ezio said handing her a flute of champagne then moving quickly to one of the couches and sitting. He figured distance at the moment was best just in case Alice determined throwing a punch made her feel better. Being from the neighborhood, and being Sicilian just like Carlo and he, gave Alice a distinct and hardened 'Survivor's' mentality. It was why he acquiesced, that and the fact they were intimately involved, to go into the brothel and spy. Alice was one of the few people he trusted with his life...his heart and soul. Ezio had long lost any privileges a birth right from the Old Country awarded. There was no 'Family' work or such for him; it all disappeared as soon as his Magi ability showed. The moment he joined the Society the final connection to his old life was broken as his family and friends stopped being just that, family and friends. He was a witch to the old ones in the neighborhood and thus evil, a disgusting thing to be feared by the adults, and an object to be hated by the young children. No, the only thing from the neighborhood and that old life Ezio kept was Alice because she was the only one who looked on him as a man and not a Magi...someone with a soul.

"And just what 'detestable' thing would that be?" Alice asked walking over while sipping the champagne.

"If I tell you my angel then there is no going back, no closing the door and claiming ignorance, understand? I cannot un-ring the bell once it has been struck my sweet Alice." Ezio asked as she walked up to him.

Without a second of hesitation she moved up and sat down in his lap, an indication she was going nowhere and this was her decision, much like the night she told him about her decision with the brothel. "What have you gotten yourself into now my sweet beddu?"

Now he felt safer, from being punched at least, at hearing her say the loving pet name she had called him from that first night they found each other again. He was still a young apprentice in the Umbra those days walking along the streets of Manhattan at night after completing a task when he looked up and there she was, his sweet Alice from the old neighborhood looking back. "There is a cabal of sorts, buried deep and high in the Protectorate. It was this secret alliance that had ordered the Marines to assault the brothel this morning, until we the Umbra were dragged into their plan."

Alice looked deep in his eyes, her way of judging if what he said was true, though she knew there was never a need to do so. Her Ezio had never once lied to her, not even when the rumors of his powers with magic were circulating through the neighborhood in despicable hushed rumors forcing him to live an ostracized life. When she asked Ezio that morning long ago when they were so young if he was a witch like her mother said he was, the most handsome boy she had ever seen never blinked and never tried to hide from her when he answered yes. It was that exact moment, when he cared enough to be truthful with her, that Alice fell in love with him. Even after he was taken away and no one seemed to care she had never forgotten or turned her devotion away from her sweet beddu making the night she came across him again so unbelievably sweet. "A secret group in the Protectorate...but what would a bunch of soldiers want with Weavers?"

"I do not know my angel, but I think the conspiracy extends to the upper Rings of the Society as well."

She sipped her champagne then nodded, "That's not good, but a secret group in the Protectorate and the Society would explain those two shadowy men showing up the other night."

"What two men?" Ezio asked with a tilt of his head and concern in his voice.

"They had to be Protectorate," Alice replied leaning up against him more getting comfortable, "the way they both carried themselves, it screamed military."

"What did they do?"

"Both picked girls on the lower level, disappeared for the hour they bought, and then both left as quick as they could. Strange thing, the girls didn't come back for a bit and when the guards went looking for them they found the poor things drugged in their rooms." Alice answered before sipping more champagne.

"The men slipped them a 'mickey' huh? The pair needed access and time to look around I'd say, confirm the Weavers were there, which is why they chose the girls on the lower level." Ezio sighed. The brothel worked on a tier kind of system when it came to 'price', the higher up in the levels you went the more you paid for the time spent which meant the girl was more 'adept' at what she could do for you...or to you if that was your thing. These men chose the lower level to keep the eyes of the guards off of what they were trying to do.

"Yes, well I was just happy they didn't try and pick me. It seems your 'advice' kept me from being asked back to the rooms more than once." Alice smiled with a small wink.

The tall Umbra only sighed again and shook his head. "Not everyone I'm afraid. I'm sorry for what you had to endure my angel, so very sorry."

The atonement wasn't needed Alice said with her smile as she reached up and caressed his cheek with her palm. She did everything for him, would do anything he asked. When he needed someone to go in and send back information on the brothel in the search for the two Weavers he was sure was inside Alice had immediately volunteered and would hear nothing about changing her mind. She wouldn't trust anyone else to watch over her beddu and no one else would she trust to do the task of spying and not turn on him if caught. So, begrudgingly, Ezio allowed her to be the spy but before he let her go in he had one piece of advice that would help her stay away from the men who came looking for pleasure. When he told her to let her hair grow, all of her hair and even the ones around her private area, Alice had almost laughed herself to death. He told her most of the men who visited Carlo's were looking for 'clean' girls, little girls with pure bodies, and if she wasn't then it would help her from being asked to go back to a room. Carlo only dealt with the higher class of individual which meant most if not all had certain...eccentric standards. Alice thought it was total crap, she knew men and a bunch of hair down there was not going to stop any from...well you know.

Only it did, because every man who came through the doors took one look at her 'garden' and bolted the other way with a scared look. Damn, my beddu was right she had thought feeling much safer now in the brothel even if it took all her composure to keep from scratching herself down there wildly. That safe feeling disappeared a month after she had successfully ducked every attempt to be taken back to the rooms. Carlo had called her into his office and Alice knew it was because she was making hardly any money for him, what she had given to the till of the place was what she had smuggled in. Damn, I'm going too kicked out before I can find these Weavers Ezio needs me to she assumed in a panic as she walked into his office. It was quite the opposite she discovered because it seemed Carlo had an affinity for a woman who let hair grow...down there. The boss of the brothel never tried to have sex with her, never tried to bed her, just made her stand by his desk and let him slip his hand into her bloomers and slide his fingers around for a feel. As long as his hands took a stroll through her 'garden' then she no longer had to worry about certain things either. As perverted as it sounds the fact was his obsession was good for her. It was quickly passed through the brothel that Alice was Carlo's main girl and as such she got to go where she wanted and never had to worry about putting her due in the till. It was after one of the nights when the brothel came alive and every person that came through the doors paid double to sleep with one of the girls that Alice finally found the pair of Weavers. They were downstairs in the basement; kept apart at all times except for the nights when Carlo wanted business to run wild.

"Is Carlo dead?" Alice finally asked though she had guessed the answer all ready.

"Yes," Ezio nodded leaning into her touch, "the conspiracy couldn't afford to leave him alive."

"And that strange little man Bentley?"

"I'm afraid we will never see Mr. Bentley again. It was the Shaman Greywolf who paid Carlo a visit this morning wasn't it?" Ezio asked with a smile while reaching under the robe and rubbing Alice's leg high on the inside of her thigh.

"The man wearing the big black hat and Eagle feather...yes it was him. But how did you know though? I didn't get a chance to send a note." Alice responded while reaching down to cover his hand on her leg with hers and then pushing both higher. They passed notes to each other through the kitchen staff, specifically one dish washer who acted as a messenger for a price in coin Ezio paid happily to keep tabs on his love.

The tall Umbra just shook his head still smiling, "I saw the large IP, the shaman's friend, running on the street below during the raid. From what I understand where one goes the other will be close by."

She just nodded from her seat and sighed, "He's as big as a house that one, not as big as Gino, but still pretty big. They took the Weavers you know, carried them right out the front door before all hell broke loose in that place."

He just nodded again and sipped the last of his champagne. "I assumed as much, though why I have no idea. I'm not even sure how he got his hands on a Joris stone to draw us to the brothel. And how did he know the Protectorate was coming for the Weavers? He drew us there with almost perfect timing...I think?"

Alice nodded and then took a sip of champagne before speaking, "he saved me this shaman fella. I was caught on the second floor with bullets bouncing all around me and out of the blue he comes running up and carried me out of there. Then, with a chivalrous smile, he drops me off by the Museum...a strange but interesting man."

"Then I will have to thank him the next time we talk." Ezio smiled.

"We both will beddu, we both will."

He only nodded watching her drink the last of the champagne before standing up quickly and turning to him. She slid out of the robe slowly, seductively, letting him stare at her naked body for a moment, just a second or two, as she spoke. "Come to bed, tonight I want you to make me very happy for all that I suffered in that brothel."

And then she was gone walking back into the bedroom stopping just long enough to take the bottle of Champagne from the ice bucket. Ezio watched her perfect rump shake as she walked away before bending down to pick up the robe and head back to the bedroom himself. Just like Alice said, tonight he wanted to do something else than search for his answers.

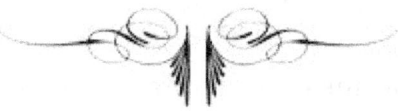

She stood in the middle of Fade's personal stateroom naked with the exception of a bed sheet wrapped around her body looking at a small set of shelves that held the personal knick-knacks of the Sky Pirate. There were so many small oddities it might have seemed like a junk pile to anyone else, but to Camille it told the story of Fade, her personal journey. There was a pair of dice, for what game and where it was played Camille had no clue to either question, but the pair looked worn and the Magi could easily see the Sky Pirate throwing them in some game of chance on the deck above with her crew. Then there was an eye patch, an honest to goodness eye patch complete with a leather strip to tie it in place. Camille wondered who it might have belonged too, maybe a mentor like another Captain who had taken Fade under his wing and taught her the ways of the Pirate. There were other objects as well, some easy to discern why Fade kept them and others not so, but a pair of small handmade dolls left Camille completely stupefied. The Sky Pirate wasn't someone to be sentimental and it was easy to understand why she kept the dice and even the patch, but a pair of dolls a little girl would play with? What possible story the two small effigies could tell about Fade eluded Camille as she stared at the pair, even slowly reached out and with a careful touch ran a finger down one feeling the aged canvas give just a little under her touch.

What do you mean to my dear friend you pair of raggedy dolls? What importance are you to my dear Fade?

There was no answer, no matter how hard Camille wished for one, and there wouldn't be one at the moment as the door to Fade's room threw open with a violent push. The Magi had just enough time to look away from the shelf to catch sight of Fade storming up as angry as she had ever seen the Sky Pirate Captain. The fact Fade slammed her belt, which still held her cutlass and long gun and knife, on the small table in the room as she passed wasn't necessary to show Camille how upset her friend was. The Magi clutched the bed sheet tighter around her body as the Sky Pirate stopped a foot from her with a raged filled bluster.

"What the hell were you doing on that cruiser?" Fade growled so low and ominous it would have made a grown man wet himself while pointing her index finger menacingly at the Magi, only Camille wasn't fazed by the show one little bit. She knew the reason her friend was attacking in such a way and it had little to do with any true anger. The real reason was actually quite touching as the Umbra sighed.

"I was doing what I have been tasked to do by the Society."

"And what is that? Put yourself in harm's way!" Fade bellowed, a voice filled with more fear than anger Camille could tell as she let the Sky Pirate continue. "Do you know how close you came to being hurt?"

There it was, the whole reason Fade was in this vicious mood. Camille had an idea what was the cause, it formed the moment the Sky Pirate came rushing in, and now it had been proven to be so. She looked at her friend and smiled just a little at the corners of her mouth. "I'm fine Fade. I was never in danger and so was most of Brooklyn."

"I don't give a damn about Brooklyn, not one damn whit!" Fade screamed again, only lower and with a gasp this time, as if she were fighting to regain some control of herself. Camille stood quietly letting her friend get what she could under control as the Sky Pirate hissed. "I could have hurt you...or worse!"

All right, there was only one way to deal with this Camille thought, one way to snap Fade out of this moment. With a deep exhale and a growing smile the Magi clutched the bed sheet holding on to just edges meeting the Sky Pirate's gaze with a raised eyebrow. "I am not hurt my friend, you can look me over if you'd like. You took all of my clothes so it should be very easy. I'm as naked as the day I was born, or so I'm supposed to be as Mr. Hayes explained it to me. By the way, how is he? The man almost had heart failure when he had to order me to undress."

The move, with a playful intent meant to disarm, began to draw the Sky Pirate down from the angry perch she had taken upon entering the room. Even though Fade's eyes never lowered or left Camille's the move had the effect it was supposed to as the Sky Pirate began to ease, her finger dropping slowly with her arm down by her side as the fire in her eyes began to ebb. After a moment more Fade finally spoke, "I could have killed you."

"And yet you didn't," Camille said with a empathetic tone trying to soothe the fear her dear friend felt as Fade walked past her ducking behind an ornate wooden tri-fold dressing screen, "you didn't kill me or any innocent people in Brooklyn Fade. You knew exactly where to hit the cruiser to disable it but not damage it enough to have it fall from the sky into the borough. Only you have that kind of ability."

"I wasn't trying to take the cruiser from the sky. I was..." Fade said from behind the screen as her jacket went over the top before letting the last of her words go the way of her namesake. Camille pulled the sheet tight around her again while talking and trying a different tact with her friend, a question she already knew the answer to.

"What were you there for anyway my friend? Why did you risk being captured?"

Fade's boots flopped over in the corner suddenly as she spoke, "I was there to help John."

"John," Camille sighed shaking her head on the outside while smiling slowly on the in, "what was he doing there, wait, how did you John was even going to be there?"

This time Fade's pants went up and on the screen followed by her corset and the long red sash she wore round her waist. "One of the crew came up to me this morning talking about a dream he had last night, and mind you this man isn't one to talk about dreams believe me. He said he saw a strange looking air ship no one else but his own eyes could see flying into Brooklyn."

"The Tiānkōng," Camille whispered shaking her head. She had a feeling, an intuition, as to why and how the crew man had the dream. It was a seed you could say, a single message provided and planted by the one who helmed the mythical but very real Junk, the ghost Zheng Hui. He was the one who had called for Fade knowing full well the Sky Pirate would come to help John...her other close friend the shaman. There was just a few who knew of the past between Fade and the shaman and the ghost was probably the most knowledgeable of the special relationship.

"Exactly, it took me less than a minute to turn the Moon around and put in a course for Brooklyn. Then, just as we're high in the clouds keeping an eye and ear out for something and anything that would lead us to the Tiānkōng the same crewman sees the flying boat off our starboard bow settling in right between those buildings...and a second later that damn cruiser set its keel right over John's ship." The Sky Pirate captain remarked tossing a second belt over the top of the screen to hang there by her corset.

The Tiānkōng arrived by the brothel just before the cruiser showed up Camille thought, so it was true? John had led them right to the building and then used the Umbra to block whatever it was this cabal Ezio hinted at was up to. Only, he hadn't called Fade to help out so the shaman must not have known how many

Protectorate Marines there were on the cruiser, or did he? When it came to John one never really knew what to expect. Camille looked at the screen and sighed, "Do you know if Wallace is all right? Was he hurt in the fracas?"

"It was more than a 'fracas' Camille," Fade answered with a chuckle as she stepped around the screen dressed in just her shirt now and with the light of the room the silhouette underneath the blouse showed off the Sky Pirates slim body. "It was a full on fight, if the Old Rebel had caught me I'd be in irons right now in some cell."

"You were never in trouble my friend. From the beginning you had the advantage. But truthfully, have you heard from John or Wallace?" Camille pleaded needing to know what had happened to the engineer, hoping her friend could give her some bit of news.

Fade sighed and walked over shaking her head sending her long red curly locks swaying as she spoke, "No, I have not heard from any one on board the Tiānkōng. I do know, because it was John down there and Wally and Wahkan at his side, that no marine or air sailor could have taken them. I bet all three are safely flying around somewhere resting and getting ready for tomorrow."

It was true the Umbra told herself silently, the very thing all three men were probably doing at that very moment, and yet Camille didn't want to accept it. She sighed just as Fade had done and walked over taking a seat on the edge of the bed with a dejected expression. The fact she put her elbow on her knee then her chin in her hand to support her head was more than a dead giveaway to the Sky Pirate captain of her friend's depression. Fade walked over and took a seat next to her friend letting their bodies touch and letting the Umbra know she was there and had no intention of leaving her in this time of crisis. She knew the last thing her friend needed was to drag out this foul cloud, this mood of uncertainty, and yet Fade had to ask a question that had been nipping at her all day.

"What do you think John was doing at that place this morning? What the hell have those three lovable fools for men gotten themselves into this time Camille?" She whispered looking to the Umbra with her own concerned expression.

When the Umbra turned and looked to her friend Camille could easily see a perfect reflection of her own unease though the reason was as much a mystery as the dolls. Ever since the pair started down this road of friendship Camille had noticed Fade was never one to hide her feelings, unflinchingly honest with her heart, to anything she had asked with one exception, the Shaman Greywolf. When it came to the man, and the affection for John that was easy to see, Fade had refused to give an answer ducking and parrying any question of how she felt for him with the same skill she possessed with her cutlass. She did the same when it came to inquires about the history between the two, especially any intimacy. Yet with answers like the last and the fact Fade had risked certain capture to come to John's aid Camille was more than sure about her dear friend's feelings for the shaman. Fade's heart sought love and affection just as any others, only with the Sky Pirate it was always on her terms. The Umbra detected the closeness and desire for Greywolf the first time she observed the way the Sky Pirate interacted with the shaman. She didn't even try to hide the looks of longing till Fade noticed the Umbra's eyes taking note of every little twitch. Camille had spotted the attraction easily because she was feeling the same with Wallace and just minutes after the first time she had seen and spoken to the engineer. Fade had detected it just as easy as well and inquired about it. Maybe being asked straight out by her new friend on her feelings was why Camille had finally spoken of her longing for the Scotsman one night, a white man, and her fear of what such a pairing might bring. Unlike the Sky Pirate the Umbra needed to speak her heart to let go of the apprehension, a colored woman and a white man, coming together in this day and age, it was frowned upon on both sides and yet Camille couldn't stop thinking about Wallace. Fade had been the one that introduced the pair one night to one another and started the longing in Camille's heart and soul. It was why she held nothing back when she answered her friend with the truth.

"John and Wahkan rescued two Weavers from that place, two very important Weavers who the Protectorate already had planned on taking themselves. I have no idea why the shaman took them but I'm afraid...he has stepped in the middle of something very corrupt and vile."

"Great," Fade whispered closing her eyes for a moment to take in what her dearest friend had said before speaking again, "Why would John rescue Weavers? He doesn't need them like you do."

Camille only shook her head indicating she had no clues that would lead her to a reason why the shaman did what he did. The look she received for the motion from Fade was just a small smile from the Sky Pirate, a weak grin that said it was all right, I'll be fine after a moment or two. And yet the Umbra knew her friend was hurting just as bad as she was on the inside, so with a small move she leaned over and put her head on her friend's shoulder. The hand holding her head slowly crept over and took Fade's in warm hold as Camille felt her friend lean her head over against hers and squeezed her hand back.

"Why did you make me take off all of my clothes?" The Umbra asked with a small chuckle.

"It was the only way I knew to make sure you wouldn't walk away from me before I said what I wanted to say...the way I needed to say it. I knew if you were dressed you might have left the room to let me cool." Fade confessed with the same small chuckle and the small amount of mirth loosened the mood just a bit more, enough to speak easier.

"What are we going to do now that we know what we know?" Camille whispered.

"I'm going to find them, all three, and demand an explanation from all of them, especially John! Then I'm going to decide how hard I'm going to hit him just before hugging the man with so much force I'll break a rib." Fade answered quickly, the unflinching honesty shining through the dark clouds both felt. It made Camille smile and ready for the next question her friend asked after a long moment of silence.

"How are your nips?"

The Umbra smiled finally moving the bed sheet she was covered with, opening it just enough to look down inside to her breasts then back up to her friend. "The swelling has gone down a little, but not that much. Both of the poor things are still bigger than before...getting skewered."

The Sky Pirate couldn't help but smile at her friend's words as she pulled back on the collar of her shirt and looked down inside. "Mine stayed swollen after I had them skewered, but doesn't it feel 'nice' when you pull one?"

The intent from Fade, that hidden meaning, was like a smoldering ember setting off a rising flash of desire, drawing an immediate response from Camille as she smiled more and actually giggled. "Oh yes, the sensation is very 'nice'. I find myself doing it

unconsciously at times, starting things I don't have time to finish

you might say."

"I do know what you mean...certainly I do. And the

tattoo...has it healed nicely?"

The question made Camille smile more as she leaned away

from her friend and then forward just bit letting the sheet droop

exposing her back. The large tattooed images of angel's wings

graced her skin, wings that were full and open looking to gather the

wind and take the Umbra high into the sky. Fade slowly reached

out and ran a finger along one of the lines tracing it with the tip of a

single finger. The touch sent a shiver through Camille as she looked

over, "it looks good doesn't it?"

"It looks perfect, fits you perfectly" Fade whispered noting

the tattoo was large just like the one on her own back. Would her

friend get others like she had done, still did? Have I led you astray

my dear Camille the Sky Pirate thought with a sudden pang of guilt

as she whispered. "Have I totally corrupted you now?"

The tone of the moment totally changed and Camille felt it

immediately, reacted by sitting up and looking her friend in the

eye...with unflinching honesty. "No, you only showed me there is

life beyond the walls of the great Magi Society. All I ever knew

before you woke me to this fabulous world were grey walls and

harsh directions from others, but now I see colors and I know the warmth of a touch. My soul wants another now when before it only knew the coldness of learning from tomes and that glorious feeling is because of you my friend."

Oh such pretty words Fade thought, words that instantly made her feel so much better. She still missed John and may soon that road would come to its head Fade thought. For now though, with such inspiration putting wind in her sails, the Sky Pirate stood and held out her hand to Camille and smiled. "Come on, we both smell like we had a long day and in need of a shower."

The Umbra didn't answer or respond. She knew it was both unnecessary and unimportant. She only stood up and took the hand following her friend out of the room to spend some time cleaning up and to just let the moment go where it wanted.

Mr. Cooper wasn't sure where he was exactly. He never did when he was called to these meetings because the men who came for him made sure he didn't and couldn't know where he was. They used a different car to get him every time. They blindfolded him and then put a hood over his head every time. They took at least forty-five minutes (a silent count he kept in his head) every time to arrive where ever it was the meeting was to take place and the car always took at a minimum forty to fifty turns. Even if he could remember all the twists and stops the car made the loud noise the men blared on each trip made it almost impossible to keep track of any kind of an idea in his head. So, when the men removed the hood and blindfold there was little surprise for Cooper to see he was in some plain and unrecognizable warehouse. The large space was dark and empty except for a thirty foot by thirty foot spot in its center, dead ahead, lit up by lanterns and electric lamps powered from a source he could not see. There were seven individuals, some standing and some sitting on plush chairs that were brought in for the meeting, in the lighted area. Cooper started for the area while in the dark, in the shadows, he could sense other eyes. Guards were all around, probably carrying the latest in arms, ready to shot anyone acting suspicious towards the ones he was walking towards. Better keep my movements to small easily identifiable ones he thought as he walked up.

The seven individuals were easy to recognize, it was the same group from the other meetings. There was Major General Silas Samuels dressed in his starched green uniform, the man in charge of the Intelligence wing of the Protectorate, standing by a chair leading the meeting as he always did with short grunts that emanated from his thick body. "Are we all cleaned up in Brooklyn?" He asked the Colonel on his staff standing just a few feet away.

"Yes sir, all possible leads to our cause have been taken care of." The man answered.

"What of the news reporters?" A man dressed in a crisp navy blue uniform complete with gold sash and medals asked from the chair he sat in, his distinct British accent cutting the air like a knife. Cooper knew General Samuels counterpart, Major General Thales Hamelin of the Royal Guard, just from the sound of his voice. Just like Samuels, Hamelin was the man who ran the Intelligence division of the Royal Guard for the Brits and had garnered the reputation of being the human embodiment of a tough English bulldog. There were very few things that scared the British Major General and even fewer men.

"We have the local reporters declaring the operation was a standard raid to bring Carlo Troisi's illegal business to an end, nothing of more interest and no need to report any further." The same Colonel responded quickly as Cooper stepped into the light with his hands at his side. Had to be careful with all those guards out there in the dark he thought, safety first you know.

"And Carlo's ties to the 'Family'?" Hamelin asked a second time just as quickly.

"We ensured his ties were severed before the operation was carried out. No one from the 'Families' will be looking for him or inquiring about him." Hamelin's aide, a Colonel with the usual military style short cropped hair, answered while standing perfectly straight in his blue uniform with gold sash as he spoke.

"Good, good." Hamelin replied taking a sip of his scotch as Samuels finally looked over and greeted, in his own gruff way, Cooper's arrival. Even though the Major General was just past his mid-fifties his body was still as fit as a piece of steel and his demeanor was as mean a two hundred pound junkyard dog.

"Well Mr. Cooper, you're just in time to explain to us why the hell the Umbra stepped all into our operation."

At any other time the directness of the Major General would have unnerved practically anyone and yet Cooper just locked eyes with Samuels. He was well past being intimidated by the Protectorate officer, well, almost. He still felt his mouth go dry with fear as both Samuels and Hamelin's eyes bore into him with slow surgical precision. "The Umbra simply followed already well established protocol-"

"What protocol gave you permission to interfere in our operation?" Samuels growled cutting Cooper off meaning to send the young man running. The young Magi froze for a second, not out of fear but to let the small gathering quiet down. He was no longer the whiny boy from the cruiser, the one crying out in dismay at Fade's attack. No, the necessity for a facade had ceased, being here among the cabal there was no need. Cooper stood tall and kept his eyes locked with Samuels as he continued on.

"The same protocol established in the Society's charter, article 112 to be precise. The same rules set forth by the US government in the Magical Legislation Act of 1923, the law of the land you would call it. Whenever a confirmed presence of Joris energy is detected, by whatever means, the Umbra must be informed and sent forth to determine the source of the energy and, when possible, acquire said source to prevent harm to the public trust."

The Major General didn't look away at what he saw was an obvious challenge. Samuels had never and would never stand down to another man, no matter how young. The gathering grew quiet again with the two men staring at each other, waiting for the other to break. Only neither had the intention of backing down and it was only when the soft Mid-Western voice of someone else breaking in did the silent war end. "Mr. Cooper is right General. The secret operation was compromised the moment someone brought the Joris stone to the brothel."

The two men finally broke their test of wills and looked to the one who spoke, the one with the soft voice. She was sitting just a few feet away with two others, Magi all three. Her flowing red hair, once crimson, was shot through with grey now lightening it while providing a contrast to the black coat with tails she wore. Buckles lining the front of the coat sparkled in the low light of the meeting as her brown eyes settled on the men. "I still think we need to hear what happened this morning Mr. Cooper, if you don't mind?"

"I doubt I have more to add to what the Marine Commander on the ground told you I'm sure ma'am." Cooper answered the lady whose name he had never been given. The woman was an elder member of the Society, climbing almost all the way to the top of its hierarchy, to the third Ascension, with expertise and efficacy but never once being called to sit on a council or Ring, the collective who determined the ascent of the Magi in the Society. There are nine Rings and each one control's two levels or Ascensions of the Society, 18 levels in all from the base to the very top. It doesn't matter where a Magi enters the Society, from what country or at what age, as all who arrive start at the first level of Ascension, a Novitiate. Each member then moves up through the Ascensions of the Society being promoted by the members of the council who make up the Ring for those levels. Only now, with the geo-political climate being one of sub-zero relations, how long this grand Magical Society with its open and free exchange of knowledge across borders would last was anyone's guess Cooper thought. The wonders which were to herald from minds working as one and the miracles that were to be might never happen now. The political strain was already forcing a few Magi who were used to choosing knowledge over ideology when given the chance to stand with Nationalism...choosing sides almost...and that saddened Mr. Cooper very much. Where would the Society be in ten years...twenty? Would there even be one or would every Magi hunker down behind walls of stone just like Governments and never speak to one another again?

"Then let's say this time it is for confirmation then senor." A man stated in a strong Spanish accent standing off to the side of the woman who had spoken earlier. His black hair was also shot through with grey giving the appearance of some state of priestly wisdom. Cooper knew different though. He knew the man was from Spain, just outside of Barcelona traveling in secret to avoid detection from his and the US Government. Cooper was never given a name just like the woman and just like her the man was also a high ranking elder.

There was no saying no, the choice to turn away and leave long gone now Cooper knew as he swallowed hard and spoke. "We were told this morning early a substantial source of Joris energy was detected in Brooklyn by our Hounds, and then almost as quick it disappeared, momentarily."

"Someone had the stone masked, unmasked it, and then covered it again...almost?" Hamelin asked with a stoic cold face.

"Yes sir, the Hounds never lost the scent but could not zero in on the source. The Umbra determined someone was taking the stone out of hiding and masking it so as to transport the source to a place to sell it. For that reason Miss Camille invoked Article 112 and the Magical Legislation Act of 1923 taking control of the cruiser from the Admiral. She felt the chance of losing the source was too high to not act. It was just unfortunate the ship Miss Camille took was the exact one the operation was going to use."

"It sounds more like a plan then an 'unfortunate' circumstance. This source of Joris energy, now faint, moved around the borough of Brooklyn until you converged on it at the brothel, correct?" Samuels asked this time.

"Yes sir, random movement until it stopped at the brothel where within minutes the source returned to its full state for what we assumed was the sale. Someone had removed the object from what was hiding it signaling our chance. At that time Miss Camille gave permission to commence the acquisition of the source. It was during the operation that we were attacked by Fade and the cruiser severely damaged. We barely made it back to the yards." Cooper finished looking straight to Samuels.

"Well,' the red haired woman from before smiled and nodded to the young Magi, "that was exactly what we were told by the Marine Commander. I think it's time General to let Mr. Cooper in on our enterprise. I think he's proved himself quite competent and trustworthy."

Competent...enterprise...this was sounding extreme, deeper down the rabbit hole then I was prepared to go Cooper thought as he continued to look at Samuels who took over the conversation. "What do you know about an object called the 'Philosophers Stone' Cooper?"

The Philosophers Stone...now I know I am way out on a very thin limb here Cooper thought suddenly, "Only what I've read in tales and heard in bed time stories sir. It's...a myth."

"No Mr. Cooper, it is not. We were just about to make one." Hamelin nonchalantly remarked from his seat as Samuels walked over to the young Magi. The news, the sheer enormity of what the General in charge of the Royal Guard's Intelligence Division just said made Cooper's mind go literally blank as the gruff Samuels stepped up right in his face.

"And what do you know about splitting atoms Mr. Cooper?"

The question made the young Magi blink, or maybe he was still trying to comprehend the fact these seven individuals were talking about making the mythical Philosophers Stone, which couldn't be done by the way. Whatever it was the General asked Cooper could only lick his lips and whisper confused, "Splitting atoms sir?"

"Yes Cooper, splitting of the atom, you know...the smallest of anything that there can be." Samuels quickly retorted and when Cooper was unable to answer the gruff man carried on just as quick. "A little over a year ago a group of scientist, a mix from the United States and our ally the British, wrote a paper and published it without a single thought of what they were doing. It was nothing really, this silly idea they had. The paper was a lot of jargon about scientific principles, theories, and such that only a handful of people on the planet could understand. Yet it was enough to send a shockwave through every government and its military, a God Damn tidal wave Cooper."

"What did it say?" The young Magi asked looking away from Samuels to Hamelin and the British man only smiled. He's always as emotional as a statue Cooper thought, and now he's smiling...this can't be good.

"If one could split a single atom the resultant release of energy could be measurable, though very small. So theory states it is feasible that if one was to build a large enough container to hold a greater number of atoms and then split just one the resultant release of energy will cause a chain reaction splitting the other atoms in the container and thus exponentially raise the output of energy released to a number that can only be scientifically assumed."

Now his mind was blank and completely blown and Cooper felt like a man hanging on the edge of a cliff by his fingertips. What did...this atom splitting...have to do with a Philosopher's Stone? The final Magi by the man and woman, a second woman of the same age and rank of her colleagues, with her blond and grey hair braided came to his aid speaking with an English accent as sharp as Thales. "Science can theoretically build a bomb powerful enough to reduce an entire city to ash in a mere second Mr. Cooper."

"Wha-ha-at?" Cooper stuttered as he tried to kick start his brain again.

"Yes Mr. Cooper, a bunch of men in lab coats can destroy a city, on paper at least. Imagine how the President and the Supreme Commander of the Protectorate reacted when they were told what these scientist claimed could be done, now imagine the reaction after being told the Russians and the Chinese and everyone else who read the same paper were now mobilizing their own scientist to try and reproduce what those foolish scientist said could be done." Samuels stated quickly, direct and to the point in his own special way.

Cooper exhaled, like someone punching him in the stomach, a bomb that could destroy a city, an entire city his mind wailed. He looked and felt sick as Hamelin took the baton and raced on with it. "We of course have our own men and women dedicated to testing what the scientist theorized in their paper, put them in place before the ink was dry on the directive from our superiors. Our scientists say we're at least ten to fifteen years away from any type of available weapon, which matches every other country's timetable our intelligence has obtained. This race was already a draw and we barely got away from the starting line."

"So everyone has the possibility of having a bomb that can destroy a city?" Cooper asked finally wrapping his brain around what was being said.

"Thanks to those fools in their lab coats, in due time yes, which means we're at a militarily stalemate again. And that is why we need to create this Philosophers Stone Mr. Cooper." Samuels stated turning to walk back to his original spot.

Wait, wait a moment Cooper told himself silently, he needed a moment to gather his thoughts and when he did he finally spoke. "Why do you need a Philosophers Stone, even if we could make one? What purpose would the Protectorate or Royal Guard have with it?"

"It's an extremely obvious reason Mr. Cooper, because no one else would have one." Hamelin explained with a huff at the end, as if the question were asked by a child with who little time could be wasted on.

The world spun again but on a tighter axis this time because he was ready for it. Cooper's mind worked fast and now he understood why the three unnamed Magi were here, had been from the very beginning. "That's why your here...the Society is going along with this?"

"Yes," the woman with red hair, the leader it looked to be, answered, "the Society has decided that helping the Protectorate to create the stone would be advantageous to all. We have an alchemist ready and up till six months ago we had a pair of Weavers ready."

Advantageous to everyone....how Cooper thought? What kind of an advantage would a Philosophers Stone be? Did anyone in the Society even know how to use one let alone identify when one had been successfully created? Then he started to think about the statement concerning the Weavers and a single name came to his mind and when it did the acts and happenings of this last half year hit him like a brick. Did this group have Isaac killed to get his Weavers only to lose the pair, was that the reason the Protectorate hit that brothel like a steam-driven hammer, to get them back at any cost? These Weavers had been brought together for a single purpose, joined by Isaac for that purpose, but why have him killed...unless he was nothing but a means to an end in this thing and with his part done so was his need to be 'involved'. Cooper had been pulled into this conspiracy for familial reasons and now he felt like he was drowning with what he learned, so much so he licked his lips again trying to breathe and whispered. "What do you need from me then? I don't understand why you need me?"

"All we need you to do Mr. Cooper is keep providing us Intel as to what the Umbra is doing and you'll be fine. You pass along any and all information concerning all those Magi in the conclave, especially the ones in charge, and you'll be one step closer to getting your father freed from prison." Samuels remarked with a wicked smile.

Why did they need him to report back on Umbra activity when there were three Elders and obviously higher ranked Magi than himself involved? That should have been the question Cooper was asking himself but upon hearing the mention of his father everything else was dropped to the wayside without a second thought. "My father, he's alive and safe?"

"Oh yes Mr. Cooper," Hamelin stepped in answering the question, "I saw him just the other day. He is being taken well care of in spite of his present circumstance."

"He was framed! My father would never commit treason. He was unjustly accused and put in a prison." Cooper snapped suddenly looking back and forth between the Generals with an angry eye and his right hand raising slightly, the fingers almost forming to a point to jab at the pair of officers. The other Magi didn't move, and the guards out in the dark either thankfully only sat watching the exchange intently making mental notes.

General Samuels just sighed and shook his head at the display before making his remark, "it's a little late to argue the case Mr. Cooper, that horse has already left the barn...for the both of you."

There was a secondary meaning to the statement and Samuels wasn't even trying to hide it. No, he wanted this young man, this Magi, to understand perfectly well his role in all of this and to stick to it. He wanted Cooper to realize he was neck deep now and he wasn't getting out, that the only way through was forward and that meant following orders. Next to Samuels the stoic figure of Hamelin sat and watched, observed with a discerning eye and when he saw Cooper's hand begin to lower he took control.

"I assure you he will be kept safe Mr. Cooper as long as you continue to cooperate with us, remain calm and obliging."

"As long as I'm your spy," Cooper retorted with a hard whisper.

"Yes," Hamelin said letting a low growl roll out of his chest now, a growl that he knew would grab Cooper's full attention. "Do not think for an instance Mr. Cooper we will not have your father secretly transferred to a deep dark hole of death to never see the light of day again if you try and free yourself of this arrangement. Do you understand?"

Cooper only nodded once, just once, but it was enough for Hamelin who only replied with a cold air. "You may go now."

That was it. That was my dismissal, I can go now Cooper thought as his hand and arm went slack by his side while his shoulders slumped and sank. He looked to Samuels expecting the General to add one last kick before letting him slink away through the dark, but the man only stared at him with a stone face. The deed was done, Cooper knew exactly where he stood and that was nowhere good. I'm all in now, whether I want to be or not. The young Magi turned and started to the long walk of leaving when the male Magi called out.

"Mr. Cooper, one more question, concerning Miss Camille Brousseau."

The young man stopped and turned and looked to the Elder with a confused expression. "Yes sir?"

"When the cruiser had completed its 'landing', she exited with you and Mr. Ezio. Do you happen to know where she went?"

"No sir, Fade's whip came flying about after I left the cruiser though so I assumed she boarded it, but I can't confirm she was aboard. Why do you ask?" Cooper answered with haste, seeking a quick response to his own question in return.

"Nothing important Mr. Cooper," the third Magi answered this time for the man, her smile both beautiful and sinister at the same time. It reminded Cooper of the Tigers at the Zoo, beautiful creatures from a distance but get too close and the beast will just pull you into the cage and eat you alive on the spot. That smile haunted him as he walked away from the clandestine meeting. It bothered him when the men put the blindfold and hood on him, and every minute of the long confusing drive he took to return to the outside world.

They waited till a signal was given that the area was clear, their 'guest' gone, before Samuels spoke up. "All right, I'll say it, today was a setback."

"More than a setback my friends, those Weavers were the only chance to succeed with this plan, with Joris gone we need them to create the necessary energy to infuse our stone." Hamelin sighed giving a wave of his hand. His aid went quickly to work pouring a glass of special whiskey brought along for the General.

"I know General Hamelin," the read haired Magi stated from her chair sighing just like her male conspirator, "the Commander on the ground is sure of his information."

"Hell yes Addison," Samuels cut in quickly with a snap using the lady's name for the first time tonight, "I trust the man. He was handpicked by me and Thales here. He knew what was to occur and that it was to be of top priority."

The male Magi turned quickly and looked to his colleague with the long braids with a puzzled look, "Excuse me Miss Corinne, but I did hear right that the Commander said the Shaman John Greywolf took the Weavers."

The question, the way it was worded, may have seemed a little off or simple to anyone else, but to Corrine it was just the way her counterpart Eloy thought. "Yes Mr. Eloy, we were told that. Specifically that his companion was seen leaving with the Weavers just moments before the operation started."

"Si and the Umbra followed a source of Joris energy to the brothel, which we found and the source...it was a stone infused with Joris energy?" Eloy asked quickly.

"Yes, it was." Addison acknowledged turning slightly to view her fellow Magi.

"Hmm, very interesting...very interesting indeed." Eloy whispered reaching up and stroking the small beard on his chin while he thought.

The make shift room was quiet for a moment, just a second or two, before Samuels looked to Hamelin exasperated. The Major General of the Protectorate Intelligence Group was just about to his breaking point, and after this day's complications his patience was not exactly steadfast or protracted. Then Eloy smiled and looked to both of the officers. "We will need to alert the Protectorate in all the major cities from here to Denver, but mostly in Chicago. Those units will need to be ready to respond at a moment's notice."

"Prepared for what exactly?" Samuels asked with a snort.

"Yes, ready to respond to what?" Hamelin added with a frustrated shake of his head. His usual cold and calm demeanor was starting to change as well, must have been a bad day all around.

Eloy turned from them to Addison and Corrine, "the shaman introduced himself into our plans...but I think for other reasons. I think he has not a thought of what the Weavers were to be to us."

"Other reasons?" Samuels and Hamelin stated this time.

"Si," the Magi smiled and yet never did he look away from his fellow Magi, "follow me please, he used the stone to lure the

Umbra to the brothel we can assume. The random movement, the faint scent for the Hounds to follow, it was all just to prolong the hunt until he was ready for the Umbra to show. The Shadows arrived just in time to upset some other nefarious business I think. Maybe Mr. Troisi was going to try and have the shaman shot to back out of some bargain and senor Greywolf used the Shadows to stop that? He took the Weavers we know, but why he did we do not."

"Yes Eloy, we all know he took them away and no, we do not know why he took them." Addison sighed.   She enjoyed Eloy's company and his curious mind, but the man had the potential of riding the train off the tracks every once in a while, this seemingly one of those times.

Hamelin shook his head and whispered before taking a sip of his whiskey, "This is what we get for working with Magi...total random confusion."

"Give me a soldier with a rifle any day," Samuels hissed drawing a quick nod from his counterpart.

"We can make many assumptions of the day's events, but I think one very strong one is the shaman knows the Weavers are being hunted, tracked, so he'll be heading to a place of safety. I have heard from sources that Chicago has several places he has been seen at. I think he'll be going there to hide." Eloy finished and when he saw the small smile on his fellow Magi's he knew his quick assumption had been accepted, by some.

"How do you know he'll run to Chicago? It sounds like you're going on pure conjecture here." Hamelin asked.

Eloy shrugged his shoulders and smiled looking at the officers. "It is simple logic really. No one really understands the shaman's magic, how it works, but we do know it does not come from Weavers. So he took the Weavers from Carlo for a specific arrangement other than what they were truly brought together for and in turn I think once he has seen his business through he will let them go."

"He'll just set them free, two of the most powerful Weavers next to Joris. He'll just let them go?" Addison asked with a raised eyebrow.

"Si, he has no use for them and he is not a man who intervenes unless asked to from what I have been told, which makes me wonder a little as to what or who had him take the Weavers, but I do know he will not keep them. We need to make sure when they are set free that we are ready to take possession of them Generals." Eloy added, finished with the usual flair of a small nod with his head.

It all made about as much sense as a Billy Goat eating a tin can to Samuels this theory by the magic man, but he never hesitated before looking over and giving his aid the order to have

Chicago and other major cities on the lookout for the Weavers. The Order was to be disguised in the form of a special request to pick up the pair, both on the run, for questioning on committing some small offense. The more discreet the better but it was a TOP priority the Major General told his aid who acknowledged and disappeared to take care of everything. Samuels turned back just in time to hear Hamelin speak up.

"Why did you ask about this Camille?"

"She leads the same Umbra conclave who found their way into our operation...and she is known to associate with one Fade, the Sky Pirate." Addison returned. She knew what would happen the moment she answered and wasn't surprised one bit when the response was just what she received.

"Really, than I want her picked up and placed in Protectorate custody as soon as she shows up Addison. We can't afford to have her running around at this point in our plans." Samuels ordered quickly.

The directness of the command seemed to sit uneasily with the three Magi, and Hamelin moved in with a swift reminder of just what they all were here for. "We are not playing some game here ladies and gentleman. We are here to obtain a weapon, a very powerful weapon, and the price of failure if we do not is the distinct possibility of another war this world may not survive."

"That's right people," Samuels adding stepping right in the footsteps of the British Officer, "if we want to stop another 'Great War' then we need a stick big enough to scare everyone away with. Now, are you still willing to do what is necessary, what you came here to do?"

The group was quiet again, only it was just long enough for Addison to cock her head to the side and grin just a little before blinking and responding. "I will have Camille picked up as soon as she steps inside any of our buildings."

"Good Addison," Hamelin nodded, "there can be no hesitation now. We have come too far to be turned back."

Yes, we have to come too far now Eloy thought to himself, maybe too far.

His room swam in the sweet scent of smoldering sage, sweet grass, and cedar cleansing his spirit with every breath John took in. The incense, specially made for him by an old friend in Chicago, helped him, soothed his soul, and gave aid when he crossed on his journeys, like he was doing now sitting on a small handmade carpet in the center of his room with his hands resting on his knees and folded in legs. The quiet of his sanctum, bombarded earlier by the emotions of the empathic Weavers as they played, gave way slowly to the sound of a gentle wind as what he knew was the middle world, the reality of everyday, faded with each slow breath he took. As all things around him slipped away John's senses shifted to accept that which only a few knew existed and yet all would come to experience one day. As his spirit began to fly from his body and travelled through the veil between the middle world to the waiting one, to the place all men and women pause to be judges before moving on, John let go of all that was his body in his room on the Tiānkōng.

When he felt his energy calm, the travelling done, John opened his eyes to see a gloomy sun overhead as he sat in a vast field of knee high grass now, the floor of his room long left behind as he journeyed. There was nothing special about this field that would catch one's eye, no hills or mountains or obstructions for as far as the eye could see, only the endless sea of people wondering in it...for as far as the eye could see. This is where we all come when our time is done in the Middle World, where man and woman and child come to wait until called to have ones past life examined, weighed, and ultimately resolved. John stood and as he did those souls around him began to whisper with far-away voices when they saw him. As he looked out from under his black hat searching for one soul in particular those around him began to plea and beg, what was this place they asked? Why am I here? Where is my family and loved ones? They've just crossed these few, so new to this place they still don't realize they have died. It was that way for some at first John thought as he ignored the questions and began to walk toward a glowing point on the horizon. Taken so fast from what they knew these souls had yet to realize life was over for them in the Middle World. He couldn't stop to talk with these lost ones, not now, or he would be here forever conversing with these wandering pitiful souls. Hands reached out to touch him, grab and keep him close, but each appendage broke as he touched it, falling apart and back into vapor as he walked on. I could stop and try to explain where they were, maybe try to help them understand these who have just arrived, but really that wouldn't be of any help to them now. They're only hope, those abruptly new to this world, was to wait now and let this place keep them until called to the One Tree.

John walked on with a quick step and the farther along he went the more the souls began to change from lost ones to those who had come to be aware of where they were now but not what was to become of them. As he passed along some souls stopped, their ghostly voices calling to him to ask who he was. Was he the shaman they inquired, the one who comes and talks? Why do we wait here like this, like cattle in a field they asked over and over? What is to become of us?

Again he never answered the souls who looked to him. John knew it was the same with these souls as it was with the lost ones.

To stop and talk would only hinder him; keep him here walking and talking among them so long he would literally loose his other self in the Middle World. No, John just moved on ignoring each call until he saw the one he needed to speak with. He walked faster now and with each step closer the souls around him grew more cognizant yet again as to where they were and some even knew what awaited them. The shaman walked up to one man, a single ghostly soul who looked to be older than John with short grey hair and a tired face, dressed in the robes of a Magi. When the man looked up from watching his foot falls on the grass below a small smile of recognition crossed his shimmering face. "Good...is it day or night now John?"

"It doesn't matter Isaac, not here at least." John answered as the souls around the still pair began to move past on the right or left. We're like a rock in a stream. We can never stop the great walk to the One Tree. We barely even redirect this infinite flow of souls.

"No, I guess it does not, here in this place at least does it John? It is strange how I can't tell time yet I know you rescued them, my Boles and my Wells. You saved them John...I can feel it. Even here, on this field with all of us who have crossed, I can feel their energy...like a small shiny line of bright energy tying us together." Isaac the Magi remarked with the same smile of recognition.

"I took them from Carlo's grasp Isaac, nothing more." John replied.

The Magi, speaking in a voice that sounded Northeastern...maybe Maine, stepped closer with eagerness. "What I told you, all that I knew...it helped you didn't it?"

"Yes Isaac, your information was very helpful." John answered truthfully locking eyes with the spirit. From the all the background on the Weavers to who had them to the darkness coming to take them to all their likes and dislikes, it was all details provided by Isaac. In the end it had helped more than the shaman could or wanted to tell the spirit at the moment. "And per our agreement Isaac you now owe me my due in our barter, the name."

"I know John, I know what I owe you, but please...tell me they are safe now. Tell me you will look after them."

The shaman only shook his head 'no' coldly and answered, "The name Isaac. Tell me the name of the alchemist who made you the potion that aided in binding the Weavers."

"Please John, they need-"

"The name Isaac,"

"-someone to look after them-"

"Isaac," John growled stopping the spirit's plea instantly. He didn't want to feel this anger, not now here in this place, but the former Magi was trying to change the barter they had agreed to and that was not acceptable, especially with the request the shaman knew Isaac was about to ask. "Boles and Wells are free now, free to go where they wish. That was all I agreed to do for you, take them from Carlo and set them free."

"But they will never be free John, you know this and yet you won't help them!" Isaac spat. The emotion between them began to heat more, anger flaring and sparking, and as it did the souls moving around the pair began to take notice. Some began to cry, wail in fear, while others took the feeling into their ghostly forms and devoured it hungrily. They had been on this field for so long these old ones, deprived of anything living that even the bitter taste of anger was a feast, and as such they stopped now hanging close to the pair in hopes of taking more.

"And who is responsible for their station in life now Isaac? You knew what would happen when you bound them, two strong empaths, soul to soul. You knew what it would mean to commit such an act and yet you still did it." John countered. With his voice calm and tranquil he hoped to reign in the Magi's spirit, the anger it felt, here on the field, wouldn't help and neither would guilt unfortunately, which the shaman knew might be next. Yet Isaac had to see the truth of what he had done...the terribleness of his actions. The One Tree waited and there all would be laid bare including this.

The Magi's eyes changed as the shaman's last words were fact, a truth honed to such sharpness that it cut to the bone. He looked down to his hands with a small sigh, the palms turned up so he could see them, as if both were covered in some vile substance he could never wash off. "I know John...I know what I've done..."

"Do you Isaac? Do you truly understand what you've done now? If you do then tell me why you would bind them so deeply that if one were to die the other would follow shortly. They are tied to each other forever, in life and in death because of what you've done. One can never leave the other now, to be apart for just one night hurts them." John asked as the guilt he felt from the Magi was attracting even more souls now. Ghostly spirits were standing around them in a large circle stealing the bits and pieces of emotion that passed between the men, feeding on what they used to know...what they remembered and longed for.

The Magi looked down at his hands for a moment before looking up and speaking softly, finally answering. "Hubris John, simple and meaningless I know...I understand that now, but those days when I was alive I had no inclination of the ghastly outcome of my act. I was asked by the First Ring to see if I could find a way to match the energy Joris could produce, a task which had all the indications of being impossible and they told me so at first, vehemently. Only I had ideas John, theories, and I knew I could do it, the pride in me refused to give up. I just had to find the right Weavers and I could make a pair as powerful as Joris. I was so sure it could be done, by my hand alone, it became an obsession. I knew binding two Weavers as one was the only way to succeed and I knew I was the only one who could do it."

"So you took two beautiful young souls and sacrificed their free will to prove you could do it."

"Yes John, yes...I did exactly that...but it was only after I did that horrendous act that I began to regret doing such a hateful thing. I started to see them not as Weavers but as young sweet girls, as Boles and Wells. I started to notice how they liked me to read to them, how they laughed and wandered around the mansion and its gardens, and every day the guilt and regret pulled me deeper into pain. You see John I knew what purpose they were to be used for and at the start of it all that meant nothing, only the success of my endeavor was my concern. To climb the mountain at any cost, that was my intention and my folly. Then, only after the pair began to look at me like a father did I begin to care for them and knowing what would happen next with Boles and Wells...that realization, that truth, it tore my heart in two. It drove me to make an even worst decision concerning their safety."

John shook his head thinking this is how it always comes to pass, that men like Isaac only see the trees and never the forest until it is too late to change. "And that truth is when they are made to create the Philosopher's Stone it will kill them. It was why you were asked to create a second Joris; the energy needed to create the fabled stone is so immense it will consume any Weaver who tries to infuse said stone. You knew Bentley was going to try and make a Philosophers Stone because he recognized your work with Boles and Wells. He knew of their power and you knew if he succeeded that meant both Boles and Wells would die, one taken quickly when making the stone and the other slowly from being left alone."

"You remember our talk well John. That boy Bentley, he had no clue what the consequences of his actions would be. He would have killed them both and for what, a mythical piece of rock? No, I put them both in danger and I had to make sure both were safe. I had to get them away from the mansion...from...when they killed..." Isaac stated with animated hands, his guilt subsiding as he spoke. In his haste the spirit had mixed up two events of his former life, maybe a simple mistake or a sign of what was to come. The One Tree must be near now for him John thought, judgment and the cleansing.

"Is that when you were killed at the mansion, when you tried to sneak them away Isaac?"

"Yes, they killed me for them...to take them and leave no loose ends...but I do not know who exactly did the deed. I do not know a name or a face. It is all blank, grey to me now."

"And these people, you know they still hunt Boles and Wells. They will always hunt them Isaac, to their very last days if it comes to that very dark end." John stated low.

Isaac nodded with a sad look and whispered, "I damned them John, cursed them to be as one forever and to be hunted. It is why I need you to protect them, care for them, because neither can survive the ones who come for them now. I cannot see a face yes, but I can see the dark pursuing Boles and Wells and neither will live long if it takes them."

The shaman looked at the Magi and wondered, the pain from his former life, this realization that tears his heart in two, would the remorse be enough when he was finally at the One Tree standing ready to be judged? Would it be enough to let him go up or would it weigh him down to fall below? Such things mattered little at the moment, there was still walking to be done here in the field for Isaac. "I will not be their protector Isaac. I will not be their master either."

"But John-"

A raised hand cut off the spirit as John shook his head again, "I will be their friend, as I am to Wahkan and Wally, if they wish to stay on the Tiānkōng. If they wish to leave that is their choice, I will not influence them to stay or go."

A small smile began to form at the corners of Isaac's mouth as he nodded once and spoke low, "that is all I ask for John, mercy for those young Weavers because of my damnable act."

"I will help if that is what they wish, now the name of the alchemist who made the potion to bind the Weavers Isaac."

"I don't have the name of the alchemist who made the potion John, but I have the name of the one who I purchased it from. He, or she, lives in Chicago...you know who I speak of do you not?"

"Yes," the shaman answered with a long sigh. He wasn't a bit happy for this sudden twist which ended in not garnering the name of the alchemist, but he had the next best thing. The 'twin' that Isaac spoke of was a well-known entity among the Underground, a dealer and procurer of sorts. "You worked with Laken Malus."

"That is the one,"

"Then our deal is done Isaac, may you find you way to the One Tree and your journey from there an enlightened one." John replied one last time. He nodded and turned walking away, through the mass of ghosts who had gathered to feast on the emotions of the two. Their forms broke into vapor again as he passed through them only to swirl in the air and reform back into spirit. As he walked away John heard one last question from Isaac.

"How did you come by two Joris stones so fast John, to find one would be a miracle but two in such a short time...that seems beyond the fortune of luck?"

The shaman stopped and turned just enough to look over his shoulder at Isaac and grin a little as he answered. "There was no luck Isaac, I just asked Joris nicely himself to make them for me of course." John didn't wait for a reply, only turned and began his trek back to his body, the journey home. He walked away from the Magi and as he did his form began to slowly fade from this world, with each step his body turning into a wispy trail of smoke till finally the shaman was gone. Behind him Isaac watched and when there nothing left to see he only smiled contentedly knowing his Boles and Wells would have a chance now at a new life, and the fact John had obtained two Joris stones in one day by asking the dead Weaver to make them...well that just made the Magi smile a little wider. Oh the mystery that is John Greywolf.

"Thank you John...for all you have done and will do...thank you."

Then Isaac simply turned and continued to walk, step after step, as he travelled onward to a point he knew was still far away. The others around him followed suit, the feeding of emotion now over they too settled back into the walk to the One Tree. Only one soul remained still on the field as the others wandered past, a lone dark one that looked with evil to the last spot where the shaman departed from. This figure hissed like a snake and the souls around it retracted in fear and apprehension, then it left the field the same as John had, in a wisp of smoke. The souls left behind smiled and nodded happily as this dark one was gone now. They continued to walk along waiting...walking and waiting...

With a small blink John 'awoke' back in his room on-board the Tiānkōng. He took in a deep breath and noted his incense had burned out, the sweet smell of sage now barely clinging to the air around him. The shaman stood feeling it was late now, later than when he began his journey. He stretched his stiff back and shoulders letting the blood flow again through the joints before slipping on an A shirt and then walking over to pick up his coffee cup and heading out of his room. He was going to the kitchen to get some coffee when he stopped at the door to the Weavers room. John stood for a moment staring at the portal before finally opening it just enough to look in. There, under the blankets in the bed holding each other tightly Boles and Wells slept peacefully. He smiled small and then closed the door quietly before continuing on to get his coffee. After pouring his cup full John walked up to the main deck and over to the rail to stare out at the stars. He was sure he wouldn't be alone for long and he wasn't as the ghostly form of Zheng appeared by the rail next to him.

"We are headed to Chicago so you may speak to Laken Malus?"

"Yes," John said after taking a sip and looking over, "eavesdropping on me in the Waiting World again Zheng?"

"No, but it is not hard to see where this path we travel will take us."

"And where is that my friend?"

Zheng looked up and out at the star filled sky and then back to the shaman. "You retrieved the Weavers from that place in order to garner the name of an alchemist who poisoned a loved one of yours John. I know you seek the ones who threaten your brother and sisters my friend, but do you wish to protect them or take revenge?"

"A little of both Zheng, maybe, but I won't end up like Isaac, blind to where I walk. Your worry for that happening is not needed."

"Good, then I will take us to Chicago. Will we be dropping off the Weavers there?"

A small chuckle escaped John's lips as he smiled. "We'll have to see what happens when we get there. A choice will need to be made but only afterwards."

"Yes it will," Zheng smiled.

"Thank you by the way my brother, for contacting Fade." John nodded before sipping his coffee.

The ghost only nodded in reply, as silent as ever. There were no other words passed between the two, Zheng disappearing only to reappear at his helm to guide the Tiānkōng. John sipped his coffee looking out into the vast dark that was the night and felt it mirrored his soul these days. When he learned of his sister Sara's sickness and the fact it was brought on by a poisoning from an alchemist's concoction he felt a rage and a dark drop over him like never before. Now though, even as that dark still clung to him with a powerful force, John felt like it would end. Night must give way to day as it always has and this pall would lift from him as well...as soon as he got the name of the one who threatened his family and he settled the debt with that person.

###The End###

About the Author...

*R.Kane lives in the Southern US with his family where he was born. He enjoys the occasional fishing trip for bass and throwing the ball with his Golden Retriever. He is the author of other independent titles like '**Runner**' and '**Little Wolf**'.*

Please visit his website for updates and his other works - http://www.rkanepublications.com

www.ingramcontent.com/pod-product-compliance
Lightning Source LLC
Chambersburg PA
CBHW071304170626
46809CB00001B/336